# THE LEGEND
# OF
# WAPPATO

# THE LEGEND OF WAPPATO

## CHIEF CASSINO OF THE MULTNOMAH

Donald Wilson Bruner
Marilyn Howell Bruner

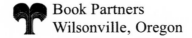 Book Partners
Wilsonville, Oregon

Library of Congress Cataloging-in-Publication Data

Bruner, Donald Wilson, 1919-
    The Legend of Wappato : Chief Cassino of the Multnomah / Donald
Wilson Bruner and Marilyn Howell Bruner.
      p. cm.
    ISBN 1-58151-039-X (alk. paper)
      1. Cassino, Chief, ca. 1780-1848--Fiction. 2. Multnomah Indians--
Kings and rulers--Fiction. 3. Frontier and pioneer life--Oregon--Fiction.
4. Indians of North America--Oregon--Fiction. 5. Oregon--Fiction. I. Bruner,
Marilyn Howell, 1930- II. Title

PS3552.R79965 L47 2000
813'.54--dc21
                                          99-053593

Cover design by Richard Ferguson
Text design by Aimee Genter

**Book Partners, Inc.**
P.O. Box 922
Wilsonville, Oregon 97070

*To the Multnomah—*
*who were never able to tell their story*

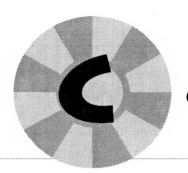

# CONTENTS

# PREFACE

Throughout history, certain individuals have distinguished themselves as quite unique in their achievements. Often it is difficult to explain how they have developed their particular insight, skill or ability—it seems to come naturally. These singular men and women have appeared in every era, in a variety of circumstances, and many have emerged from simple and humble roots. For his time and in his way, Chief Cassino of the Multnomah tribes was such a person.

Born around 1780 along the Columbia River, Cassino lived sixty-nine or seventy years and died at Fort Vancouver in December 1848. He is mentioned by most of the early fur traders and explorers, and by many famous visitors to Fort Vancouver. His portrait was painted by the renown artist Paul Kane, and he was a friend to botanist David Douglas, the "Great Grass Man."

In these early records, his name is spelled variously as Cassino, Casino, Kaesno, Casinov, Koesnov, Kiesnov—and other creative ways. All who knew him agreed that his intelligence was extraordinary, his acceptance of the white traders and settlers was remarkable, and his influence upon his people was a great factor in the peaceful settlement of the Oregon Territory.

# LAND OF THE CHINOOK

WASHINGTON

OREGON

Chinook Village
Wahkiakum Village
Cathlamet Village
Cowlitch Tribe
Loowit
(Mt. St. Helens)
Klickitat
Tribe Area
Cape
Dissapointment
ASTORIA
(Fort George)
Fort Clatsop
(Lewis & Clark)
Clatsop Village
Kalama
Klickitat
(Mt. Adams)
Columbia River
WAPPATO
(Sauvie Island)
Ft. Vancouver
Wallamt
(Oregon City)
WyEast
(Mt. Hood)
CASCADES
(Bridge of the Gods)
Multnomah (Willamette) River

Callapooyah

# LAND OF THE MULTNOMAH

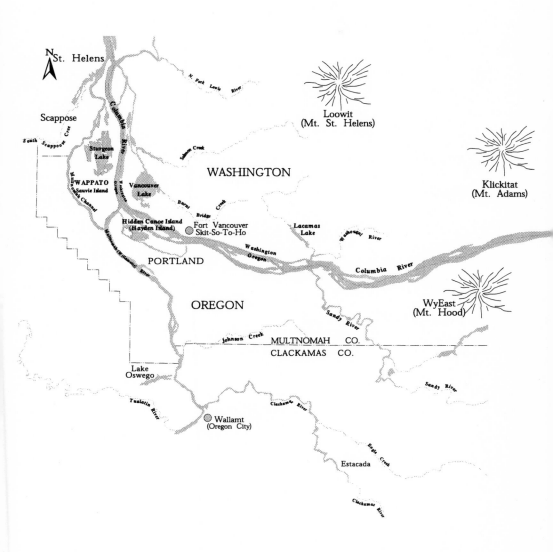

N
St. Helens

Scappose

Loowit
(Mt. St. Helens)

N. Fork Lewis River

Klickitat
(Mt. Adams)

South Scappoose Cree

Columbia River

Salmon Creek

Sturgeon
Lake

WASHINGTON

WAPPATO
Sauvie Island

Vancouver
Lake

Multnomah Channel

Burnt

Creek

Bridge

Hidden Canoe Island
(Hayden Island)

Fort Vancouver
Skit-So-To-Ho

Lacamas
Lake

Washougal River

Willamette River

PORTLAND

Washington
Oregon

Columbia River

OREGON

Sandy River

WyEast
(Mt. Hood)

Johnson Creek

MULTNOMAH CO.

CLACKAMAS CO.

Lake
Oswego

Sandy River

Tualatin River

Clackamas River

Wallamt
(Oregon City)

Eagle Creek

Estacada

Clackamas River

xi

# WAPPATO TRIBAL AREA

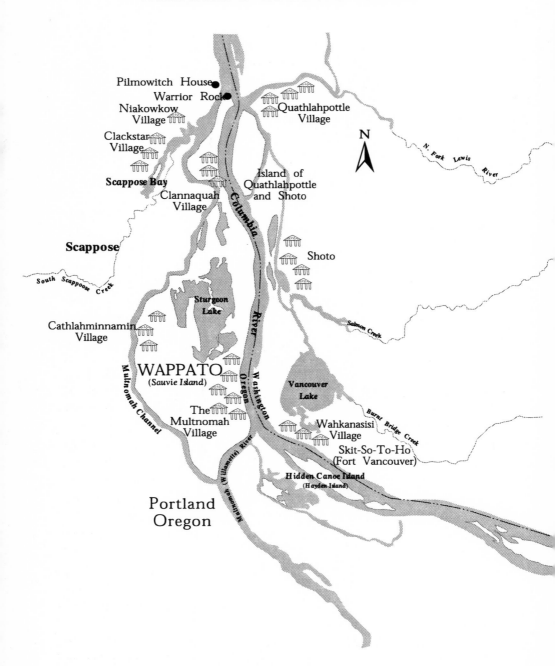

Pilmowitch House
Warrior Rock
Niakowkow
Village
Quathlahpottle
Village
Clackstar
Village
N. Fork Lewis River
N
Scappose Bay
Island of
Quathlahpottle
and Shoto
Clannaquah
Village
Columbia
Scappose
Shoto
South Scappoose Creek
River
Sturgeon
Lake
Salmon Creek
Cathlahminnamin
Village
Oregon
WAPPATO
(Sauvie Island)
Washington
Vancouver
Lake
Burnt Bridge Creek
Multnomah Channel
The
Multnomah
Village
Wahkanasisi
Village
Skit-So-To-Ho
(Fort Vancouver)
Hidden Canoe Island
(Hayden Island)
Portland
Oregon
Willamette (W illamette) River
Multnomah

# WAPPATO
# BEFORE THE
# WHITE MAN

In the cool mist of the late summer morning, the two boys slid their prized canoe into the Great River. As they began to paddle north, they talked excitedly about the adventure that lay ahead. Although both boys were familiar with the Great River from its mouth at the ocean all the way up to the summer trading place above the cascades, in the past they had always traveled with family. This trip was their first opportunity to try the downriver journey on their own. The boys were strong, healthy, and fast becoming young men. As they pulled out into the mainstream, the strong current moved them quickly downriver.

From his seat in the stern, thirteen-year-old Cassino paddled and steered expertly through the rolling surge of the river. In the bow, his closest friend, Monsoe, who was also thirteen, set a smooth and steady rhythm with his paddle.

Even though Cassino's mother was a roundhead, which marked her out as a slave, Monsoe had no reservations whatsoever about his friend. When the boys were younger, there had been some competition between them, but Cassino was so adept at everything he tried, so clever and wise in all his choices, and such a natural leader among his peers, that their rivalry was soon set aside and Monsoe's admiration for Cassino grew to near hero worship. The pair had become inseparable. When they weren't exploring together up and down the river, or roaming through the woods hunting, Monsoe was either staying with Cassino in the Niakowkow village or Cassino was staying with Monsoe's family at their camp above the Great River.

As a result, Cassino became like another son to Monsoe's father, Pilmowitsh, and there was no doubt of the youth's admiration and

1

affection for his best friend's father. A close bond was established between the two that would become an important factor in both their lives.

The morning passed quickly and the boys reveled in their newfound freedom. As the sun reached its zenith above the river, hunger pangs began to gnaw at Monsoe's belly. He stopped paddling for a moment as he turned to look at Cassino over his shoulder. "We should eat so we will have the energy to go faster and longer."

Cassino agreed, but added, "If we stop now and make a fire, we will spend too much time while the sun is up. Let's stow the paddles, except to steer, and eat while the river carries us along."

Monsoe conceded and the two boys made lunch out of the dried fish and berries that were packed near the top of the basket of provisions. When they had finished their sparse meal, they leaned into their paddles once again and propelled the canoe quickly downriver.

Back at his camp, Pilmowitsh busied himself preparing for the journey upriver to visit Chief Taneeho of the Multnomah. He turned to his most favored wife, Lopahtah, who would accompany him to see her father, and said with a frown, "I'm worried about our son Monsoe making the trip downriver at such a young age. When I was a boy, we were never allowed to go to the mouth of the river unless we went with the men of the tribe. But Monsoe said that Cassino was determined to make the trip alone, if necessary, and I feel much better knowing that they are together to watch out for one another."

"I'm worried too," said Lopahtah, "but both boys are strong and capable canoe handlers, as you well know, and Cassino is able and wise beyond his years. There is no one I would trust more to look out for Monsoe."

When the canoe was ready, Pilmowitsh and Lopahtah pushed away from the shore and paddled toward the tip of Wappato Island. Wappato had long been a favorite place of the mid-river Chinook tribes, because it sat at the juncture of two large rivers, the Multnomah and the Great River. The island was a sylvan paradise that furnished most of the necessities of life, including an abundance of wappato—the bulb that was a staple food for the Chinook. Watching over the river basin were three impressive mountains: the bewitching, snow-capped Loowit; the ruggedly handsome Klickitat; and the sharply pointed Wyeast.

Passing along the length of Wappato, Pilmowitsh and Lopahtah soon reached the large main village of the Multnomah tribe and beached the canoe. As they approached the cluster of cedar houses, the old chief came out to greet them. He held aside the plank as his daughter and son-in-law ducked through the doorway, then clapped his hands to have mats spread out.

"Pilmowitsh, my son," said Chief Taneeho, "let my daughter sit with us. Let me do honor to the mother of my grandsons!"

The chief and his visitors sat around the firepit and shared stories about the childhood exploits of Monsoe, and his younger brothers Tanohah and Sohowitsh, until it was time for Taneeho to attend a council of chiefs in the village longhouse. Pilmowitsh and Lopahtah returned to their canoe and continued their journey to a favorite camping spot a short distance up the Multnomah River.

As the sun disappeared behind the tall trees lining the Great River, two stiff and sore boys pulled their little canoe onto an island in the middle of the channel. Their youthful exuberance returned as they set up their first camp, making sure that every detail was correct and all was secure in the proper Chinook way. Although they soon had a nice campfire going, they didn't spend much time preparing a meal, and before the flames had died down to embers, they were both asleep, dreaming about the next day.

The next morning, the boys were up early, and pushed off as soon as the canoe was ready. At the point where the river swings west on its final turn toward the sea, they picked up a strong tailwind from the east and felt the current subside into an ebb tide. At first, they thought the conditions were favorable and would help them along, but the water soon turned choppy and the wind began to buffet the small canoe, making steering almost impossible. To make matters worse, the wind was not steady in one direction, but gusted and veered erratically. The boys tried desperately to reach the south shore, but the ragged wind and churning water overturned the small boat and tossed them into the chilly water. Both strong swimmers, the pair managed to stay with the canoe and push it toward the shore. They reached dry land tired, cold, and wiser—but without most of their food and equipment. They managed to start a fire and dry out, and they scraped together a meager meal before settling in to wait for conditions on the river to improve. Monsoe couldn't help but wonder what his younger brother

Tanohah, a consummate canoe handler, would have done in this situation.

As often happens near the ocean, the next day dawned calm and fair. The boys had no problem handling the current and they reached the large Chinook village on the north shore of the river near the mouth with no further incidents.

Almost immediately, Monsoe realized that this trip had a much deeper meaning for Cassino than just two boys on a canoe adventure. He moved confidently around the village, making new contacts and renewing old friendships. Everywhere they went, Cassino and Monsoe were well received, and Cassino seemed to be well known.

During their first few days in the village, the boys fished and hunted and played games with the other Chinook youths. They enjoyed learning the best fishing spots and trading stories with the other boys about life near Wappato Island versus life at the mouth of the river.

One day a group of older Chinook boys took Monsoe and Cassino along as paddlers in a large canoe, going out over the bar into the ocean. At first, the great ocean swells were frightening. The canoe dipped into a trough and the waves towered overhead. The experienced Chinook paddlers showed the two upriver boys how to steer into the waves until they reached the relative calm away from the bar, and soon Cassino and Monsoe became an integral part of the crew. Before long, they were all whooping and hollering as they crested each wave and slid down the other side. When they returned to the village at the end of the day, both boys agreed that they had enjoyed their most exhilarating day ever.

Soon it was time to make the return trip upriver to Wappato. Shortly before they left, Cassino was summoned to the house of one of the main chiefs. Monsoe was not invited, and he passed the time outside, impatiently scratching pictures in the dirt with a stick. When Cassino finally returned from his audience with the chief, he had a small bag with him and told Monsoe they would have to stop at the Cathlamet village along the way. When Monsoe asked why, all Cassino would say was that he had a message and the contents of the bag to deliver to the Cathlamet chief.

Paddling upriver against the current took much longer than the down-stream journey, but by staying close to the shore, the boys found calmer water and were able to make good progress. They were in no hurry, enjoying the time together and stopping to explore many inlets and islands along the way. They had an adequate supply of food, so they only spent time hunting and fishing when they wanted fresh meat.

When they reached the Cathlamet village, Cassino asked to meet with the top chief. The prospect of two youths expecting an audience with the chief of the most powerful Chinook tribe between Wappato and the mouth of the river was unthinkable, and the people laughed at the boys' request. Cassino was undaunted and eventually arranged to see the chief. He managed to have Monsoe included and both boys were received with honor and treated as warriors.

Monsoe listened in rapt silence as his friend passed along greetings to the Cathlamet chief from the Chinook chief at the mouth of the river and chatted knowledgeably and ably about news and other matters of importance. Monsoe had always admired Cassino's intelligence and self-assurance, but this was the first time he had seen his friend in action before such a powerful audience. Cassino seemed to regard the incident as a matter of little consequence.

The two boys also stopped at the Cowlitch camp and visited a young chief named Soleutu. Monsoe began to see how Cassino was carefully establishing connections with the downriver tribes, but he wouldn't understand the significance of these ties until much later.

When the two travelers finally pulled their canoe up on the beach below Pilmowitsh's house, they were surrounded by Monsoe's family and besieged with eager questions. Pilmowitsh soon arrived and ushered the boys up to the house, where a hot meal was hastily being prepared. As they ate, they told the stories of their adventure, but Cassino said little about his visits with the chiefs on the return trip. As soon as he could politely leave, he slipped away from the house and returned to the Niakowkow village to report to his mother.

As soon as she saw her son, Tenastsil said, "Did you speak to the chief?"

"Yes, Mother," Cassino replied, "and he asked me to visit the Cathlamet village with a message and a gift on the way home."

"Very good," his mother said. "I think the time is right for you to pursue your destiny."

# 2 TENASTSIL

Cassino's mother, Tenastsil, had been born and raised a Yakima, the daughter of a sub-chief. As a girl, she learned the ways of the eastern tribes. When she was fifteen, her father was killed in a skirmish with the Klickitats, and Tenastsil, her mother, and several other Yakima women were carried off as prisoners. A Klickitat brave, struck by the young woman's beauty, thought to take Tenastsil as his wife, but it was near the trading time at the cascades of the Great River, and he decided instead to take her there in hopes of selling her for a high price. He was not disappointed. The great chief of the Chinook bought her at first sight. Though she knew she would never see her mother or people again, Tenastsil did not fear for her future, because her value was secured by the high price that had been paid for her.

Her memories of the long voyage down the river to the ocean remained vivid. It was the first time she had been in a canoe, and her emotions as they moved quickly downriver ranged from fear to delight, and from thrill to total relaxation. Although she found the strange, flat-headed Chinook very different from her native tribe, she felt comfortable with the large number of other "roundhead" slaves in the party.

The Chinook chief, who was about the age of her own father, was infatuated with her, and his patience and gentleness soon endeared him to her. He had kept her separate from the other slaves and made it clear to everyone that she was to be treated with respect.

When the trading party reached the Chinook village at the mouth of the river, Tenastsil was delighted to see the ocean for the first time. She was placed under the care of the chief's numerous other wives, and accorded similar privileges. Although she was a slave, the chief considered her as one of his wives and kept her away from all other men. Soon there was talk in the village about the great chief and his roundhead consort.

The great chief had the rare distinction of being responsible for all the Chinook people, from the mouth of the Great River to the cascades, and he had always fulfilled his role with great care and wisdom. But now he was troubled. Never had he been so completely and inexorably captivated by one woman—and a slave and a roundhead at that. Although she was a girl, barely sixteen years old, she was by far the most intelligent and uniquely special woman he had ever known—and he had known many. He became preoccupied with her and distracted in his duties. His dilemma deepened when he discovered she was pregnant.

When the child was born—a strong and healthy boy—he was named Cassino and the chief ordered his head to be flattened in the traditional Chinook way. The cradleboard was brought and the process begun, but when word filtered out into the village, many nobly born Chinook expressed their disapproval. The thought that the son of a roundhead would have his head flattened was repugnant. Only children whose parents were both Chinook were entitled to this honor, and many feared that other slaves might get the wrong idea.

The chief hoped that the passage of time would defuse the tension, but his continued passion for Tenastsil and the increasing pride he showed in his son did little to help the situation. He tried to disguise his feelings, but no one was fooled. By the time Cassino was a toddler, it was evident that he was exceptional. He always played with older children and diligently investigated everything that came to his attention. As he grew and began to demonstrate his natural leadership ability, his Chinook detractors in the village became even more resentful.

Finally, the great chief realized that a long-term solution must be devised. For many nights, lying side by side, he and Tenastsil discussed the problem and gradually formed a plan. Once the decision had been made, Cassino's father went into considerable detail describing to Tenastsil how the boy was to be raised to eventually become the great chief he was destined to be.

"There is need for strong leadership in the mid-river area around Wappato Island. Though they are brothers, all the tribes there are divided. With cooperation, much could be accomplished, but they need a leader to pull everyone together. I will find a small village where you and our son can go, where Cassino can grow up and gain the respect and trust of the people.

"He will become the greatest chief in the mid-river area, and perhaps someday he will even take the place of his father as chief of all the Chinook. You must see to it that he receives the proper training, my little Tenastsil. I will help in every way I can." He embraced the young woman—the mother of his most favored son—and tried to forget that she would soon be gone from him forever.

When the weather began to turn warm and the blossoms gave way to leaves, Tenastsil and Cassino were sent to live with the Niakowkow. The arrangements were made quietly, and two of the great chief's most trusted friends escorted the Yakima girl and her young son upriver.

Several days passed before the members of the large Chinook village noticed that the slave girl and her boy were gone. None of the great chief's wives would talk about it and no one dared to ask the chief. As time went on, the episode was forgotten, except for an occasional vague rumor from upriver that no one could substantiate. Cassino's father never again turned from his duties and his leadership remained unquestioned.

Tenastsil was welcomed into the home of the elder chief of the Niakowkow and quietly devoted herself to raising her young son. Only the old chief knew the full story and he was sworn to secrecy. Due to the chief's status in the small village, the Niakowkow never questioned the status of the beautiful young roundhead mother and her precocious, flat-headed Chinook son.

Cassino's earliest memories were of his mother telling him about the great chief who was his real father: how he loved them, but how he had to be far away. Tenastsil faithfully trained him and taught him his father's words and wisdom, and planted in his heart the desire to someday be a great chief. Cassino could not remember a time when he did not know what his destiny would be.

Tenastsil never saw the great chief again, but he provided generously and kept himself apprised of the progress and growth of his son. One day, he sent word to the Niakowkow village that he was setting Tenastsil free. He wanted her to find her own happiness, which he would never be able to supply. She was still young and beautiful, and the great chief wanted her to be free to love another man. At first, Tenastsil resisted the idea, but as time went on, she became accustomed to her freedom.

Like most of the Chinook women around her, Tenastsil learned to be free and uninhibited with her sexual favors. Over the next few years, she had liaisons with several prominent men from neighboring Wappato tribes. She bore three daughters and raised them with Cassino.

Six summers passed, and though Tenastsil was now thirty years old, she was still a great beauty. Her fine, shiny black hair was naturally curly—which was unusual for a native woman—and the random strands of silver only made her appearance more striking. She had a full yet delicate face; a warm, soft mouth; and even, white teeth. Her smile and laugh could be shy, suggestive, or dazzling—sometimes all three—and her lovely body remained that of an exquisitely formed young girl. Though she could be irresistible to any man she chose, surprisingly she was not resented by other women. Instead, they envied her, admired her, and liked her.

# THE
# YOUNG
# ONES

One afternoon late in the summer, a canoe put in to shore below Pilmowitsh's house and a young chief of the Quathlahpottle came over to where Pilmowitsh was directing the work on his latest canoe.

Although the chief's face showed concern, he followed the usual protocol by making small talk. "Is this the new canoe everyone is talking about, Pilmowitsh, the one that will be big enough to carry your entire family? How long before you can visit our village so we can see it?"

"We're almost through shaping the bottom," Pilmowitsh replied, "but we still need to finish hollowing out the inside of the hull. It will take us quite a bit longer to completely finish the work, but then it will be the largest we have made. Of course we will come to show it off when it's done," he said with a smile.

Pilmowitsh walked slowly around the upside down canoe. "The prow will be pointed," he explained to his visitor, "and the sides of the hull will curve gradually back to here," he continued, indicating the location he had determined. The bottom of the log at the bow had also been worked back in a slight curve so that when the hull was turned over and in the water it would cut through riffles yet provide lift in swells. There was no curve in the bottom of the stern, but the sides tapered back to a modified blunt point that would cut swells from a following sea. The sides at the stern were somewhat flared to provide a trailing keel for stability and maneuverability.

"I can see why you are called Pilmowitsh the Canoe Builder," said the young chief. "And this will no doubt be your finest yet."

"I am fortunate to have skillful slave artisans who can accomplish much of the work," Pilmowitsh said modestly. "Now, welcome to my house."

The two men walked up to the cedar house, where Pilmowitsh's wives had arranged soft furs around the firepit. They brought Pilmowitsh his pipe and tobacco as the canoe builder and his guest sat down. After a smoke and some more polite small talk, the chief set forth the purpose of his visit.

"The Quathlahpottle and the Multnomah are about to go to war," he began. "Some of the Clannaquah Multnomah came across the river a few days ago to a lodge belonging to one of our sub-chiefs. They killed two slaves and stole two of the chief's wives. We have sent an ultimatum to the Clannaquah that either the wives are returned and the slaves paid for—along with gifts to compensate for the insult to our honor—or we will go to war. Of course, we will parley first, and we have agreed with the Clannaquah that you will make a suitable mediator." He paused to gauge Pilmowitsh's response, then continued, "The parley will be tomorrow at the Clannaquah village, when the sun reaches the top of the sky. Pilmowitsh, will you serve your brothers in this way?"

Pilmowitsh nodded. "I will serve," he said quietly.

When word of the parley reached Pilmowitsh's sons, the excitement in the camp began to build. Monsoe made sure that Cassino was informed, and he joined the brothers around the fire that evening as they talked of war and asked Pilmowitsh questions.

"Father, do you think there will be war?" Monsoe asked.

"The Chinook have an honorable way to wage war," Pilmowitsh replied. "First we try to settle our differences by parley and peaceful negotiation."

"But there is great antagonism between these two tribes," Cassino observed. "The parley won't satisfy them."

"You are right, Cassino, but we are still Chinook and we will follow a certain formality. One never attacks without first informing his enemy of the place and time, and there is no fighting after the sun goes down."

"I have seen the war canoes," added Tanohah. "Why is the fighting done on the river?"

"Each tribe has its land, but we are a water people and the river is a neutral place to fight," Pilmowitsh patiently explained. "The fighting will continue until one or two men are badly hurt or killed. The side that suffers the first casualties loses, and the fighting stops. The losers give presents to the victors and everyone has honor. That is the Chinook way. But let us hope that my words can prevent war."

The next day, Pilmowitsh set out mid-morning to paddle to the Clannaquah village on the river side of Wappato Island. He was received with respect and ushered to the village meeting lodge. The Quathlahpottle canoes arrived a short while later and the parley began when the sun was directly overhead.

Pilmowitsh worked diligently, trying to negotiate a settlement of differences between the two tribes, but the Clannaquah were proud and unyielding, and their ranks were bolstered by a number of young Multnomah warriors who were eager to do battle. The Quathlahpottle representatives became angrier as the parley dragged on, and each time Pilmowitsh thought he was bringing the talks to a successful conclusion, the younger hotheads on both sides would shout down the agreement and undo what he had hoped to accomplish.

By late afternoon, the Quathlahpottle had lost all their patience and announced that they would attack the Clannaquah the next morning. They withdrew abruptly from the parley and pushed off in their canoes, shouting insults as they paddled across the river.

Pilmowitsh returned home, weary and disappointed. His sons greeted him on the beach and peppered him with questions about the parley. "The battle will take place in the morning," was all Pilmowitsh said before he walked slowly up to the house.

Tanohah and Sohowitsh left immediately for their grandfather's house in the Multnomah village. Pilmowitsh knew he didn't have to worry about them. He knew the old chief would keep the boys out of harm's way. Cassino had other ideas, however, and calling for Monsoe to join him, he headed toward the main Clackstar camp. Just before ducking through the door to his house, Pilmowitsh turned and shouted after the two young men. "Stay away from the flying arrows, my sons!" They waved to acknowledge his admonition as they pushed their canoe into the water. Pilmowitsh sighed as he watched them go; his sons were growing up too fast.

Cassino outlined his plan as he and Monsoe paddled quickly up the channel. At the Niakowkow camp, Monsoe jumped ashore and spread the news to any of the young men who wanted to see the battle. Cassino continued alone into Scappoose Bay to the large Clackstar village, where he brought the same message. The Clackstar youths quickly gathered canoes, food and other provisions and followed Cassino back down the bay to meet Monsoe and the Niakowkow group. The entire party crossed the channel and paddled up the slough nearest to Big Rock and cached the canoes.

As the sun was setting over the Scappoose Hills, Cassino led sixteen young braves across the marsh to the Great River side of Wappato. They carefully worked their way up the shore, as close to the Clannaquah village as Cassino deemed safe, and settled down to spend the night. From their vantage point, they would have a good view of both warring camps and the river in between, where the battle would take place. They could already hear a continual stream of shouted insults, war cries, threats and other fearful noises coming from the two camps. The barrage of noise was both frightening and exhilarating.

The Quathlahpottle had established a war camp directly across the river from the Clannaquah, and both sides had begun preparations in earnest. The warriors daubed their faces and bodies with war paint. To indicate that they were a sub-tribe of the Multnomah, the Clannaquah painted themselves one color down one side for the Clannaquah, and another color down the other side for the Multnomah. Both camps readied their bows and arrows, protective wood corsets, tough cassocks of eelskin, and headgear. The corsets were made of rounded sticks of hardwood, interlaced for flexibility and to allow movement, but strong enough to protect against arrows. As soon as the sun went down, fires were lighted on both sides of the river and the two camps increased the tempo and volume of their noisy intimidation to a blood-curdling frenzy that echoed through the night.

When the boys on the bluff had recovered from their initial panic, some wanted to join in the excitement by shouting and cursing. Cassino quickly nixed the idea and put the boys to work. He instructed each one to find a place along the high bank where he would be concealed but could see the entire scene. Cassino and Monsoe distributed food and told everyone to eat and then settle down for a long night.

As the boys ate, a series of terrifying shrieks from the Clannaquah side pierced the night. Cassino turned to Monsoe and whispered, "This will keep us up all night, and it's only going to get worse. Both sides are trying to frighten and discourage their opponents and keep their own warriors on edge and ready to fight. We must keep control of our group. Some of those boys are a lot more frightened than they care to admit. Why don't you move down to the other end of the line, so that everyone else is between us. Tell them all not to leave their places. We must study the battle carefully and learn all we can."

Pausing for emphasis, he added, "Listen to me, Monsoe, and remember this well. It comes from deep in my heart and in my spirit. One day, the Wappato tribes will no longer fight each other. There will be one strong chief over all the tribes—and he will settle all disputes."

Motioning for Monsoe to go, Cassino settled in for the night. Monsoe moved quietly down the line, cautioning each boy along the way. He found it hard to settle himself as he reflected on Cassino's statement. Who would this single, great chief be?

There was little sleep to be had along the river that night as the nerve-wracking bedlam continued. As soon as it was light, Cassino passed out more food and motioned to Monsoe to join him at the top of the bluff. The sun was well up in the sky when suddenly an eerie silence fell across the water. Then, without warning, a deafening crescendo of battle cries split the air like an explosion and canoes from each side came racing out into the river. As was customary, women paddled the war canoes, freeing the warriors to fight. The shrill voices of the women added to the din.

Each group of canoes kept to its side of the river as taunts and challenges were hurled back and forth across the divide. Suddenly, one of the Quathlahpottle canoes darted out of line toward the center of the river. A Clannaquah canoe sped out to meet it. The two boats maneuvered parallel to each other as each side tried to gain the upstream advantage. In a sudden flurry, both sides let fly their arrows as the canoes danced and dodged in an effort to protect the occupants. The canoes moves swiftly and except for their passes at each other kept a safe distance apart. The battle waged back and forth, as one canoe after another joined the fray. Sometimes, after making one pass, a canoe would turn quickly and try to surprise the enemy with a second pass.

The sun was nearing its apex, and still the battle raged on. Cassino, with Monsoe wide-eyed at his side, noted each maneuver and flurry of arrows with a cool detachment. He regularly checked the other boys to make sure they were staying under cover and bearing up under the stress of watching the pitched battle. Everyone along the shore appeared completely enthralled. Cassino and Monsoe analyzed each action and tried to understand the strategy. Suddenly, Cassino stopped talking and pointed to a pair of canoes that were making an unusually close pass. A terrible wail arose from the Clannaquah canoe as a warrior pitched out into the river, an arrow through his neck. The Quathlahpottle warriors were jubilant and the battle was over.

The Clannaquah put down their weapons, fished their fallen comrade out of the water, and returned to the shore. The triumphant Quathlahpottle warriors milled around on the river for a while longer, hooting and hollering. After removing all their war paint, the victorious Quathlahpottle approached the Clannaquah camp and were received with honor. With much ceremony, the Clannaquah and Multnomah presented many gifts and made restitution for the wives and slaves.

After the dispute was settled, life on Wappato returned to its normal serenity. The battle had settled the differences between the Quathlahpottle and the Clannaquah for the time being, and the animosity between the two tribes gradually died down. But in the Clackstar and Niakowkow villages, where groups of young boys reenacted the battle endlessly in their games, the sound and the fury of the great battle lived on.

# PILMOWITSH
# THE CANOE
# BUILDER

As summer faded into fall and the day to leave for Wallamt—the falls on the Multnomah—drew near, Pilmowitsh worked steadily to complete as much of the new canoe as possible. He used controlled fires inside the hull to speed up the hollowing out process—completing the work with tools made of stone and bone. Soon, the finer work of finishing the canoe would begin.

Nanalla's parents came to visit and stayed for several days. They were looking forward to the trip to Wallamt, because the fall run of salmon was always plentiful. One night by the fire Pilmowitsh asked, "Father, do you hope to do any trading at the falls this year?"

The older man looked away from the fire, shifted his weight to make himself a little more comfortable, and replied, "We have taken many birds at the lake this year, so we have plenty of feathers to trade, but we have few skins or furs to spare. Our supply of wappato is sufficient for our own needs, but not for trading. We have some fine bone needles the women will want." He paused for a moment, nodding his head pensively as he considered other wares that might be bartered. "We have all the slaves we want for now," he continued, "but it would be good to trade for some furs. What are your plans, my son?"

"We will spend our time fishing," Pilmowitsh replied. We need a good supply of fish for the winter. The women will trade for trinkets with the people who live around the falls, and I will keep my eyes open for an iron knife—as always. Traveling to Wallamt always reminds me of the first time I saw a Konapee iron knife that would be the perfect tool for building canoes. In fact, you were the one who found it."

"Yes, we Shoto tried to trade for that knife with the Molalla chief, but he would not part with it."

17

The memory of the unsuccessful barter still irritated Pilmowitsh. "He only wore it around his neck as an ornamental weapon of war. What a waste of a priceless tool!"

As they leisurely passed the pipe between them, the men took turns retelling the story of the legendary Konapee for the benefit of the younger men gathered around the fire.

"Many moons ago, the Clatsops pulled four strange men from the sea. They called them 'those who drift ashore.' The men had arrived in a huge canoe with trees and many ropes on it. The canoe burned and from the fire came many strange and wonderful things. The most wonderful of all was the shiny hardness they called iron. Konapee, the "Iron Maker," had the *tamanowos* to make knives and hatchets from this iron. The men also brought copper, from which the Clatsops made bright ornaments to trade with the other tribes along the coast, but the most highly prized tools were those made of iron. Later, but still many winters ago, it was said that Konapee came up the river and married a woman near the Cascades."

The next few days were busy with preparations for the journey. The women packed five canoes with food and tools that they would need, clothing and coverings for sleeping, and poles and mats for two lodges. Pilmowitsh and the men continued to work on the new canoe and had it almost ready for stretching. A uniform thickness to the hull had been achieved by feeling with one hand on the inside of the canoe and the other hand on the outside. Such was Pilmowitsh's skill that the variance from stem to stern was undetectable. The men turned the canoe bottom side up and smoothed the outer surface with fine beaver-tooth chisels. Then the process was repeated on the inside of the hull. When evening fell, they covered the canoe with soft mats and left it for completion when they returned.

That night around the fire, after the men had finished passing the pipe, Tsultsis remarked, "My husband, do you know what the people are saying? They say, 'There goes Pilmowitsh the Canoe Builder.' We hear it everywhere, from all the Wappato tribes; isn't that right, Lopahtah?"

Lopahtah answered with a gentle smile. "It is true, my husband. The Multnomah want your canoes, and we are very proud."

Pilmowitsh was pleased but tried not to show it. He gazed into the fire and made no comment, but his wives understood. Canoe building was his *tamanowos*, which no Chinook man would ever speak of.

As the smoke swirled around his eyes and the flames danced in the fire pit, Pilmowitsh let his mind wander back to the day he left the Clackstar village as a youth and came back as a young man. He had purified himself in the sweat hut and then plunged into the cold water of the channel to complete the process. When he became weak and hungry from fasting, he left the village and hiked alone into the Scappoose Hills. He traveled as far into the woods as his weakened condition would allow, then cleared out a little place under a fallen tree and crawled in. The effort made him hot, but soon he was shivering from the cold of the impending evening. His stomach was cramping and his mouth was parched. Before long, he fell into an uneasy sleep, with unsettling thoughts racing through his head.

His fitful rest was followed by a deeper sleep—and with it, a vivid vision. He saw a cedar tree and three beavers, two large and one small, and the beavers were working to cut down the tree. The beavers changed into two men and a boy, and the boy was Pilmowitsh. After the tree was felled, the two men disappeared and only the boy was left to work on the tree; and when the cedar had been transformed into a beautiful canoe, only the boy was paddling it. Finally, he saw a succession of finely crafted canoes, and in each one sat a solitary boy, and that boy was always Pilmowitsh.

When Pilmowitsh awoke from his sleep, the sun was out and his time of fasting was over. He ate his fill of berries that he found nearby, and reflected for a long time on his vision. His *tamanowos* was clear; he had no doubt. From that time on, he learned and practiced the art of canoe building. Now they were calling him "Pilmowitsh the Canoe Builder." The recognition was gratifying; it meant he was realizing his *tamanowos*. What more fulfillment could a man want from his life? Still, he must not become complacent; he must continue to improve, to perfect his craft, to express himself in wood—the noble cedar—according to his *tamanowos*.

The next morning, everyone was up early for their departure to Wallamt. The children were laughing and running excitedly about. Pilmowitsh divided his family and slaves equally among the canoes, making sure that the ablest paddlers were placed to the best advantage. Shoving off in the lead canoe, he looked back with satisfaction at the procession behind him—each canoe an example of his craft, and each one cutting smoothly through the water of the channel. He decided that they would need to camp one night along the way. Even though it was late summer, with low water and a relatively weak current, the journey was still long and entirely upstream.

The day was perfect—warm but not hot, with just enough breeze to keep the paddlers from overexerting—as they slipped along the back side of Wappato Island. There was not a cloud in the pale blue sky for as far as the eye could see. Birds of all sizes and descriptions were everywhere—scuttling along the beaches and skimming low over the water in search of their next meal. A vivid gold and black butterfly fluttered across the channel from the green, sun-drenched bank.

Each village they passed seemed deserted, a testimony to the general migration toward the falls. There was no sound except the cries of the birds, the dip of the oars, and the occasional subdued voice from one of the canoes.

They passed the deep river leading into the main lake on Wappato and skirted the little island in the channel. Deer stepped from the cover of the trees along the bank to drink from the shallow edges of the water. Further on, a bear perched on a rock outcropping studied the rippling current, poised to swipe at any fish that dared to swim within reach. Pilmowitsh began to watch for a place to beach the canoes, so the group could eat and rest. Before long, he saw a tiny creek coming from the mainland side of the waterway, and a sandy beach nearby. He signaled the others to put ashore, and the women began to prepare a meal in the shade of some large trees clustered along the shore.

When everyone had been refreshed, the small group pushed the canoes away from the bank. Back on the water, with the sun stretching toward its zenith, the day was warmer but still pleasant. The travelers knew they were approaching the upriver end of Wappato and the Multnomah River. The Multnomah at this point was nearly as wide as the Great River itself. The densely forested hills to the west seemed to run straight up from the river, hiding the afternoon sun and making a cool, dark edge on the water.

Pilmowitsh kept on until they were some distance up the Multnomah before looking for a suitable place to spend the night. He spotted a high bluff on the east side of the river. Rich bottom land, which was covered by water much of the year, extended out from the bluff and away from the river in a great semicircular basin. It was a delightful and secure place for the children to play in the water and explore the edges of the river while the elders made camp.

After the evening meal, everyone settled around the campfire ready for story time. In the background, two mat lodges, where the travelers would sleep, were silhouetted in the waning light of dusk. Pilmowitsh gazed up at the sky, which was beginning to reveal its glittering treasure of stars. After a moment, he looked around the campfire at his family and began to speak:

"All day we passed alongside our beautiful Wappato Island. You know its simplicity and its grandeur in every season of the year. You know its grasses and roots; its berries, nuts and trees; its rivers and its lakes. You know the fish, the birds, and the animals that make their homes on this great island. And you know the people. Most of us were born on or near this island, and we have lived our lives there. It is well that we remember how we came to be here in the valley of the Great River, and of the Bridge of the Gods that was located where the Great River cuts through the mountains. Above that place is the summer meeting ground where all the tribes who live beyond the mountains come to trade with those of us who live on this side of the mountains.

"Our fathers have told us—just as they were told by their fathers, and by their fathers' fathers before them—of a time long, long ago, when the Great Spirit Sahale had no people on the Great River. Then the Great Spirit caused a father and his two sons to come from the east. When the father and his sons arrived at what is now the summer meeting grounds, they were overwhelmed by the grandeur and magnificence of thsurrounding land. The two boys began to quarrel and fight bitterly over which part of the land each should possess. Finally the father settled the dispute in this way: He took two arrows and shot one far to the north, and the other far to the west. Then he told one son to seek the arrow to the north, and when he found it to settle and raise his family in that place. He told the other son to seek out the arrow to the west, and to settle and raise his family in that place. The son who went to the north founded the Klickitat nation." Pilmowitsh paused for emphasis, "The son who went to the west was our own forefather, who established our own great Multnomah nation."

Pilmowitsh signaled to one of the female slaves to put more wood on the fire. When the flames were again leaping high, Pilmowitsh continued his story.

"Sahale, the Great Spirit, thought it well to separate the two great nations, so he raised the mountains between them. These were ordinary mountains, without the snowcapped peaks you see today. He formed a massive rock bridge over the Great River from one mountainside to another. Our fathers tell us that the bridge was so towering that many men in canoes could pass under it on the Great River.

"Now, at this time, man did not know about fire. The Great Spirit Sahale placed a witch woman, Loowit, on the *tamanowos* bridge to tend the fire and guard it. As time went on, Loowit felt sorry for the people, because she knew how much better their lives would be with fire. She begged Sahale to allow her to give fire to the people. He finally agreed and the lives of the people improved greatly. Sahale was pleased with how carefully and well Loowit had guarded the sacred fire, and he decided to reward her with a gift of her choosing. After much thought, she asked Sahale to change her into a beautiful young maiden.

"Soon all the young chiefs were in love with Loowit, but she paid little attention to any of them. Then two strong and handsome young chiefs became interested in Loowit at the same time. One, called Klickitat, was from the north, and the other, called Wyeast, was from the west. Both young chiefs began to court the favor of Loowit, but they began to quarrel when she could not choose between them. They led their people in war against each other, and soon there was much destruction, suffering and misery. The people were worse off and more to be pitied than before they received fire.

"The Great Spirit Sahale was very angry. He caused the *tamanowos* bridge to collapse into the Great River, which backed up its waters and caused the roaring cascades you see there to this day. In his fury, Sahale had Loowit, Klickitat, and Wyeast put to death. But when his anger had subsided, he remembered the purity of their love and their desire to do what they thought was right. He decided to erect permanent monuments to the fallen trio, so they would never be forgotten by the people.

"On the south side of the Great River, Sahale raised the sharply pointed monument called Wyeast, which touched the clouds and was seen by everyone. He caused this great monument to be covered by pure white snow year round.

"On the north side of the river, he raised the ruggedly handsome Klickitat, which also stretched to the clouds and was blanketed with the purity of snow.

"Then, within sight of the two great chiefs, but off to the west by herself, Sahale raised the softly rounded Loowit, as a monument to the beautiful young maiden forever."

The children around the campfire were enchanted by the telling of the well-loved story, and everyone was reluctant to break the silence when Pilmowitsh was finished. Finally, the long day and a healthy fatigue from the paddling took its toll, and one by one each went to his place in the mat lodges. The fire soon died down, and only the soft sounds of the night could be heard beneath the lush blanket of the stars.

The next morning, before the sun had cast its rays into the bottom lands, the procession of canoes again plied the waters of the Multnomah. By mid-morning, as they neared the falls, they began to see families and tribes camped along the river. From the mouth of the Clackamas River to the falls, every available spot along both sides of the river was taken. When the roar of the falls began to echo along the rock walls of the canyon, Pilmowitsh motioned for his followers to turn the canoes around to seek a suitable campground to the north, downstream. When at last they had settled on the high side of a sandy knoll, the women set about establishing the camp while the men took the canoes back upriver to survey the fishing prospects.

The days spent at Wallamt were enjoyable and profitable. The Chinook families took home all the dressed-out salmon they could load into their canoes, along with other goods they had received in trade. It was an exciting time, especially for the children, but it was always good to return home and settle back into the daily routine.

After he returned to Wappato, Pilmowitsh focused his attention on completing the canoe. Each step was meticulously planned, the slaves who would assist in the work were instructed, and all the materials were made ready. Pilmowitsh was busy. He sent slaves to haul many large stones from the river, which were placed into two large fires kept burning in the clearing. Pilmowitsh retrieved the stretcher boards he had fashioned to use as thwarts and carefully checked their lengths.

The canoe was set on two logs, one near the bow and the other near the stern, and the hull was partially filled with water. Between the logs, small bark fires were kindled under the entire length of the canoe.

As the stones in the large fires became hot, they were carried on boards and dropped sizzling into the water in the canoe. Hot stones replaced cold ones as needed. The heat and steam generated through this process gradually softened the canoe so that the stretching and final shaping could begin. Pilmowitsh instructed several slaves to pull the sides of the hull apart at the center and he deftly inserted the longest thwart. Progressively shorter thwarts were inserted on each side until every one was in place and the canoe took on its final shape. Then the rocks were discarded, the water was dumped from the hull and the drying began.

While the canoe was drying, Pilmowitsh spent his time carving paddles and finishing the headpiece. When the inside of the hull had dried sufficiently, slaves were put to work smoothing out the bottom and removing any scars caused by the fires. Lava and sandstone were used to sand the entire canoe. Then the outside was painted black, using a mixture of burnt rushes and oil, and the inside was stained red with an oil-based, red ochre paint. The edges of the hull were trimmed with shells.

The final step was to secure the headpiece, a custom-designed, intricately carved piece of cedar that Pilmowitsh had begun crafting about the same time he started the canoe. Long evenings of careful carving were now impressively displayed in the splendid figure of a bear. Pilmowitsh secured the headpiece to the body of the canoe, using wooden pegs and passing the tapered ends of cedar limbs through holes drilled in the hull. The entire family followed in procession as the slaves carried the beautiful canoe down to the beach and carefully slid it into the water. The graceful bow cut through the water with scarcely a ripple. Murmurs of praise and admiration rippled through the small gathering and Pilmowitsh sighed with satisfaction at the perfectly balanced work of his hands.

The canoe was large enough to hold everyone, so they climbed aboard and set out up the channel to show it off at the Clackstar village.

# THE IRON KNIFE

One day, not long after Pilmowitsh had completed his masterpiece canoe, his fourth wife, Shenshina, came to ask permission to visit her family among the Cowlitch. They had not traveled to Wallamt earlier that year and she had not seen them for some time. The Cowlitch lived a fair distance downriver and Pilmowitsh was reluctant to let her go without him, but he was preparing to stretch a new canoe and didn't have time to travel. Her apparent anxiousness was perplexing, but he finally gave his consent for her to go, as long as she was accompanied by a male and female slave.

At daybreak the next morning, Shenshina and the two slaves paddled quietly down the Great River. She was excited yet apprehensive at the thought of going home. Although she was happy living among the Multnomah, she had never quite thought of "home" as anywhere other than the Cowlitch village. Pilmowitsh was a fine and sensitive husband, and she was proud of him, but she knew deep in her heart that he did not love her in the same way he loved the others, especially Lopahtah. Still, Shenshina wasn't jealous, because she too loved the cheerful, warm Lopahtah, who had always found ways to make her feel comfortable and content.

The Cowlitch were the most influential tribe between the mouth of the Great River and the Multnomah. Shenshina was accustomed to the large village and many friends. Her childhood friend Soleutu had become one of the leading young men in her tribe. He was highly esteemed by the chiefs and elders and it was thought that he would soon become a chief. When she was younger, she had always thought that Soleutu had looked upon her favorably and she had secretly hoped he would take her as his wife. Even after her marriage to Pilmowitsh, she had held a soft spot in her heart for Soleutu, and it was Soleutu who would figure prominently in Shenshina's unfolding plan to find an iron knife for her husband Pilmowitsh.

Shenshina reminded herself that she must be careful in how she went about her mission, but if all went well, everyone concerned would be happier and richer.

When Shenshina and the slaves arrived at the Cowlitch village, she went quickly to find her mother before her presence in the village could become widely known. When her mother saw her, she pulled her daughter quickly inside the family lodge, and the two women had a joyful reunion.

Shenshina told her mother about Pilmowitsh's skill as a canoe builder, his great gift for working with wood and the excellence of his canoes and carvings. She described the beautiful new canoe he had just completed and explained his great desire to have an iron knife. She knew that in the past the Cowlitch had owned several of the coveted iron tools, and she asked whether anyone in the village might have one to trade. Next, she told in great detail the story of her life among the Multnomah, including her relationship with her husband and with the other wives, especially Lopahtah. Finally, she told her mother the secret desire of her heart.

When Shenshina had finished her story, her mother promised to speak to Shenshina's father and ask him to approach Soleutu.

Shenshina spent several happy weeks renewing old acquaintances before the time arrived to begin the journey back upriver.

One clear, cool day in late fall, a lone warrior with six slaves beached his canoe below Pilmowitsh's house. The renowned canoe builder went down to greet the newcomer, and showed him samples of his work before bringing him into the house. When his wives had gathered to meet their guest, Pilmowitsh said, "This is Soleutu of the Cowlitch. Our house is his house. Make him welcome and comfortable."

The women quickly placed mats in front of the fire for the two men. The best food in the house was brought out and Pilmowitsh cooked and served a meal for his guest. The pipe was then offered and the men enjoyed a leisurely smoke. Finally, Pilmowitsh said, "Tell me the news of the Cowlitch. Has it been a good year?"

"Yes, my friend," replied Soleutu. "The summer was bountiful and we are well prepared for the winter. We have plenty of food and many furs from trading with the Clatsops and other Chinook tribes along the coast. Many of our families went upriver to the great trading time at the Cascades, but most traded downriver this year. The salmon were so plentiful in the Great River by our village that few went to the falls of the Multnomah."

Pilmowitsh nodded in agreement. "We saw no Cowlitch at the falls, though there were many from the Wappato tribes and many more from the south: the Clackamas, the Molalla, the Calapooya, and the Tualiti; but very few from downriver. What do you know of the Cathlamets?"

"Much peace and goodwill exists between the Cowlitch and the Cathlamets at this time," replied Soleutu. "But it has not always been so. It is good to be able to trade with them again." He paused for a moment and looked into the fire before he continued, "I've heard many good words about Pilmowitsh the Canoe Builder and the excellence of his work."

Pilmowitsh was pleased, but he replied quietly, "Many of the tribes have fine canoe builders."

Soleutu nodded. "The men of our tribe heard from some of the Clackstar about your new large canoe. We were told there is no better canoe on the river and now that I have seen it myself, I know they did not exaggerate. The men of my tribe desire such a canoe and will give many slaves to acquire it."

When trading, it was customary to be less direct, so Pilmowitsh was cautious and a bit puzzled by Soleutu's straightforward approach. To test the younger man's strategy, he said, "The new canoe is large enough for my entire family and several slaves. It represents a lot of time and a lot of work. With winter coming on, I do not wish to acquire additional slaves. It is a poor time to talk of a trade."

"Any time is a good time to trade if one has something that the other desires," Soleutu said with confidence. "Pilmowitsh, let me show you something."

From a bag at his side, Soleutu withdrew a long, slender bundle of doeskin. With great care, he slowly unwrapped the skin and with a dramatic flourish withdrew a heavy-bladed iron knife.

Pilmowitsh was astounded. He had never before seen an iron knife and he didn't know what to say. He wanted to touch it, feel it in his hand

and imagine what it would be like to work with such a fine tool. It was hard not to show his emotions, but he managed to nod his approval while maintaining an impassive expression on his face.

Soleutu smiled and carefully handed the knife to Pilmowitsh. "Take it, examine it, just as I have examined the canoe. Then tell me if we cannot discuss a trade."

Unable to conceal his eagerness any longer, Pilmowitsh took the solid, substantial knife into his hand for the first time. He felt its strength, the cold blade honed smooth. His fingers curled around the handle and he nodded in appreciation of the finely balanced weight. The knife was superior to any tool he had ever used. He had to have it.

Soleutu noticed the subtle change in Pilmowitsh's expression and he smiled inwardly. He knew the advantage was his for the moment and he reminded himself to be shrewd and cautious. The stakes were high and he must be careful to strike the proper bargain. He waited quietly for Pilmowitsh to begin the bargaining.

As he turned the knife over in his hand, Pilmowitsh tried to slow his racing thoughts, to concentrate on the deal that would have to be made. How had Soleutu known that he coveted an iron knife? Shenshina! Of course, she had told the Cowlitch when she visited her family. He had her to thank for this opportunity. But could he manage the trade? The advantage was with Soleutu and both men knew it. Pilmowitsh would have to begin the bargaining, but he delayed for a few moments to collect his thoughts.

Raising his eyes from the knife, Pilmowitsh nodded in agreement. "You were right about this being a proper time to trade. For the right price, this iron knife would be very useful for building canoes." Soleutu smiled but said nothing.

Pilmowitsh paused, then pressed on. "A trade of the knife for the big canoe might be possible."

Soleutu pursed his lips and appeared to be weighing the proposition. Finally he said, "With the canoe, we would need much wappato in exchange for the knife."

Pilmowitsh felt a rush of exuberance wash over him and he spoke a second too soon. "For the iron knife, I will give you the big canoe and half of my winter store of wappato."

Soleutu hesitated. He knew the moment of truth had arrived and that his next words would either seal the deal or set the negotiations back—

perhaps irreparably. Softly, he said, "Your offer is generous, but as I told you, we have an adequate supply of food for the coming winter." He paused again, as if to gather his thoughts. "For such a fine knife as this, I must have the large canoe—and—your wife Shenshina to become my wife."

Pilmowitsh felt the blood drain from his face and for a moment he could not find his breath. The practice of trading wives was customary among the Chinook, but he had never considered the possibility for himself. He wanted the knife—he must have it!—but the proposed price was too high. He was about to shake his head with regret when it suddenly occurred to him that Shenshina might have arranged the terms of the trade as well as proposing the idea to Soleutu. To Pilmowitsh, this new thought was like a dagger in his heart.

Finally he said to Soleutu, "Such a great trade must be carefully considered. I need time to think." With great reluctance, he handed the iron knife back.

Soleutu carefully wrapped the knife in the doeskin and placed it in his bag. He felt compassion for Pilmowitsh and sought to convey his understanding. He said, "Shenshina is a fine woman. She is Cowlitch. We played together as children and I watched as she grew into a gentle and dutiful young woman. She always made her father proud. Of all the young women in the village, none was more careful or painstaking in her work. Shenshina brings much honor to you and to the Cowlitch.

"Please consider my offer of the iron knife in exchange for Shenshina and the large canoe. I must visit the Clackstar village nearby before I go home. I will return in two days and I will hear your answer then."

Soleutu arose from beside the fire and Pilmowitsh accompanied him down to the beach. He was grateful for the time to think about the trade and he told Soleutu, "My house remains your house. My father and brother will be honored to receive you as their guest in the Clackstar village. I will have an answer for you when you return." He summoned one of his slaves and sent him on ahead of Soleutu with a message to his father.

When Pilmowitsh returned to the house, he heard the chatter of his wives subside and they quickly busied themselves with activities outside to give him his peace. He knew they had heard the entire conversation with Soleutu, but he chose to keep his own counsel.

That night around the fire was unusually quiet. There was no story time and even the children felt the tension as the adults found things to do that did not require conversation. Pilmowitsh sat in his customary spot shaping a stone tool. He imagined what it would be like to carve with an iron knife. Then thoughts of Shenshina flooded his mind. How could he send her away? He had often worried about whether she was happy, though she had never complained. She had always worked hard and had been a faithful wife. They had grieved together when she lost her child, but she had seemed to recover and was hopeful that someday she might again conceive. Pilmowitsh sighed and set down the stone tool he had been absently working. "Tonight I will sleep alone," he said quietly. "In the morning, I would like Shenshina to accompany me in one of the small canoes."

The morning broke gray and cold. Shenshina and Pilmowitsh were dressed warmly against the chill and Shenshina carried an extra blanket with her down to the beach. Pilmowitsh had his firestick and a slave loaded extra kindling into the canoe. Instead of venturing into the Great River, the two set out up the channel, paddling past Big Rock. Pilmowitsh steered up a little slough that was partially hidden by a sand bar and beached the canoe. They walked away from the shore to the shelter of a large oak tree and Pilmowitsh built a fire. When the fire was well established, the two sat silently for a long time, warming themselves and thinking about what to say.

Shenshina began to speak, but Pilmowitsh raised his hand to silence her, then reached over and pulled her close to him. Sheltering her in his arms, he said softly, "My precious wife, there is something that has troubled me for some time, which I have never mentioned to you. You have been a good wife—no man could ask for more—but you have not seemed as happy as the others. Often I have thought to speak to you about this, but I kept silent because I feared the truth in my heart."

Shenshina looked up at him, returning his smile. "No woman could have a kinder husband," she said, "but there have been so many times when I have missed my family, missed the others in my village. I am not like the others because I am the only one not from Wappato—the only one of your wives who was not born and raised on or near the island. No matter how hard I have tried, I have never felt that I belonged here among the Multnomah. My place is with the Cowlitch.

"Also, I have struggled to find my place with you. A woman wants to do for her husband what no other woman can do. Tsultsis gave you your first son, and Lopahtah has also given you a fine son. And we all know that Lopahtah gives you the best of what a man desires most from a woman. Nanalla is the youngest and she will find her way, just as...just as I have at last found mine." She looked intently into his eyes, then dropped her gaze and continued before he could interrupt. "Pilmowitsh, my dear husband, I can give you the iron knife. I can give you what no other woman can. I know in my heart that you desire this knife, and I want you to have it, because I know the wonderful work you will do with it."

Pilmowitsh was stunned by the depth of her love for him and he struggled to control the emotion in his voice as he responded. "Shenshina, my heart is overflowing. But what about you? Would you go willingly with Soleutu?"

"Soleutu is a kind and noble man," she replied. "He is not a great craftsman like you, but he expresses his creativity in leadership. In many ways he is an artist when it comes to influencing and leading our people. I have known Soleutu all of my life, and I know that someday soon he will be a respected chief among the Cowlitch."

Pilmowitsh started to speak, but Shenshina placed her fingers on his lips to stop him.

"Now," she said, "I am going to tell you something that I have never mentioned before. Since I was a little girl, Soleutu has desired me in much the same way you desire Lopahtah. I can tell you this because I know you will understand and will not be angry with me. And Soleutu has only one wife and no son. Perhaps I will be honored to give him a son. So you can see, this trade will be good for both sides; everyone will gain. Please give me the honor of presenting you with the iron knife that you desire, and allow me to return to my place among the Cowlitch."

Pilmowitsh drew her closer to himself. "You are a wise and wonderful young woman. You are worth far more to me than the iron knife, though you know how much I desire to own it. I wonder if Soleutu knows that he is receiving by far the better half of the bargain."

"He knows," Shenshina said gently.

# THE
# WHITE MAN
# COMES

L ate the following spring, when the weather turned mild, Pilmowitsh and his sons repaired their nets in anticipation of the first run of salmon in the Great River. New strips of white cedar bark were woven into the gaps, and round, flat rock sinkers were drilled or notched and then tied on to the edges of the nets with fiber cords. The nets were of various sizes, and the largest was longer than Pilmowitsh's house.

When the salmon began to run, the catch was so bountiful that the family was kept busy catching, cleaning and smoking the fish.

One day, Pilmowitsh called his sons together, along with Cassino, and said, "The river has been good to us and we have abundant food from the forest as well. It is time that we prepare a feast to honor our family and friends. Chief Taneeho will be our guest of honor, Nanalla's parents will have a special place, and we will invite our Clackstar relatives. Cassino, your mother will of course be included, as well as some of our Niakowkow friends. Who else should be invited?"

The young men added their suggestions to the list of guests, and the group began planning and preparing for the celebration. Firepits were dug for roasting venison, birds and fresh salmon. A separate hole was dug to hold the stones that would heat the stew pots, and yet another pit for steaming wappato and other foods. The young men cut planks for skewering the salmon, and fashioned spits to roast the meat. The women brought tightly woven baskets to hold the stew. The younger children gathered fresh berries and herbs to supplement the dried herbs and nuts from the storehouse. Pilmowitsh's camp was a beehive of activity for several days.

The feast day dawned clear and bright. As the sun began its ascent in the southeastern sky, the guests began arriving. Soon a row of canoes lined the shore. Monsoe and Cassino uncovered the pits and brought out steaming baskets of wappato. Tanohah and Sohowitsh tended the spits, broiling salmon and roasting fowl. They selected choice pieces to serve to the guests of honor. Pilmowitsh ladled a hearty venison stew into wooden bowls while his younger sons served such delicacies as dried berries, nuts, wild onions, and fresh wild strawberries. The guests talked and laughed and carried on merrily while stuffing themselves with the delicious feast.

A quickly moving canoe rounding the tip of Wappato Island went unnoticed by the revelers. When the canoe reached the shore, a young Multnomah warrior jumped out and sprinted toward Pilmowitsh's house. Not pausing for any of the customary greetings or invitations, and glancing neither right or left, he made a beeline for Chief Taneeho. In shocked silence, everyone stared at the urgent newcomer.

"Chief Taneeho," the young warrior gasped as he tried to regain his breath, "the chiefs of the Multnomah are meeting in tribal council. Astonishing news has come from down river. Two days ago a great canoe, greater in size than anyone can imagine, came across the bar into the Great River. This great canoe has trees on it that soar into the clouds, and it travels through the water without paddles. This canoe carries many of 'those who drift ashore,' as in the Konapee legend. They are strangely dressed and their faces are pale as the moon. They trade for furs—nothing else!"

Taneeho rose quickly and turned to Pilmowitsh. Making his apologies, he said "I must go to the council and decide what we should do. Will you go downriver, my son?"

Without hesitation, Pilmowitsh replied, "Yes, my father. I will depart as soon as the canoes are made ready. I will take Monsoe, Tanohah and Sohowitsh—and also Cassino if he wishes to go."

The guests, who had gathered in clusters around the warrior and the chief, al began talking at once. Chief Taneeho thanked Pilmowitsh for the feast before leaving quickly with the young warrior. The others mingled for a time discussing the news before leaving for their homes. Pilmowitsh gave instructions to his wives and slaves to prepare provisions for the upcoming journey.

Cassino was pleased that Pilmowitsh had suggested that he accompany the group downriver. It would be an honor to travel with the best canoe builder on the river to see this strange new canoe. He was also happy that they would have Tanohah's expertise to navigate the rough waters of the Great River.

Tanohah suggested that they take one of the canoes that would be easily handled by the five of them, but Pilmowitsh said, "There will be many others who will come to see this sight. We must plan to camp out and not depend on the hospitality of our brothers in the lower villages. We will need our largest canoe to carry enough supplies in addition to the slaves we will need to work."

Tanohah readily agreed. "We can save some space by cutting the necessary poles at the place where we establish our camp," he said. "That way we can carry enough mats for two lodges."

"We have plenty of food left over from the feast to feed us for several days," added Monsoe. "I will ask the women to pack some for our journey. I know my mother wishes to straighten up the camp and she will be pleased that nothing will be wasted."

"Yes," said Pilmowitsh. "Do that and then you and Cassino gather the other supplies we will need." Turning to Tanohah, he continued, "Have you thought of which slaves we will need? I know you will select the best canoemen, but remember that we will be downriver for several days and we will have other work to be done." The two men discussed the merits of each slave and finally agreed on seven men and three strong young women, good paddlers who could also do the cooking.

Cassino and Monsoe had their own agenda in mind. As they collected supplies for the trip, they also gathered all the furs they could find. They even went so far as to send slaves to the Clackstar and Niakowkow villages to get more pelts for trading.

Pilmowitsh felt uneasy about leaving his wives behind, because he was certain they would want to see this curious canoe as much as he did. But Tsultsis insisted that she would stay behind to straighten the camp and keep things in order while the men were gone, and Nanalla was reluctant to leave the smaller children behind for an unknown length of time. When Lopahtah realized that the other wives were staying behind, she asked Pilmowitsh if she could go along. Pilmowitsh was delighted to include her in the traveling party.

The addition of Lopahtah brought the size of the party to sixteen, all of whom were capable paddlers.

By early afternoon, Tsultsis and Lopahtah had packed the canoe with food and cooking supplies, and Nanalla had inspected all the mats before placing them inside the hull. Pilmowitsh checked all the supplies, including extra paddles, firesticks, a few cutting tools, baskets, pipe and tobacco, and fishing nets. He looked with surprise at the bundle of furs that Cassino and Monsoe had gathered, but then he nodded his approval. Cassino, Monsoe and Sohowitsh packed them into the canoe, Tanohah assigned each traveler a place to sit based on each one's skill with the paddles, and the group pushed off into the waters of the Great River.

Swelled by the melting snowpack in the mountains, the water in the river was swift, strong and cold. As soon as the canoe left the shelter of the point, the powerful current swept it along at great speed. Tanohah was exhilarated. He loved the challenge of navigating the mighty river at high water; avoiding the eddies, watching alertly for snags, submerged logs and other debris, while steering the craft to take maximum advantage of the downstream flow. Once again, he appreciated the fine craftsmanship of a Pilmowitsh-built canoe.

The travelers saw many other canoes on the river, all headed downriver on a pilgrimage to see the great canoe and "those who drift ashore." Lopahtah sat directly in front of Pilmowitsh, which made it easy for the two to converse privately. As they passed the river of the Cowlitch, Pilmowitsh said, "I am happy that everything turned out as it did for Shenshina and Soleutu. She was a good woman."

"She was brave and wise," replied Lopahtah. "She deserved to have her happiness."

"The Chinook way between man and woman is best," Pilmowitsh said thoughtfully. "I have heard that some of the tribes above the Cascades believe a woman is no good if she has been married to another. No man will take her as his wife. What a crazy idea! And how unnatural. Once a man takes a wife and they belong to each other, what has gone before should make no difference."

The wind was beginning to build as it often did in the late afternoon, blowing directly downriver from the east. Tanohah took note of the first gentle swells on the river. With the strong current and all the debris in the water—including some massive logs they had passed along the way—

he knew the river could quickly become dangerous if the paddlers weren't prudent. As the wind increased, the swells grew larger, and Tanohah knew that a nasty chop was soon to follow.

Just ahead, he saw a sandy island that looked as though it might make a suitable campsite. He shouted ahead to Pilmowitsh in the middle of the canoe, "Father, let's make camp up ahead!"

Pilmowitsh turned his head quickly and nodded his agreement without missing a stroke. Tanohah expertly guided the canoe out of the mainstream and soon the craft was beached in a small, sheltered lagoon protected by a strip of smooth white sand. As the group made camp, it started to rain. The wind increased and the rain came down in torrents.

*On the evening of the thirteenth of May, 1792, Captain Robert Gray checked the security of his ship, the* Columbia Rediviva, *as it lay at anchor about ten miles up the bay opposite a large Chinook village on the north shore. Three days prior, they had sailed past Cape Disappointment, discovered the channel and proceeded over the bar at approximately eight o'clock in the morning. The weather at the time had been calm, but today had turned miserable. The rain was a constant drizzle with an occasional downpour. The wind whipped in every direction, with the strongest gusts coming in from the southwest. The strong outgoing current carried with it a steady cargo of debris, which only added to Captain Gray's concern about the safety of his vessel. He gave orders to move further upstream at the first opportunity.*

*Up on deck, Captain Gray inspected the ship's guns and cautioned his men to remain alert and keep an eye on the hordes of natives who had paddled their canoes alongside the ship. Although he was certain that most of them had never before seen a white man, they seemed to be familiar with iron and copper. When he was satisfied that all was in order, Captain Gray instructed his mate to summon him at the first sign of a disturbance and then retired to his cabin.*

*Alone in his quarters, the captain weighed the situation. As the first to trade with the natives, Captain Gray enjoyed the advantage of acquiring extremely fine furs at a low cost. The unusually large number of natives in the area indicated they had come from great distances up and down the coast, and also from upriver. His men had remarked about the finer, more stately appearance of these natives compared to the ones they had traded with up north around Nootka Sound. The captain's main concern was that news of the incident at Gray's Harbor might have reached these parts and would cause trouble.*

*Captain Gray bitterly regretted having to use force—against his own principles and his orders—but there had been no alternative. The* Columbia *had been anchored in a lovely inlet about fifty miles north of its present position. At the insistence of his mate, John Boite, the bay had been recorded on the chart as Gray's Harbor in the captain's honor. But the natives had become warlike and began approaching the ship in great numbers. The crew had fired on one canoe of warriors, leaving no apparent survivors. The other canoes had immediately turned away, or the carnage could have been much worse. The natives here in the river had thus far been very friendly and did not seem to fear the* Columbia's *crew. He hoped that nothing would happen to change the situation for the worse.*

*Captain Gray was proud of his ship. At first, he had regretted giving up the helm of the* Lady Washington, *but after taking command of the* Columbia *and sailing her to China and then home to Boston—the first American ship to sail around the world—he believed there would never be another ship like her! Now on his second voyage, she had brought them over the bar into the "Great River of the West." He had decided to name the river after his beloved ship, and already the men were calling it "Columbia's river." He determined to sail upstream the next day at slack water—before the beginning of the flood tide—to find a more protected anchorage.*

After a wet and chilly night, Pilmowitsh and his party were grateful for the leftover food from the feast. The quick onset of the rain had prevented them from setting up an adequate shelter the previous night and the soggy conditions on the island made it difficult to keep a cooking fire going.

Although the wind had slackened somewhat, the rain continued unabated. The rest of the journey promised to be wet and rough, but everyone was eager to continue as soon as the morning meal had been completed.

As soon as the canoe ventured out from the protection of the island into the mainstream, it was swept along at an alarming pace. Tanohah became uneasy when he saw no other boats in the water. The strong current, along with the outgoing tide, created riffles and swells, making the water unpredictable. With the winds beginning to increase once again, Tanohah knew that approaching the final bend in the river at this stage would be too dangerous. He steered the canoe on the slack side of the next island and shouted above the wind, "Father, we must wait for the changing of the tide." Pilmowitsh nodded in agreement.

Once the canoe had been pulled ashore, everyone pitched in to erect a shelter of mats on the tree-lined shore. A fire was kindled and the group settled down to eat. Cassino turned to Tanohah and said, "Where do you think we will find the great canoe? Down by the Chinook village, as the Multnomah warrior said?"

Tanohah looked at the wind bending the tops of the trees and whistling through the branches. "The Chinook village sits near the mouth of the Great River, which is open water. The poor weather might make 'those who drift ashore' seek a more sheltered place. Suppose you were guiding this great canoe. Would you stay out in the open bay? Even if this canoe is as large as they say, it still might navigate upriver. Perhaps we shall see it sooner than we think."

Sohowitsh interrupted excitedly. "You mean we might meet it up *here*, Tanohah? Hadn't we better cross to the other side of the island to watch for it?"

Tanohah laughed and said, "The tide is wrong for the great canoe to move upriver. Didn't you notice this morning that we were the only canoe on the water? When the tide turns and the wind dies down, there will be many canoes in the river and then we can cross the island."

Around midday, the heavy rain turned to mist, the sun tried valiantly to burn through the clouds, and the wind slackened to a stiff, intermittent breeze. The travelers quickly packed the canoe and launched back into the river, joining the many other canoes headed downstream. The excitement grew at each turn of the river. Everyone leaned forward, straining their eyes to peer into the distance, only to settle back with a disappointed sigh as the river stretched before them with no sign of the fabled canoe. As the next bend approached, the excitement began to build again, and the rhythmic dipping of the paddles increased ever so slightly.

Well into the afternoon, as they finally rounded the last major bend in the river, Tanohah held the canoe close to the north shore. Suddenly the cry went up, "There it is! There it is! The great canoe!" Away in the distance, shrouded in the mist, great white clouds appeared to hover on the water. As they drew closer, they could see scores of smaller canoes milling around—far more than they had ever seen, even at trading time. The scene was at once exciting and unsettling. The delighted chatter in Pilmowitsh's canoe soon gave way to silent anticipation as the paddlers picked up the pace in unison.

Lopahtah's impassive face showed no trace of the uncertainty she felt as she pulled her paddle firmly through the water. She had an unsettled feeling that life would never be the same after this day. She tried to put aside these thoughts by reminding herself that she always felt uncomfortable when she was away from Wappato. She turned her mind to her husband and her two sons and knew the excitement they must be feeling at this moment.  She knew how keenly Pilmowitsh wanted to know about this great canoe. She hoped he would not be disappointed.

For Sohowitsh, the trip was the greatest adventure he could imagine. What would the big canoe be like? How would "those who drift ashore" look? Would they put ashore, and where? He could hardly contain himself as their canoe began to close quickly with the great ship, which was moving upstream toward them. When he could control his excitement no longer, he shouted to Tanohah, "Steer close to the great canoe!"

"We will do as our father decides," Tanohah replied quietly. He was apprehensive about the approaching vessel and wary of drawing too close.

"Father, father," shouted Sohowitsh, but Pilmowitsh was so engrossed in his own thoughts that he didn't hear his son's voice. "Father!" Sohowitsh persisted. "Can we steer close to the great canoe?"

Gathering his thoughts, Pilmowitsh at last replied, "Yes, my sons, we will go in close. Tanohah, steer in as close as you think is safe, and we can drift alongside. Then turn in behind it and we will paddle up the other side."

The enormousness of the ship astounded them and they had to crane their necks to see it all. "Look at the tree trunks that go straight up to the sky," said Cassino. "They have clouds fastened with ropes and the wind blows against them."

"There is another tree in front, over the water," added Monsoe.

"Where are the paddles that make it move so rapidly?" asked Sohowitsh.

"The canoe is too tall; no paddle would reach the water," said Monsoe.

The young men's excited observations spilled out in a jumble of interwoven words. "Look at the funny men!" "They have clothes that cover everything but their faces and hands." "Some of them have hair on their faces like animals." "They are all roundheads; they must be slaves." "They seem friendly. See how they wave their arms?"

While his sons chirped along, Pilmowitsh tried to study this strange new vessel, but he was awed by its massive size. As a boat builder, he could see that the bow was correctly shaped and the craft was evenly balanced, but the composition of thick planks somehow tightly fastened together was unfathomable. And the amount of iron staggered his imagination. Were the great iron pieces protruding from the sides part of the construction? As he gazed in wonderment at the soaring trees and the billowing clouds, he knew that these pale-skinned men had a greater magic than his people could ever hope to possess.

Tanohah managed to pull behind the great canoe, but it was moving through the water at such a speed that it was difficult to keep up paddling against the current. The group finally fell back to visit with their fellow Chinook and learn about the trading. They saw iron nails that they could acquire for two salmon, and strips of copper for making ornaments, but they marveled most at the blue cloth, the first they had ever seen.

Suddenly a cry went up across the river. The great canoe had come to a halt in the water and the billowing clouds were jumping about in a most frightening way. "Look, look," cried Sohowitsh. "The clouds are angry and trying to get away!"

As great numbers of "those who drift ashore" swarmed up the trees, Cassino said, "The Konapee are fighting with the clouds. They have climbed the trees and don't seem afraid. Do they have greater strength than even the clouds?"

After a short struggle, the clouds were gone and only the bare trees remained. The natives were certain they had seen the magic of these strange men.

*About four-thirty in the afternoon, Captain Gray was dismayed when the* Columbia *ran aground on a sandbar. The men were able to strike the sails quickly enough to avoid harm to the ship. The captain ordered a large kedge anchor to be put into a boat and lowered over the side. With the anchor securely positioned away from the ship, the sailors kedged her off the bar fairly easily. A sounding was taken of the river and deep water was reported south of the ship's position. Captain Gray realized they had strayed from the main channel, but decided to anchor for the night and return the next day to their former anchorage.*

As dusk descended on the river, the canoes that had been clustered around the great ship began to disperse and head for shore. Pilmowitsh reluctantly decided that they must make camp before it became too dark and he instructed Tanohah to steer the canoe across the river to an island on the south side. The found a good campsite and the male slaves were put to work cutting small saplings for lodge poles. Before dark, the men had erected two mat lodges for protection from the rain, and the women had built a large fire and prepared a hearty meal under Lopahtah's supervision.

When the men were well fed and warmed by the fire, they discussed what they had learned from speaking with the other Chinook. They heard that the great canoe had been in the river for four days and much trading had been done. Pilmowitsh said that tomorrow they would arrange to trade the furs that Cassino and Monsoe had packed in the canoe.

The young men laughed at the strange things done by "those who drift ashore." The pale men had poured barrels of saltwater over the side of the great canoe and many from the Chinook village made a game out of paddling their canoes under the streams of water. Then the barrels had been lowered into the river and fresh water was taken up. Some of the men had spread a black, sticky goo on the sides of the great canoe. The goo had an odd smell and formed soft, sticky wads when dropped in the river. Other men pounded something into the cracks high up on the sides of the huge vessel.

Pilmowitsh told the tale he had heard about the warriors who had been killed in the large bay to the north. A terrible thunder, fire and smoke had come from the great pieces of iron sticking out from the sides of the large boat, and the war canoe had been destroyed.

"We must learn all we can about these people," said Cassino. "We must meet their chief and learn the source of their great magic. We must make them our friends, for surely to oppose them would be madness. More will come now that they know about the Great River. What do you say, Pilmowitsh?"

Pilmowitsh nodded. "You speak well, Cassino. Their magic is beyond anything we have seen along the river. The great canoe seems like something only the Great Spirit Sahale could make, just as he made Wyeast, Klickitat and Loowit. Even though I have seen this great canoe with my own eyes, I can scarcely believe it."

Monsoe stood up and walked to the beach away from the light of the fire. He soon returned and said, "Father, little fires are burning all over the great canoe, but the wood is not consumed—and some fire the men carry close without burning themselves. It is a sight never to be forgotten." The other men nodded and murmured in agreement.

Tanohah had studied the actions of the ship's crew and he said to the others around the campfire, "When 'those who drift ashore' took the small canoe out into the river, they were looking for the deepest water. This strange craft must go down very deep in the water and it cannot travel where the river is shallow. If this is so, they will not take the great canoe farther up river. Do you agree, Father?"

"There is so much magic in all of this, my son, it is hard to understand," Pilmowitsh replied. "I believe we must have seen the great canoe touch the bottom of the river. And the massive iron hook that they dropped to the bottom of the river seems to hold the canoe so that it doesn't drift with the current. But how it moves upstream without paddles is a mystery. There is so much to know, we can only wait and see."

The talk and speculation continued long into the night. It was hard to sleep with the mysterious object so near. Occasionally, one or another would leave the fire and walk to the edge of the shore to peer at the great canoe looming in the darkness. Eventually, however, fatigue won out, and the men settled down to sleep.

At first light, everyone was up. The great canoe was still there. After breakfast, the women were left behind to tend the camp and the men shoved off in the canoe and paddled toward the big boat. Cassino and Monsoe took their bundles of furs, but Cassino was reluctant to trade until he had more information about how to negotiate well with "those who drift ashore." The men soon discovered no shortage of people willing to talk about what they had seen and heard.

Lopahtah stayed in camp with the slave women and mulled over the events of the previous day. She was concerned about Pilmowitsh. He was usually so sure of himself and confident in his actions, but after listening to the men talk around the campfire, Lopahtah sensed a growing bewilderment and perhaps a bit of fear in her husband. He seemed shaken and that made her uneasy.

Out on the water, Tanohah studied the men on the great canoe closely. When the tide was at its highest, the activity on board suddenly accelerated. "Watch it now," he shouted to the others. "The iron hook is coming up." As the pale men scrambled up the trees, Tanohah shouted, "They are letting loose the clouds!"

With the sails unfurled, the massive vessel slowly turned and began to move forward. Back in the main channel, the ship caught the current and quickly picked up speed. It was a stirring sight and Pilmowitsh was in awe. He was seeing and experiencing events far beyond his imagination, but he resisted the urge to call out at the wondrous sight. As head of the family, he reminded himself, he must remain calm and in control.

"We will not follow the great canoe," he said quietly to his sons. "We will return to camp, pack the canoe, and move near the village at the mouth of the river."

The men returned to the island and quickly broke camp. When they paddled downriver, they found the great canoe, as expected, moored across from the Chinook village. The entire area was crowded with campsites and canoes. Pilmowitsh and his family had to paddle quite a ways back up along the north shore before they found a suitable place to make camp.

While the slaves set up camp, Pilmowitsh and Lopahtah settled down to rest. Cassino and Monsoe were eager to visit the Chinook village. They took Tanohah and Sohowitsh along, and Pilmowitsh knew it would be a long time before the young men would return.

As they hiked along the beach, Cassino outlined his plans. "First we must seek out young Comcomly and my other Chinook friends. If they are trading out at the great canoe, we can go with them. Then we must go to the chief's house that we visited before, Monsoe, and tell him where to find Pilmowitsh and our camp. We must also look for other Wappato tribes and see who is here. Tanohah, you look for the Multnomah. See whether your grandfather, Chief Taneeho, is at the village. He may wish to speak with your father, because no one knows more about canoes than Pilmowitsh. Sohowitsh, you will serve as our messenger. We have many things to do when we reach the village. Monsoe can help me find lodging for us with some of our Chinook friends, in case we decide to stay the night."

Cassino continued to explain his ideas as the young men climbed over large rocks and driftwood along the shore. When the group reached the village, each went his own way to accomplish the tasks Cassino had assigned. They arranged to meet later to plan their strategy for the next day.

Back at the camp, Lopahtah became concerned when the young men had not returned by nightfall, but Pilmowitsh assured her that all was well. The next morning, Sohowitsh returned to report that Chief Taneeho was in the village and wanted to see Pilmowitsh and Lopahtah. He added, "Cassino and Monsoe believe the time is right to trade the furs. With your permission, we will take the furs with us in the canoe when we go to see Grandfather."

Pilmowitsh nodded. "Cassino has friends in the Chinook village. He will know when the time is right. Stow the furs in the canoe while I select slaves to paddle us downriver."

When they arrived at the village, Tanohah was waiting to take command of the canoe, and Pilmowitsh and Lopahtah went to see Chief Taneeho. They learned from the old chief that "those who drift ashore" came from a place called Boston. The Boston Men knew the Nootkas and could speak jargon. The Boston Men called their great canoe a "ship," and some of the Chinook had been told that more ships would soon come into the river.

Taneeho and the other Chinook chiefs who had gathered were eager to question Pilmowitsh about the great canoe. Pilmowitsh shared some of his theories, but he was reluctant to say too much. He had heard that the magic of the great ship was in the wind—and he knew how the wind could move a canoe—but it was hard to imagine how the wind could have much effect on such an enormous ship. Pilmowitsh listened as the chiefs speculated about the clouds and the trees on the great canoe, but there was so much yet to learn and he needed time to sort it all out. He and Lopahtah were glad when it was time to return to camp.

Late in the afternoon the two walked down to the riverfront to look for the young men and the canoe. A shout from the water caught their attention and they looked up to see the four boys, waving wildly from the canoe and all wearing blue coats like the Boston Men. Spaced evenly between the slaves, they made a colorful and impressive sight.

When the canoe reached the shore, Sohowitsh came running and shouting, "Look what Cassino and Monsoe have given us! Each one of us has a jacket. Cassino would not trade the furs for one, two or three jackets—only for four!"

"Here, look at it closely, Father," said Monsoe as he removed his jacket and handed it to Pilmowitsh.

"It is heavy and warm," Pilmowitsh said approvingly, "but there is a fine, light cloth on the inside. What is the purpose of two pieces?"

Lopahtah was astonished at the fine sewing. "Their needles must be very small. And look, the little stones down the front are not stones at all, but shiny yellow copper. They are so smooth and capture the sun."

"We have been offered many things in trade for our jackets," Tanohah said proudly, "but nothing is as fine as these."

Cassino had heard a rumor that the Boston Men would be leaving soon, so Pilmowitsh decided that everyone would go out to the ship the next day, because it might be their last chance.

The next morning was overcast and the river was rough, but with Tanohah's expert guidance, the men were able to draw the canoe close to the great ship. They spent a good part of the day watching the activity on board. It was evident the Boston Men were preparing to leave, and when the river had risen to its highest level, they pulled up the iron hook, let out the vast white clouds, and started downriver, followed by dozens of native canoes. To the surprise of everyone, the great ship stopped just inside the bar and sat there for two more days.

*May 19, 1792. While awaiting proper conditions for crossing the bar, Captain Robert Gray officially named the great river after his famous ship, the* Columbia, *and recorded the name in his log. He also named the southern point on the shore Point Adams, and the northern point he named Point Hancock. Both names were officially entered in the log.*

The tenth day the great ship had been in the river dawned bright and clear with a gentle breeze. Pilmowitsh realized that the time of departure had arrived and the group hurried to paddle the canoe to the mouth of the river. When the sun was directly overhead, the great ship cut through the breaking waves at the bar and sailed slowly away. A silent flotilla of canoes bobbed in the breakwater as the natives watched the magic ship disappear.

*May 20, 1792. Just after midday, when the tide was full, Captain Gray ordered the anchor hauled and the sails set, and the* Columbia Rediviva *made its departure. By three in the afternoon, the ship was nearly across the bar, and by five o'clock she sailed in water over twenty fathoms, well beyond the treacherous currents of the Great River of the West.*

# THE KING GEORGE MEN

**A**fter the great ship left, Pilmowitsh and his party remained near the mouth of the river for two more days and learned more about the Boston Men. A comely young slave girl of the Cathlamets reported that she had been intimate with one of them. The Cathlamets were camped above the village, where a number of the Boston Men had gone ashore. The girl had been collecting firewood when she was met by a tall white man. He had golden hair and deep blue eyes and his skin was very pale. He gave her a necklace of blue beads and began fondling her. When she didn't protest, he removed his clothing and pulled her down in the grass. Except for his pale skin, she reported, he was like any other man and he had his way with her. When she returned to camp with the beads, everyone had to believe her story even though she was a slave and a roundhead.

For Pilmowitsh and his family, the return trip upriver was accomplished in easy stages and it was good to be home. Tsultsis and Nanalla wanted to hear every detail of the great adventure. Lopahtah told all she could remember, though she was careful to say nothing about Pilmowitsh's reaction to the great ship. Pilmowitsh returned cheerfully to building canoes, but sometimes at night by the fire, he got a faraway look in his eyes, and Lopahtah knew he was seeing the huge ship moving across the water. He never said a word, but Lopahtah knew.

Not long after their return, Cassino and Monsoe decided to go hunting for fresh meat. They tracked a deer for several hours before bringing it down and then stopped to rest before carrying the carcass back to their canoe. As they sat leaning against a tree, Cassino began to talk about the plan that he had been formulating in his mind. "After learning about the Boston Men and seeing their ship, I have an idea. When the next ship

49

arrives, as it surely will, they will be wanting furs, and we must be ready to supply the finest ones. We must form a group of strong young men who will listen to commands and obey them instantly, just as the Boston Men obeyed their chief. These men should be from different tribes and be selected from those who may someday be chiefs themselves. But first, we must talk to your father and seek his advice. He can help us in many ways."

Monsoe was surprised by Cassino's idea, but he could see the possibilities. "I will follow you, Cassino, and others will too. Your plan is a good one, but who will you select and when will we start?"

"Tanohah, for one," replied Cassino. "Do you think he will follow me? He is favored by Chief Taneeho and could easily become a chief of the Multnomah some day."

Now Monsoe was shocked. He had never imagined his younger brother as a chief of the Multnomah. He was jealous, but he showed no sign of it when he responded, "Tanohah is independent and a leader, but I think he would follow you, Cassino. Do you want for me to talk to him, to tell him that he would have to obey you like the Boston Men obeyed their chief?"

Cassino considered the offer, and said, "It might be best for you to speak to him first, because he can speak freely with you." Cassino stood up and stretched, and began to truss the deer to carry between them. After a moment, he looked over at Monsoe and said, "Now listen closely. One day you will be a chief of the Clackstar. You may laugh now, but you will see. One day, you will be a chief."

Monsoe knew better than to question one of Cassino's pronouncements, but he mulled over his friend's words as they carried the deer back to the canoe. He had seen Cassino's wisdom and had learned to accept his friend's prophecies as possibilities—but a chief of the Clackstar? They were one of the largest tribes; how could he become a chief? His family had lived apart from the tribe for so long that their house and camp seemed independent; yet both his father and mother were Clackstar. It was possible.

That night, after eating his fill of fresh venison, Monsoe spoke to Pilmowitsh. "Father, Cassino and I would like your advice and counsel. Cassino has a plan and he would like for you to hear it."

Pilmowitsh nodded his head and Cassino began to explain his plan.

"My father—for you have always been as a father to me—when we were downriver, you noticed that the Boston Men traded only for furs. They traded for some salmon to eat, but what they really wanted were furs. They told us that more ships will come seeking furs. Suppose we were to gather many furs in preparation for the arrival of the next ship? Then we would have the most furs to trade and perhaps we could get a better price. Remember our jackets? What a bargain! We could trade those jackets upriver for many more furs than we gave the Boston Men. And we would trade for only the best furs. We would start around Wappato, then go upriver at the great trading time, then go to the falls of the Multnomah during the late summer salmon run."

Pilmowitsh was silent for a minute, then asked, "Where would you keep these furs, Cassino?"

Cassino hesitated, then looked directly at Pilmowitsh and replied, "It must be a place away from any village, yet where the furs would be safe. Why not here—if you are willing, my father? We could keep many furs here without attracting attention."

"It is a wise plan, my son," Pilmowitsh replied, "and it could be done easily. We have room to store the furs in the house, and we can build a storehouse if needed."

"Thank you, Father," Cassino said. Then turning to Monsoe, he asked, "Have you spoken to Tanohah about joining us?"

Tanohah, who had been listening quietly in the background, spoke up for himself. "Monsoe told me about the plan. I will follow you, Cassino."

Turning to Tanohah, Cassino cautioned, "This plan must be kept to ourselves. You must not mention it to Chief Taneeho."

"If that is what you wish," Tanohah began, but after thinking for moment, he said, "but that would be unwise. My grandfather would tell no one if we asked for his silence. And if he chose to, he could help us greatly."

Monsoe looked anxiously at Cassino. He would never think to question his friend. But Cassino was smiling. "You are wise, Tanohah," he said, "and you are right. You may tell your grandfather, but speak to him in private—and respectfully request his silence."

That night, as he settled down to sleep, Pilmowitsh turned to Lopahtah and said, "That Cassino is a shrewd young man, and everything goes as he plans. He intended for Chief Taneeho to know about his plan all along, but he allowed Tanohah the honor of suggesting it. Very clever."

Cassino's plan moved forward swiftly that summer and the group began to take shape. Cassino selected the son of a Quathlahpottle chief, a Clannaquah warrior, and an intelligent young Shoto. He later added another chief's son from among the Cathlahminnamin, whose village was located about midway along Wappato on the channel side. Sohowitsh rounded out the group as its youngest member. Pilmowitsh and Chief Taneeho advanced the group goods to barter for the furs, and by summer's end, Pilmowitsh had to build a storehouse next to his house for storage.

Cassino's traders were everywhere that summer, from the Cascades to the mouth of the Great River, all over Wappato and up the Multnomah to Wallamt. They quietly traded for the choicest furs, making many new friends and contacts in the process. The entire enterprise was impressive, and the group's success was amusing to Chief Taneeho and Pilmowitsh.

On a crisp fall day, word came up the river that another ship had crossed the bar. Cassino and Monsoe hurried to Pilmowitsh's house.

"Another ship has come into the river, Father," Monsoe said breathlessly. "We must load furs and be off immediately." Pilmowitsh nodded in agreement and stood to go outside.

Cassino sent Sohowitsh to look for Tanohah, then turned to address Pilmowitsh. "Will you accompany us on this first trading trip? There is no time to gather my band, so we will need to take a large canoe and many of your slaves."

"I would be honored," Pilmowitsh said quietly, but deep in his heart the prospect of seeing another great ship stirred unfamiliar emotions. He quickly turned to the job at hand, directing his slaves, and by the time Sohowitsh returned with Tanohah, the canoe was ready for departure. Lopahtah and the other wives ran down to the beach to see the party off, and the women stood and watched until the canoe disappeared around the point. Lopahtah sensed Pilmowitsh's uneasiness as he bid his wives good-bye, and she wished that she could go along. Despite her regrets, she was happy that her husband would have another opportunity to see a great ship.

At dusk, the fur traders set up camp on an island in the river. Four young slave women had been brought along to tend to the cooking, and the virile young men found other uses for them as well. Only Pilmowitsh did not take a turn with the girls. He thought about his wives, especially Lopahtah, and settled in for the night.

The next morning, the group continued to the mouth of the river and found the ship anchored behind the cape, just inside the bar. When the men saw that very little trading was being done, they paddled over to the large Chinook village and made arrangements to stay the night. Each member of the group sought out information about the ship and reported to Cassino. They learned that even though these men looked and talked like Boston Men, they called themselves King George Men.

Around the campfire that evening, Cassino pondered this new information. "Are these men from a different tribe?" he wondered aloud. "Will this make a difference in the trading?" He carefully formulated his strategy before drifting off to sleep.

The next morning, Cassino was ready. The water was calm when they reached the ship and the canoe rocked gently beside the towering vessel. Cassino held up some choice furs to indicate that he wished to trade. The King George Men gestured to him to come aboard. At first Cassino misunderstood, but he was quick to respond when the men tossed a rope ladder over the side and motioned for him to climb up to the deck. Turning to Pilmowitsh, he said, "Come with me, my father," and the two men scrambled up onto the ship.

Pilmowitsh's heart was beating in his throat as he anticipated going aboard the huge boat. He studied the hull as he climbed to see if he could determine how thick and strong the planks were. He felt the side of the hull and pounded it with his fist. He tried to imagine how they were shaped, fitted, and fastened together. Before he knew it, he had reached the top of the ladder and was stepping onto the deck. Here he was free to observe while Cassino bargained with the King George Men in jargon.

Cassino was a careful trader. He deliberated over every proposition and was not afraid to use silence and stalling as negotiating tools. On one or two occasions, the King George Man became angry and raised his voice. When this happened, Cassino was confident he would get his price, because he knew how dearly the man wanted his fine quality furs. From time to time, Cassino leaned over the edge of the ship and called down to Monsoe to bring up more bundles of furs. The goods he received in exchange were sent back down with Monsoe, along with a stern admonition to keep them covered.

At first, Pilmowitsh stayed close to Cassino and watched the men on deck going about their business. He studied what they wore and tried to understand the use of the iron implements they used in their work. As the trading dragged on, he discovered that the pale men were as interested in him as he was in them. They let him touch the ropes and run his hand along the big pieces of iron. He saw three men sewing on a sail and realized that the "clouds" were made from a heavy cloth. He could see that living on board was like having a house in the ocean, but he shuddered to think what it would be like to be shut inside during rough weather. He had hoped that going onto the ship would make the mystery understandable, but instead he felt overwhelmed.

When the trading was completed, Cassino motioned to Pilmowitsh and the two men descended the ladder. As soon as they were in the canoe, Cassino called to Tanohah to shove off.

"Let's head up the river," he said to the group, "to some place on the south shore where no one will see us. Stay away from the villages." Turning to Pilmowitsh, he said, "My father, remember well what you have seen of the ship. I will want to hear everything. We have traded well—very well." He threw back his head and laughed with glee.

When the canoe had left the ship in the distance and no other canoes were around, Cassino motioned to the shore and the paddlers beached the canoe. The slaves pulled the boat up onto the shore and dragged it under cover of the nearby brush. Cassino gathered the group and spoke to them earnestly. "This is very important. Do not speak to anyone about our trading. If anyone asks you, tell them only that we traded for iron nails and beads. When you see what I have received for the furs, you will understand. Even when we return to Wappato—no, *especially* when we return to Wappato—say as little as possible about this trading venture and say nothing about the goods we received."

He stepped over to the canoe and pulled out six sailors' jackets similar to the ones they had obtained from the Boston Men.

"Everyone in our band will have a jacket," he said, "and one will go to Pilmowitsh and Chief Taneeho in payment for the goods they advanced to us."

Next, Cassino brought out five iron hatchets and motioned to Pilmowitsh. "Look them over, my father, feel them, try them, and choose the one you want. It's yours."

Pilmowitsh chose a well-balanced hatchet and felt the sharp edge. To hide his emotions, he swung the hatchet and severed a small tree limb.

"The King George Men were using these tools on the ship today," he said. "Thank you, Cassino. I am most grateful for your kindness."

"Here is another gift for you," Cassino said as he unwrapped eight iron knives. "You must choose the best one for yourself. I also have many strings of blue beads, strips of the shiny stuff they call 'copper,' and lots of blue cloth. Some of these goods we will save for trading next season, and some we will distribute to our families."

Finally, Cassino reached into a small pouch at his side as he said, "Here is the greatest prize of all. It is truly magic." In his hand he held a small, clear, round object, that looked like a flat, transparent stone. "The strangers call this a 'burning glass,' and it will take fire from the sun. Let me show you!"

As everyone crowded closer, Cassino placed some fine shreds of cedar on the ground and held the glass to catch the sunlight. A small, intense beam of light struck the cedar, which soon began to smoke and then burst into flame. The group murmured in amazement.

"Now, Monsoe, come here and hold out your arm. When the fire begins to burn, pull your arm away."

Monsoe held out his arm, but the fear showed in his eyes. Cassino focused the glass so that the beam hit Monsoe's forearm. Feeling nothing at first, Monsoe became bolder. "It's getting warm," he said, but held his arm steady. Suddenly he yelled, "Ouch! It's burning, it's burning," and he wrenched his arm free from Cassino's grasp.

"This is real magic," Cassino said, "but I now possess it, so you don't need to be afraid. But you can see why you must not tell anyone about our trading. We will return to Wappato and continue as usual; but no one else is to know about our success—no one!" The young men looked at Cassino with wide eyes and vigorously nodded their heads. Cassino turned to Pilmowitsh and said, "My father, are the jacket, the hatchet, and the knife a fair return for the goods you have advanced us?"

"It is more than enough!" Pilmowitsh said enthusiastically. As soon as the words were out, he wished he had tempered his response.

"We will see to it that Chief Taneeho receives his fair share, as well," concluded Cassino as he put away his burning glass.

Monsoe turned to Pilmowitsh and said excitedly, "Father, tell us what it was like to go onto the great canoe. What did you see? What did you hear? Tell us everything."

Pilmowitsh appeared bewildered and finally said, "There was so much, so many things to see, I don't know where to begin. On the way back to Wappato, I will gather my thoughts and then I will tell you what I have seen. But now, let's eat. The day's adventure has left me very hungry."

Cassino pulled out his burning glass again to start a campfire, and when the women had prepared the food, the group sat down to eat. After dinner, the young men remained to talk around the fire, but Pilmowitsh moved his bedding under a nearby tree and settled down to sleep.

*October 21, 1792. Lieutenant Broughton, in command of HMS* Chatham *crossed the turbulent Columbia River bar. He was surprised to discover the* Jenny, *another British ship, lying at anchor just inside the mouth of the river. Captain Baker of the* Jenny *told him they had been in port for only a few days, trading furs with the natives.*

*Lieutenant Broughton had recently parted company with his commanding officer, Captain George Vancouver on HMS* Discovery, *who was proceeding down the Pacific coast to Monterey. Captain Vancouver was clearly disappointed that the American Robert Gray had discovered the Great River of the West first, but he dispatched Broughton with the following orders: 1. Chart the course of the river. 2. Sound the channel. 3. Name all prominent geographical features. 4. Lay claim to all the country in the name of King George III and Great Britain.*

*As the* Chatham *lay at anchor in the river, the crew prepared for its expedition. Friendly natives were engaged to serve as guides, and Lieutenant Broughton decided to take twenty-six men from the crew. The remainder were to stay aboard the ship on standby while the expedition was upriver.*

*On October 26, the party started up the Columbia in the* Chatham's *cutter and launch, with the smaller boat in the lead. Lieutenant Broughton took great care with his charting and record keeping, entering every detail into his daily log. He used a marine compass to chart the course of the river and soundings were taken along the channel by throwing lead as they went along. Broughton named Puget Island after another lieutenant serving under Captain Vancouver, and on the third day, when he saw the lovely, rounded, snow-capped mountain that the natives called Loowit, he named it "St. Helens" after a British admiral.*

By the time Pilmowitsh returned to Wappato, he was able to describe what he had seen aboard the ship. The young men and women in his house peppered him with questions, which helped to jog his memory about the many details he had observed. He explained how the "clouds," or sails as the white men called them, were made of heavy cloth that caught the wind and somehow pushed the great ship through the water. And though he didn't see how it was possible, the King George Men had said that a big round circle with handles steered the ship. There was so much magic in everything the white men did.

Chief Taneeho was delighted by the jacket, hatchet, knife and other articles he received as his share of the payment. Later, when Tanohah brought Cassino secretly to demonstrate the burning glass, the old chief was impressed by Cassino's understanding of the white man's magic and held him in highest esteem.

A few days later, Cassino received word that a second ship had entered the river. These King George Men were not interested in trading, but wanted to come up the river. Cassino summoned the seven members of his band and asked them to meet with him in secret.

When the group had assembled, Cassino told them about the new ship, and added, "We will go down the river in Pilmowitsh's large canoe to scout the situation. We will not take any furs, because the men on this ship do not wish to trade. We must find out what they intend to do."

As the group was preparing to depart, word came that the white man's party would be moving upriver the next morning with native guides. Cassino was concerned that no one knew the size of the party.

Cassino approached Pilmowitsh and cautioned the older man. "Take care, my father, and do nothing to resist the white man. No matter what the others do, stay here and watch the Great River for their approach. Observe their actions closely so you can tell me what you have seen. Please say nothing of our departure and don't tell anyone where we have gone and what we are doing."

Drawing Pilmowitsh to the side, away from the others, Cassino continued, "Only you will know my plan. We will travel quickly downriver to intercept the white man's party and observed everything they do. Tanohah will locate places of concealment where we can see the King George Men without being seen. We will follow them as long as they are in the river, so we may be gone for several days."

Cassino and his band were able to reach the Chatham just as the exploration party was getting underway. Following carefully at a distance, the young native men were able to observe the actions of the King George Men. After three days of surveillance, Cassino decided that their main objective was to learn about the river and the surrounding country. He deduced that the sounding process was to measure the depth of the channel and he reasoned that the explorers were wanting to learn the course of the river.

As the two boats neared Wappato, Cassino and his followers concealed themselves a short distance from Pilmowitsh's camp. As the explorers came into view, Cassino watched in dismay as a great number of war canoes put out into the river. The warriors in the canoes were armed, painted, and dressed for combat.

*Lieutenant Broughton was pleased with the expedition's progress and the work completed in the past three days, but now he was greatly concerned as he counted twenty-three canoes of hostile natives surrounding his party. The native guides were quick to explain to the warriors that the mission was a peaceful one and the white men only wished to see the country. The warriors put down their weapons and invited the King George Men to the beach for a parley. Lieutenant Broughton named the point of land from which the warriors had embarked "Warrior Point," and he called the large rock just back from the tip of the point "Warrior Rock."*

As soon as Cassino saw that there would be no hostilities, he hurriedly ordered the canoe back into the water and the small band rushed to join the parley on the beach.

It was a friendly gathering, with the Wappato tribesmen eagerly examining the whites, their clothes, equipment and weapons. A brisk trading for personal possessions was soon underway. Cassino kept his eye on the leader, the one called Lieutenant, and he noticed how quickly he was obeyed. The King George Men were orderly in everything they did, and Cassino made a mental note of their actions.

Several of the warriors on the beach kept motioning at the lieutenant's rifle and seemed to know that it had special powers. Finally, the leader of the exploration party agreed to give a demonstration. An elk hide shield was propped against a bush where the beach gave way to the underbrush. The lieutenant backed up several paces, aimed his firearm and pulled the trigger. The thunderous report and smoke startled the natives, and they fell silent when they saw a hole appear in the shield. A few intrepid warriors put four thicknesses of shield together and motioned for Lieutenant Broughton to again take aim. When the firestick put a hole through everything, the natives were in awe. The smoke and the sound were true magic. Cassino never forgot this lesson. He was determined to arm his band with these "muskets" that the white men had.

*Leaving the parley at Warrior Point, Lieutenant Broughton saw a large number of natives at a spot just below the mouth of a large river that flowed into the Columbia. He ordered his men to again put in to shore. From this junction the Columbia turned east and the men could see another rugged snow-capped mountain from which the river seemed to flow. Lieutenant Broughton was enamored of the view and named the location Belle Vue Point.*

Cassino and his band continued to follow and observe the exploration party as it proceeded upriver from Wappato. Cassino would later receive a detailed report about the landing at the Multnomah village from Chief Taneeho.

*October 30, 1792. Lieutenant Broughton went ashore on the south side of the river at a point that afforded a spectacular view up through the gorge of the Columbia. A magnificent mountain the natives called Wyeast appeared to sit at the head of the gorge. Here the lieutenant raised the British flag and formally took possession of the land in the name of King George III. He named the mountain "Mt. Hood" in honor of a British admiral. Two miles further upriver, he named a point that jutted in from the north "Point Vancouver" after his commanding officer. When he was informed that a great falls lay on the Columbia not too far upriver from their location, and being short on supplies, Broughton decided to return to his ship, with his mission accomplished.*

Cassino watched the strange ceremonies of the white men with fascination. So many things made no sense. He assumed that the raising of the flag signaled the end of the journey, because the two boats had immediately headed back downriver. After the explorers had gone, Cassino's group went to the point and looked around, but they found nothing of interest. The stayed upriver for a few days to hunt. No one saw any reason to follow the white men back downstream.

# THE YOUNGEST CHIEF ON THE RIVER

assino devoted the next few years to forging his band of young men into a loyal and highly disciplined group. Each new member selected by Cassino had distinguished himself in some way and each had important connections within his tribe.

Shanum, the son of the Cathlahminnamin chief, was big and strong, and a natural leader among his peers in the upper channel area of Wappato. Shanum was unusually tall for a Chinook, well filled out and all muscle. His feats of strength were well known along the river and he knew no fear. He could be cruel, but he had learned to control himself. Many were afraid of him, but he fit in well with Cassino's tightly knit group.

Asotan was a slight but handsome youth from the Shoto. His father was the tribe's most influential medicine man and Cassino selected Asotan for his cleverness and intelligence. The young Shoto was also one of the fastest runners in the area.

Laquano came from the Clannaquah and was capable and good-natured. He was recognized as a leader among the young men of the Clannaquah and the greater Multnomah tribe. An excellent fisherman and swimmer, he was second only to Tanohah in his ability to handle a canoe. His skill with bow and arrow was widely regarded. His father was a highly respected member of the tribe and had close connections with Pilmowitsh and Chief Taneeho. Laquano had been a close friend of Tanohah and Sohowitsh since they were small.

Concomsin, son of the chief of the Quathlahpottle, was powerfully built like Shanum, but not as tall. In contrast to Shanum, Concomsin's even temper made him well-liked among his peers and earned him the respect of his elders. He was a natural leader, with a keen mind and a careful and deliberate way of speaking. An avid hunter, his skill at tracking both animals and humans, coupled with his marksmanship with the bow, made him a valuable addition to Cassino's band.

With these four young men and Pilmowitsh's three sons, Cassino had an effective group for acquiring and trading furs along the river. But his vision had always been bigger and bolder than simply becoming a successful trader, and one crisp winter day, he assembled his band to discuss his latest plans. The group met at Pilmowitsh's house, which was vacant at the time, because Pilmowitsh and his wives were visiting relatives in the Clackstar village on Scappoose Bay. A light snow was falling as the youths gathered around the fire to warm themselves.

After the customary greetings, Cassino immediately called the group to attention. "Our fur trading has been very successful, and the time has come to look ahead to what we will do next. It is not enough to acquire riches—it is what we do with our riches that will count.

"I have selected each of you with great care and purpose." He paused, and with a sweep of his arm, drew the attention of each young man to the others around the circle. "Look at one another and consider what I am saying: Each of us is in position to acquire great power and influence in his own tribe. We are young men, yet how many our age have the wealth we possess, or the slaves? How many wear the white man's jackets or carry the white man's knives? How many have a fine, large canoe built by Pilmowitsh the Canoe Builder? You know the answer. No one besides us in the Wappato area. And who along the entire Great River, from the cascades to the mouth of the river, has the power to make fire from the sun? Only I do. Only Cassino, your leader."

Everyone nodded as Cassino continued, "But this is only the beginning. The furs will continue to bring us riches, but we must use our wealth wisely. We must gain power and influence in our tribes, and each of you must find the best way to do your part. I chose you for your skill, your bravery, and your ability to think. Now is the time to put these skills to use."

A hush fell on the gathering around the fire as each young man considered his own position and potential. Asotan shifted uneasily and finally broke the silence. "What you say is true, Cassino, but what are you suggesting? We can exert certain influence by means of our wealth; but power? That is another matter. We are young men and we must show proper respect for our elders and our chiefs." He shook his head and waited for the leader's reply.

"Power comes in many ways," Cassino said. "For some it will be easier because of your family's position in the tribe. Yes, your wealth can buy some influence, but what is truly important is the respect of the leaders and the people in your tribe. It is time to think about taking wives for ourselves, and each one must be chosen with great care. You must consult with me in every case. We will decide—not your families—which women you will take as your wives."

Concomsin clucked his tongue against the roof of his mouth and shook his head. "That is easy for you to say, Cassino, but my father is chief of the Quathlahpottle!"

"And my father is the chief of the Cathlahminnamin," added Shanum. "Even a son does not tell a chief what he will do."

Cassino laughed. "You two are the least of my worries. Your fathers will see to it that you marry well. Still, you must keep me informed. Should I disagree with your father's choice, we must find ways to help him change his mind."

Tanohah, who had been sitting quietly, finally asked the question that was on every boy's mind. "Why are the wives so important? I know that taking the daughter of an influential chief can strengthen a young man's position within the tribe, but do you have ideas beyond this?"

Cassino was usually quick to respond, but this time he hesitated. When he spoke, he carefully measured his words. "What I am about to say must never be spoken outside of our group. Are we all in agreement?" He slowly scanned the group, making eye contact with each boy.

"You are right, Tanohah. There are more important considerations than furthering our position within our tribes. Most Chinook think of taking wives in only such limited terms, but chiefs must have a greater vision. We must look far beyond our own days; we think about the future. It is our destiny to control the Great River. When that times comes—and it is coming sooner than you think—we must have our alliances, our contacts, our spies already in place. There is no better way to uncover plots, unrest, dissatisfaction, rumors, and similar problems than to be able to dispatch a wife back home for a visit."

Monsoe looked puzzled. "You mean we should go outside our tribes in taking wives?"

"Not necessarily. First, we must develop strong alliances within our own tribe and with those on or near Wappato. As time goes on, we will expand our influence up and down the river. Each opportunity must be considered with the long term plan in mind. In time, we shall each take many wives—but in every case we must consider the position, prestige and power of each wife's family."

When Cassino had asked for and received a pledge of secrecy from each member of the band, he stirred the fire with a long stick before he spoke again. Finally, he looked up and said, "You have each made your promise to me. Now I will reveal my secret to you."

The young men around the fire waited expectantly for their leader to continue. Measuring his words carefully, Cassino began, "Soon I will take the youngest daughter of the old Niakowkow chief as my wife. And not long after that, I will be named as chief of the Niakowkow. I will be the youngest chief on the river, and even though the Niakowkow are one of the smallest and least influential of the Chinook tribes, it is their destiny to give to Wappato a young and powerful leader. Keep this secret locked in your heart."

There was silence around the fire. Each boy knew that this day marked a turning point in their lives. No longer were they merely engaged in a clever trading enterprise; now they were embarking upon a course of great significance for all their people. Each young man around the fire felt the added weight of a new responsibility.

Cassino stood up, signaling the end of the meeting. Without another word, he quickly left the house to return to the Niakowkow village. When the other members had also left to return to their homes, the three sons of Pilmowitsh sat by the fire and discussed what had just been revealed. Monsoe, as the eldest, opened the conversation.

"Cassino has been like an older brother to each of us, and he has been like a son to our father. Now that we have heard what Cassino expects, we must consider how to gain Father's approval. Tanohah, do you think you should go to live with your grandfather among the Multnomah? Chief Taneeho and your mother would certainly be pleased, and Father would support such a move."

Tanohah nodded his agreement. "Yes, your idea is a good one, but what about you and Sohowitsh?"

"Sohowitsh should remain here," Monsoe said quickly, "because he is the youngest member of the band. He enjoys working on the canoes and Father needs his help. I think that I should move to the Clackstar village, but I'm afraid Father wouldn't understand."

When Pilmowitsh returned from visiting the Clackstar, his sons approached him with their plan. They were relieved to see that he was not surprised. He gave his approval to the older boys, adding, "When you are ready to marry, you must choose your wife for yourself." With a twinkle in his eye, he said, "I will make the arrangements and pay for her, no matter what the cost."

Another summer and winter passed, and life on the river continued much as it had for centuries. There was a flurry of activity when a ship came into the river to trade for furs, but life returned to normal as soon as the ship sailed away. As planned, Cassino married the daughter of the Niakowkow chief and became a chief himself. Monsoe married a young Clackstar woman, the daughter of one of the leading chiefs, and Tanohah became a sub-chief in the Multnomah tribe and had two wives. All the marriages were arranged by Pilmowitsh, with the quiet assistance of Cassino.

The fur trade grew and prospered under Cassino's skillful hand. Chief Cassino was generous in distributing the collective gains, and each member of his band was able to acquire many slaves.

Cassino was careful to put the interests of his own tribe first, but he gradually began to use his wealth shrewdly to extend his influence. He became interested in the concerns of other tribes and often was able to be of assistance. With his carefully cultivated connections, he seemed to be everywhere and know everything that happened up and down the river. The Niakowkow were justifiably proud of his growing prominence among the chiefs of Wappato.

When he deemed that the time was right, he took a second wife. With counsel from his mother, Tenastsil, he chose the daughter of a Clackstar medicine man. The steep price demanded by her father was offset by the value of the important alliance.

One day, a small band of Shoto, with several slaves, came into the Niakowkow village. A young medicine man emerged from the group and strode purposefully to the house of Chief Cassino. When the chief saw the visitor standing at the door, he smiled and said, "Come in Asotan. I am happy to see you again."

As soon as the two men were seated inside, Asotan said, "I came as soon as I could, and I am happy to see that you are well. I have heard many things about the dashing young chief of the Niakowkow."

Cassino smiled. "You are sounding more like a medicine man every day, Asotan. Perhaps with some of your secrets you can help an old friend. But first, let us share the pipe." One of Cassino's wives brought a beautifully carved pipe and the two men took turns inhaling deep draughts of smoke and enjoying the pleasant euphoria.

After a brief conversation about their common interests, Cassino broached the subject that had prompted him to summon his friend. "There is a medicine man among the Clackstar, named Leutcom. He is not a friend. I need to learn as much about him as I can, especially his standing with other medicine men around Wappato."

Asotan considered his friend's request. He was reluctant to compromise the unspoken bond that existed between medicine men. With some hesitation, he said, "I've heard of this man, but I don't know much about him. I can get you some information, but it will take some time. And, Cassino, you understand that a medicine man must be cautious about things like this."

"I understand, and I am always cautious, my friend."

As the days began to wane, the Wappato families began to prepare for the annual migration to Wallamt. The festive gathering at the falls brought many tribes into close proximity and was the last opportunity to trade and exchange news—and fish for salmon—before the coming of winter. The warm, somnolent days created an ambiance of cooperation and friendship between the tribes.

When the Niakowkow canoes reached the area around the falls, Cassino established his camp in a strategic central location. His party included his wives, his mother and sisters, many slaves, and several other Niakowkow families. Tenastsil welcomed the novelty of the trip and the opportunity to observe prospective husbands for her daughters. The final decision, of course, would be Cassino's.

Shortly after the tribes began to assemble, a tragic accident marred the lively atmosphere. Olahno, a distinguished chief of the Calapooya had permitted his favorite wife and two young sons to venture out near the falls in a canoe. The young brave guiding the boat strayed too close to the raging falls and capsized the canoe. Everyone drowned and the bodies were swept away by the river. There was much sympathy for the grief-stricken husband and father, but he was inconsolable. Each morning, he climbed to a high rock above the falls and maintained a lonely vigil until the sun slipped below the western horizon. The story made the rounds of the camps, but no one dared approach the chief in his sorrow.

At Wallamt, Tenastsil had little to occupy herself besides visiting, gambling with the other women, and occasional trading. When she heard about the drowning and the lonely watch kept by the chief, she was moved to try to comfort him.

One morning, when the sun had barely offered its light and all was quiet in the camp, she slipped away unnoticed and made her way up to the big rock. She found a concealed spot and settled down to wait. The exertion of the climb and the warmth of the rising sun combined to make her drowsy. Soon she was fast asleep.

When she awoke, she saw the chief sitting like a statue in his usual place, his strong back erect and proud. From her vantage point, she studied his handsome, sensitive face, now etched with sadness. She sensed the gentleness of his spirit and her heart went out to him. Without hesitation, she quietly rose from her hiding place and walked toward him.

If he heard her approach, he showed no sign, but continued to stare impassively out over the river. She unrolled a small blanket she had carried with her and settled down behind him.

All day she waited in silence, but Olahno never acknowledged her presence. At dusk, she rolled up her blanket and walked slowly back down to the Niakowkow camp.

The next morning, she again rose early and climbed to the top of the rocks. Olahno was already seated and she went directly to his side. As before, he didn't turn or look at her. She thought she could hear him talking softly to himself, but she was unable to make out the words above the roar from the river below. Again, Tenastsil spread out her blanket, and again she waited. She was not accustomed to being completely ignored by a man, but she was determined to allow him his time of mourning.

As she sat throughout the day, she felt herself begin to take on Olahno's suffering. Although not a word passed between the two of them, she grieved with him over his loss. At the end of the day, she climbed back down to the camp with a heavy heart.

The third and the fourth days passed with no change in the chief's demeanor. Tenastsil sat behind him and he ignored her. The food and water she brought along went untouched. At the end of the day, she returned to the Niakowkow camp along the river.

On the fifth morning, as Olahno sat gazing across the river, he knew the time had come to leave his sorrow and return to his tribe. The pain of his loss would never completely go away, but he must take his place among the living. He rose from his seat on the high rock and turned to leave. He drew in his breath in surprise when he saw a strikingly beautiful woman sitting on the rock behind him. His grief had so consumed him that he had not heard her approach and he had no idea that she had been keeping his lonely vigil with him for days.

For the first time since his tragic loss, a spark of hope was kindled in Olahno's heart. Tenastsil came quietly toward him and gently touched his hand. When Olahno smiled, she said gently, "I have been waiting for you."

Taking his hand in hers, she led him down from the rock to a small meadow overlooking the river. Without a word, she pulled the chief down beside her in the grass and comforted him in the ancient way.

It wasn't long before someone noticed that the chief was no longer sitting on the rock above the falls. When he didn't return to their camp, the Calapooya were alarmed by his disappearance and several young men were sent to look for him. They soon found Olahno and Tenastsil in the meadow above the river and, without being seen, brought news of the chief's safety back to the tribe.

Word soon spread along the river that a great feast was to be held by the Calapooya to celebrate the return of their esteemed chief with his new bride. Chief Cassino of the Niakowkow was an honored guest at the celebration.

With mixed feelings, Cassino watched his mother leave the Wappato area. He was proud that his mother was the wife of a great chief like Olahno, but he did not view the relationship as a political alliance. The tribes that inhabited the river valley above the falls rarely interacted with the Wappato tribes, except at Wallamt, and Cassino saw no advantage in his connection to the Calapooya.

# THE MOVE TO THE CLACKSTAR VILLAGE

One evening while he was still at Wallamt, Cassino invited the members of his private band to a meeting at the camp of the Niakowkow. The group was in a jovial mood, because the trading at the falls had been very successful. The valley tribes had brought an abundance of choice furs, and the shrewd traders in Cassino's band had acquired the choicest ones. It soon became obvious that Pilmowitsh's storehouse was too small to house the bounty, and Cassino asked each member to take some of the surplus furs for storage.

When the young men all nodded in assent, Cassino continued, "For some time, I've wanted to turn over the accounting of the furs to one of you. Sohowitsh has assisted me until now, but I believe he is still too young to take on the entire task on his own. Because of the skill he has demonstrated in acquiring furs, I would like Concomsin to take responsibility for running the fur trade, with Sohowitsh to assist him. We will continue to operate the same way we have, but these two will be in charge. Concomsin will account for all the furs, consult with the rest of us about plans for trading, and he will be the one to divide up all the proceeds. Sohowitsh will continue to store and care for the furs, and both he and Concomsin will receive additional compensation for their efforts.

"From now on, talk to Concomsin about anything to do with the fur business. The Quathlahpottle camp is near Pilmowitsh's camp, which will make it convenient for Concomsin and Sohowitsh to work together."

Concomsin was surprised by this turn of events. He smiled at Cassino and said, "I would be honored to take responsibility for the fur business, and I am grateful that you would trust me with this task." Looking around at the others sitting around the circle, he said, "I want you all to know that

Cassino and I have never spoken about this before now. But if you all agree, I will take this responsibility and I will do my best."

Tanohah was quick to respond. "Concomsin is a good choice, and my brother Sohowitsh is an able helper. Everyone knows, Cassino, that you have many other great responsibilities. If I may say so, you are wise to pass this job on to one as capable as Concomsin."

"I agree," said Monsoe, "and I will do as Concomsin and Sohowitsh direct. Does anyone disagree?" His eyes quickly scanned the group and everyone nodded in agreement.

Concomsin turned to Sohowitsh, who was seated beside him, and said, "We will work together. I will discuss matters of business with you and we will make most of the decisions ourselves. Only on issues of vital concern will we consult with Cassino and the others."

"The responsibility is yours," affirmed Cassino, and the others nodded their heads.

When their business was completed for the evening, the members of the group rose to leave. Cassino asked Asotan and Monsoe to remain. They returned to the lodge and Cassino told one of his wives to bring his pipe. The three young men smoked in uneasy silence before Cassino spoke.

"I've asked Asotan to give us a report about Leutcom. We must be careful with this matter. Monsoe, I trust that you will keep silent with this information."

The attention shifted to Asotan, who shifted nervously and drew a line in the dirt with his finger. He looked into the fire as he spoke. "You both know that there are certain matters between medicine men of all tribes which are secret. We will not talk about these things. But Cassino has asked me about Leutcom, the Clackstar. Both of you can judge his position within his tribe better than I can, but I can say that he is not trusted by medicine men of other tribes. He is thought to be vain, selfish and overly ambitious. He seeks to undermine anyone he perceives as a rival. The goodness of his medicine is in question because he does not tell the truth. I do not wish to speak ill of another, but I am ashamed of this man." He hung his head and did not look at Cassino or Monsoe.

"You have no reason to be ashamed, Asotan," said Cassino firmly. "You have not broken your trust. You have only confirmed what we have seen with our own eyes. Monsoe and I will take care of this matter alone. Put this discussion out of your mind."

The three men sat in silence for several minutes. Finally, Cassino repeated his admonition to Asotan with emphasis. "Forget that we had this conversation, Asotan. It never happened. And you have no part in what is to come."

The following winter was the coldest anyone could remember, and the east wind whistling down the gorge punished anyone who ventured out of doors. An early freeze preceded a heavy snowfall, which piled up around the houses in the villages on Wappato Island. Normally, the snow would be gone in a few days, but the bitter weather held on for weeks. Chunks of ice floated in the Great River and where the current was weak, an ice shelf began to form. As the winter dragged on, lack of food became a serious problem for the Clackstar. The Niakowkow were comparatively well off, so Cassino marshaled his ample resources and used his many slaves to transport supplies to the beleaguered Clackstar village. His generosity kept many Clackstar from starving.

Monsoe's wife and Cassino's second wife were daughters of Chief Kinsenitsh of the Clackstar. Persuasive, wise, and influential among his fellow tribesmen, Kinsenitsh was known for his infallibility. He had used his own considerable resources to help many during the winter, but he knew that Cassino's help had been vital. At first, Kinsenitsh saw his alliance with Cassino as an extension of his own power, but he soon realized it was the other way around. Wisely, he did not resent Cassino's growing influence, but promised to help the young chief whenever possible. Kinsenitsh never wavered from this resolve.

Kinsenitsh had one rival among the other chiefs and sub-chiefs of the Clackstar, a tall, suave, and restless chief named Nobsoic. Both Kinsenitsh and Nobsoic had many wives and slaves and much wealth, but Nobsoic's influence seemed to extend beyond his position within the tribe. There were whispers that his wealth had been gained unscrupulously, but no evidence had ever come to light. His biggest supporter was Leutcom, the medicine man, and the two of them maintained an eerie sway over several of the other leaders in the Clackstar village.

Kinsenitsh was suspicious of Nobsoic and he never understood how his rival was able to obtain the necessary support of his fellow tribesmen to become chief. Once, in private counsel with Cassino, Kinsenitsh confided in the young chief. "Whenever there is trouble within the tribe, Nobsoic is behind it in some way, and he uses the disruption to gain more support and influence. When crucial decisions come up in tribal council, other chiefs will switch their support to Nobsoic without satisfactory explanation. This is a constant worry, because many of Nobsoic's ideas and plans are not sound."

"I have heard similar rumors, my father," said Cassino, "and I will have my ear to the ground."

One breezy spring day a few weeks later, Monsoe was surprised when Cassino invited him to go hunting. He knew this chore was normally left to younger braves or slaves, but when he saw the look in his friend's eyes, he immediately agreed to accompany him. When the pair had gone some distance into the woods, Cassino turned to Monsoe and said, "We're after a different kind of game today, my friend. We must keep absolutely silent and stay under the cover of the brush. When we arrive at our destination, you will understand."

The two young men continued silently and cautiously deeper into the woods. Before long they heard the sounds of a struggle, as if a wounded animal were thrashing in the underbrush. Cassino raised his hand and then pointed to the bottom of a small gully, below the place where the two men were standing. Monsoe looked and his eyes drew wide in amazement.

In a small clearing at the bottom of the wash, Nobsoic and Leutcom were brutally raping the young wife of one of the Clackstar chiefs. The young woman was clearly not a willing participant but she kept her silence as the two men assaulted her. From the snatches of conversation that drifted up the hillside, it became evident that this attack was not the first she had endured. But what Cassino and Monsoe heard next stunned them both.

As Nobsoic finished his vile assault, he turned to Leutcom and said, "Tell her what she must do for us."

With a sneer in his voice, the medicine man looked down at the young woman who was gathering her clothing and trying to cover herself. "Tell your esteemed husband that he must join with Nobsoic at the next council meeting and support his plans. If he doesn't comply or if anyone says a word about this arrangement, a terrible sickness will fall on your house that no medicine man can cure."

Gritting his teeth, Monsoe reached into his quiver and pulled out an arrow. But before he could retrieve his bow, he felt Cassino's firm grip on his arm. "This is not the time," Cassino whispered under his breath, "but I have a plan."

When the proper time arrived for the tribal council, the chiefs, sub-chiefs and leading men of the tribe gathered and were seated in their customary places around the circle. Chief Cassino of the Niakowkow was seated on Kinsenitsh's right as the honored guest of the Clackstar chief. Part way around the circle, Monsoe sat quietly and waited for the council to begin. Few noticed the unusual ornament suspended from his neck. Nobsoic sat directly across from Kinsenitsh and Cassino and regarded the two men with narrowed eyes. Shortly after the meeting began, a messenger came in and whispered urgently in Nobsoic's ear. The chief's face went pale. Cassino shot a glance at Monsoe and nodded slightly. He knew that Nobsoic had just received word that Leutcom had been found with an arrow through his throat.

The arrival of the messenger caused a momentary lull in the conversation around the circle, and to everyone's surprise, Monsoe stood up. All eyes were on him as he began to walk around the circle and speak loudly to the assembled leaders.

"Chiefs of the Clackstar—brothers—I speak as a true Clackstar, son of a Clackstar father and a Clackstar mother. There is one among us who has brought disgrace upon the Chinook and the Clackstar. For years he has tortured our daughters and wives and filled them with the most evil kind of fear. He has used them to gain wealth, power, and influence in this council."

Monsoe's words seemed to echo in the stunned silence of the lodge. He continued his journey around the outside of the circle until he stood directly behind Nobsoic. He fingered the ornament around his neck, which everyone now recognized as a "slave killer," a ceremonial club crafted of stone with two sharp blades. Removing the slave killer from his neck, he continued to speak with bitterness and resolve.

"Think, my brothers, how many of you have had a wife who has pleaded Nobsoic's causes? How many times has your wife spoken of a terrible sickness if you do not support Nobsoic? He and Leutcom, who you will notice is not here, have used their power and influence and physical strength to abuse and control your wives and daughters for their own evil purposes."

Without another word, he quickly raised the slave killer and brought the heavy stone club down on Nobsoic's head. The force of the blow split Nobsoic's skull like a melon. Blood splattered everywhere and ran down the groove on the back of the weapon and covered Monsoe's hand.

Looking down at his fallen foe, Monsoe said, "He did not deserve the death of an honorable Chinook. He deserved the death of a lowly roundhead. His carcass should be dumped in the river accordingly." He turned away, saying simply, "The honor of the Chinook and the Clackstar has been avenged."

Cassino spoke up quickly in support of his friend. Turning to his father-in-law, he said, "Chief Kinsenitsh, let us have the body removed and then please allow me to speak on behalf of the young man, Monsoe." The chief gave orders to the attending slaves and Nobsoic's body was dragged from the lodge. When order had been restored, all eyes were on Cassino.

"My brothers," Cassino began softly, "everything that Monsoe has said is true. With my own eyes, I witnessed Nobsoic's attack on the young wife of one of my esteemed Clackstar brothers, and I saw the involvement of the medicine man, Leutcom, who has also been killed today."

A murmur arose around the circle of chiefs, but Cassino spoke above the noise. "What Monsoe has done is right. His brave and courageous act has restored honor to the Clackstar and the Chinook. Such a man deserves to be a chief, and I commend him for your consideration. Also, because Monsoe is known for his fairness and his compassion, I suggest that he take charge of Nobsoic's wives and slaves and other wealth, to distribute as he sees fit. I know he will do justice to everyone." He stood and walked out of the council lodge.

In the days that followed, Monsoe was elevated to chief and redistributed much of Nobsoic's wealth, according to who had been most hurt by the dead chief's treachery. Monsoe kept two wives for himself, a Multnomah and a lovely young Cathlahminnamin girl. Cassino took as his third wife Sateena, the brave wife of Nobsoic who had informed Cassino about her husband's evil ways.

By the end of the following winter, Chief Kinsenitsh, the young chief Monsoe, and their strong ally, Chief Cassino of the Niakowkow, emerged as the undisputed leaders of the Clackstar. Cassino was soon selected as a chief of the Clackstar and moved to their village with his wives and slaves the next summer. The second step of his ascension to power in the Wappato area was accomplished. Cassino was twenty-one years old.

# 10 TANONAH

The next few years with the Clackstar were peaceful. Each year, one or two ships would appear at the mouth of the Great River, and the natives became more adept at trading and bargaining. Acting on Cassino's advice, Concomsin and Sohowitsh concentrated on acquiring muskets and ammunition, and soon the band of traders controlled most of the firearms in the mid-river region. With practice, the young men learned the skills necessary to use these new and powerful weapons.

Cassino's plans continued to move smoothly. He had married his sisters off to influential young sub-chiefs, gaining valuable new alliances in the process. Shanum became chief of the Cathlahminnamin when his father died, and he immediately declared his allegiance to Cassino. Kinsenitsh and Monsoe managed the routine responsibilities of leadership with the Clackstar, leaving Cassino free to concentrate on wider regional affairs. He now controlled the entire area along the channel on the west side of Wappato, and he had enough power and influence to achieve his dream of peace among the Wappato tribes.

In the Chinook village at the mouth of the Great River, the distinguished chief of the Chinook, Cassino's father, died and was succeeded by the one-eyed Chief Comcomly, who became chief of all the Chinook. On his first journey down the river as a youth, Cassino had befriended Comcomly, and over the years he had taken great pains to keep the alliance strong.

One evening, upriver near Scappoose Bay, Pilmowitsh finished his smoke and picked up a carving project to work on. Lop sat quietly at his side and said, "There is something that troubles me. Have you noticed how often Sohowitsh goes to visit the Multnomah these days? He has said nothing to me, but I think he is afraid for Tanohah. My father is getting old and the rivalries among the chiefs are strong. I believe the situation is becoming dangerous. A chief's daughter knows these things. Some of the older chiefs are suspicious of Tanohah's alliance with Cassino."

Pilmowitsh laid down his knife. "Does Cassino know about this?"

Lop shook her head. "It is difficult to know whether Sohowitsh understands. He has always been close to Tanohah and may only sense that he is troubled. Cassino might have a sense that something is amiss, but I am sure he has not been told."

Pilmowitsh stared at his carving. "It is hard to know how much we should interfere in our sons' affairs." Then, with determination, he added, "Cassino should be told—and Monsoe too. Then they can make their own decisions. How well do you know the rivals?"

"Very well," Lop said quietly. "That is why I am concerned."

"We must see Cassino and Monsoe at once," Pilmowitsh said, "and it is best if we speak to them here." He summoned Tsultsis and said, "Will you go and bring back Monsoe and Cassino? And make it as a mother's request. We do not want to arouse their suspicion."

When Tsultsis returned with the two young men, Pilmowitsh lost no time in explaining the situation and conveying Lopahtah's fears. "Cassino," Pilmowitsh implored, "you have been like a son to me, just as Monsoe, Tanohah and Sohowitsh are my sons. You are fast becoming one of the greatest chiefs on the river and we need your help. I am a canoe builder and I know nothing about these matters. I fear for Tanohah. What should we do?"

A plan was already forming in Cassino's mind as he replied, "Don't worry, my father. You were right to tell me about this matter, which I have been anticipating for some time. First, we must get Tanohah away from the Multnomah village for a while—but that may pose a problem. He would never leave at a time like this...unless...what if he were to receive an invitation to visit Chief Comcomly? What Chinook would refuse a request like that?"

Cassino turned to Monsoe. "You must leave for the Chinook village immediately. You must go directly to Chief Comcomly in private and tell him his brother Cassino needs an important favor. Ask him to dispatch a messenger at once to the Multnomah requesting Tanohah's presence. Explain why we are asking him to do this and let him decide what to tell

Tanohah when he arrives. He must detain Tanohah downriver until he hears from me again. Go and return quickly, and we will discuss other details when you get back."

After Monsoe left, Cassino turned to Lop and said, "Tell me everything you know about the chiefs of the Multnomah—their alliances with each other, family relationships, rivalries, and especially how each one came to power within the tribe."

Lopahtah's knowledge and insight into the workings of the tribe were exactly what Cassino needed to formulate his strategy. He appreciated her sound judgment and he knew the information she shared was accurate. As she spoke, he listened carefully, sometimes nodding his head, sometimes asking questions, until he was satisfied that he had learned enough.

"I fear the two chiefs named Posen and Immahah the most. They will cause the most trouble for Tanohah," she finally concluded.

"Yes," agreed Cassino, "Chief Posen is a renowned warrior and has shown himself to be a rival to Chief Taneeho. He is strong and brave, but he is not very clever. Chief Immahah presents a different problem, however. He is much younger and vigorous, and he possesses a fanatical zeal to further the prestige of the Multnomah and his own family." Cassino knew that Immahah considered him to be a rival as well, and that the Multnomah chief would stop at nothing to thwart Cassino, including doing away with Tanohah. Coming to power with the Multnomah was the last major step in Cassino's plan to control the mid-river region, and a miscalculation at this stage could prove very costly.

After pausing to collect his thoughts, Cassino said to Lop, "You should go to your father and attend to him in his failing health. Keep your eyes and ears open and report anything of significance to Pilmowitsh. He will pass the information to me. Do not send messengers, but return here from time to time as you normally would, but only when you have something to tell us. Say nothing to your sons. After Tanohah leaves to visit Comcomly, I will arrange for Sohowitsh to go upriver on some fur business with Concomsin. When the tribesmen hear of Tanohah's summons to see Chief Comcomly, his prestige within the tribe will be reinforced."

Tanohah was surprised to receive the invitation from Chief Comcomly, but he departed without delay. Traveling alone gave him time to think about his situation at home. There was still no better canoeman on the entire river, and he was paddling his favorite canoe. He was uncertain what he would find when he arrived at his destination, but along the way he explored some back passageways and relived his youthful exploits. As he propelled his canoe expertly through the water, much of his old joy returned.

When he reached the Chinook village, he was told that Chief Comcomly had been called away on some urgent business. Word had been left that Tanohah was to remain as his guest until his return and was to be shown every courtesy. For the next few days, Tanohah was free to roam around the village and explore the lower reaches of the river.

Upriver at the Clackstar village, Cassino and Monsoe set up a command post at Cassino's house. They knew they must work quickly. While they were discussing possible plans, Monsoe said, "Nobsoic."

Cassino looked at him and said, "Nobsoic? Immahah is pompous and vain, but he isn't evil like Nobsoic was."

"It doesn't matter," Monsoe said excitedly as a strategy began to formulate itself in his mind, "we can still use women to discredit him by making it appear that he is selling his loyalties to other tribes." For the next few minutes, Monsoe outlined a plan, and Cassino was impressed by the clever plot that his friend devised.

Cassino sent men out to comb the area for three of the loveliest, most seductive slave girls they could find. Meanwhile, he also summoned Shanum, the son of the Cathlahminnamin chief and a member of the fur trading group, and told him the plan. "We need for you to make Immahah think you are seeking favor with him by the present of the three slave girls. Ask him to arrange for trading terms that clearly favor your tribe. If my understanding is correct, he will enlist Posen's support to convince the other chiefs. When they take your proposal to the council meeting, we will use Laquano to spring the trap."

Shanum shook his head and said to Cassino, "Do you really think he would believe this?"

Cassino laughed as he replied, "Immahah is so vain and ambitious, it will be easy for you. And when you see the young girls we have bought to use as bait, you will see that the advantage is all yours. But you must act quickly. The next meeting of the chiefs is in seven days."

When the chiefs gathered to conduct the tribes business, Laquano nervously took his place in the circle. With help from Cassino he had arranged to be sent to the gathering as a representative from the Clannaquah.

When Immahah introduced the trade proposal that Shanum had made, Posen was quick to support the idea, just as Cassino had hoped. The moment of truth had arrived. Laquano raised his voice and drew the attention of the tribal leaders around the circle. "My brothers among the Multnomah, please forgive me for speaking. This proposal sounds very much like a scheme that was suggested to me by Shanum, the Cathlahminnamin chief. He offered me three very beautiful young roundheads and some other fine goods in exchange for these terms, but I could see that this proposal was not in the best interest of our tribe and I refused the bargain."

A murmur arose around the council circle as the chiefs considered this new information. The presence of the three young slaves in Immahah's house was well known.

Chief Taneeho raised his hand to call for silence. Then he turned to address Immahah. "What do you say, my brother? Were these three young girls a gift from the Cathlahminnamin?"

Before Immahah could answer, Taneeho addressed Posen. "You, Posen, are quick to agree with this proposal, but I do not see any young girls in your house. Perhaps you are persuaded without a bribe?"

When word got back to Cassino and Monsoe that the two Multnomah chiefs had been discredited, they laughed and slapped each other on the back. "We must send word to Comcomly to send Tanohah back to revel in his new good fortune," Cassino said triumphantly.

Tanohah returned to Wappato amidst much fanfare, accompanied by Chief Comcomly. They had spent many pleasant evenings discussing the fortunes of the mid-river region, and Comcomly had come to see the area for himself. He was impressed by Tanohah and decided to join Cassino in helping this young man rise to power among the Multnomah. With the support of the great one-eyed chief of the Chinook, Tanohah was made a full chief. The sullen silence of Chief Posen and Chief Immahah went unnoticed. A new balance of power had been established within the tribe.

When the time came for Comcomly to return home, Cassino accompanied him along with many gifts, including several of the coveted muskets and shot.

The following winter was cold and harsh. The howling, icy wind blew down the gorge onto Wappato, freezing everything in its path. Heavy ice formed along the shores of the Great River, some of the lakes on Wappato froze over, and much of the channel was frozen. Two incidents that occurred that winter enhanced Tanohah's standing among the Multnomah.

One morning, a great commotion erupted on the beach. Two boys had decided it would be a great adventure to go out on the swollen, ice-filled river. Now they were drifting out of control in the raging current, with chunks of ice assailing their canoe. One of the boys' fathers launched a second canoe and started after them, but he capsized in the turbulent water and nearly froze to death before they could pull him back to shore. In the midst of the confusion, Tanohah ran to his canoe and managed to navigate his way along the treacherous river. Only his prowess as a canoe handler made it possible to reach the boys and pull them into his small canoe. He returned them to shore—wet, half-frozen, but safe. The rescue was the talk of the camp for days thereafter, and the youngsters idolized the brave Chief Tanohah by re-enacting the event in their play.

Later that same winter, a small child ventured too far out on the ice on the lake behind the Multnomah camp. When the ice began to crack around the boy, Tanohah was the first one summoned. As he ran to the lake, he could hear the other children yelling:

"The ice is breaking around him!"

"Don't go out! The ice is too thin!"

"He's too far away to reach with a tree limb!"

Tanohah quickly sized up the situation and told the distraught mother, who was standing helplessly on the shore, "You must keep your child calm and tell him to stay still. We will come to him."

By now, many other adults had gathered, wanting to help. Tanohah organized the rescue effort with several crisp commands. "We need two large canoes, three fishing nets of different sizes and warm fur wraps." As several young men ran for the supplies, Tanohah continued, "We must limit the weight in the boats. I need three slim, but strong, boys to make the rescue. Who will volunteer?"

Several boys stepped forward and Tanohah selected three. "Listen carefully," he said. "This will not be easy and you must work together as a team. While you are in one canoe, push the other canoe ahead of you across the ice until it breaks through. Then, climb into it and repeat the process with the other canoe. Move cautiously so the ice will not break into big chunks. Then use the nets to pull in the child."

It didn't take long for the boys to learn how to move smoothly from one canoe to the other, and they progressed steadily across the lake. As the rescuers neared the stranded boy, the ice around him gave way and he plunged into the freezing water of the lake. He disappeared for a few seconds before bobbing to the surface, screaming desperately. With shouts of alarm echoing from the shore, the three youths in the canoe quickly maneuvered close enough to throw a fishing net to the boy and haul him into the canoe. He was crying with wet and cold, but the other boys wrapped him in furs and comforted him.

By now, everyone was tired and cold, and the return trip was nearly as strenuous as the rescue. A great cry went up along the shore when the small group finally reached solid ground, and the boys were rushed to the warm lodges.

The young rescuers enjoyed their status as heroes, but everyone knew that Chief Tanohah's quick thinking and decisive action had saved the day. His position as an important tribal leader was confirmed.

The next summer, Cassino moved his lodge into the camp of the Quathlahpottle. He lived near Concomsin and soon was elevated to the status of chief, an honor he now enjoyed in four Wappato tribes. In accordance with his growing status and influence, Cassino developed a distinctive style that reflected his power and prestige. He traveled in a large, ornate war canoe that Pilmowitsh had crafted for him, and all of his warriors wore matching sailor's jackets acquired from the King George Men. Cassino's men conducted themselves with the same crisp precision that Cassino had observed and admired in Lieutenant Broughton's party. When the warriors went ashore, they stacked their muskets in the British style and obeyed Cassino's orders quickly and efficiently.

Life on Wappato continued as it had for years, until one day surprising news came from upriver that would change the lives of the Chinook tribes forever.

# THE WHITE MEN COME FROM THE EAST

Thirteen years had passed since Cassino's first trip with Pilmowitsh to the mouth of the Great River to see the white man's ship. Over the years, an occasional ship had crossed the bar to trade for furs, but ever since Lieutenant Broughton had sailed back downriver after his expedition to the west end of the gorge, no white men had ventured up the Great River to the territory of the Wappato tribes.

The Chinook had come to know the Boston Men and King George Men as "ship's men," so it was a shock when word came from the cascades of the Great River that a group of white men was making its way downriver from the east.

As soon as the strangers reached the cascades, Cassino began to receive regular reports from his scouts and learned many details about the approaching party. The group consisted of twenty-eight men and one native woman, and they had two chiefs, "Captain Lewis" and "Captain Clark." All the men were white except a native hunter and a strange man who was entirely black. The black man's fame preceded him downriver and he quickly became a favorite of the tribes along the way. Cassino was curious to see this man called "York," for it was said that he was truly black, and when his skin was rubbed, nothing came off.

When word first came of the white party, Cassino moved to the Quathlahpottle village to be on the main river. The idea of white men coming from the east was as disturbing to him as it was surprising. He had never considered the possibility and it placed his plans in a different perspective.

*October 30, 1805. After crossing the Continental Divide on one of the most remarkable overland exploratory treks of all time, the Lewis and Clark Corps of Discovery arrived at the lower cascades of the Columbia River. The journey had been filled with danger, hardship—and always— the unknown. Along the banks of the river, Captain Clark surveyed the rapids and the portage possibilities.*

*In his journal, Captain Clark reported stopping at a native village, where he saw houses similar to others they had seen, only larger. These lodges ranged in size from thirty-five to fifty feet long, by thirty feet wide, and were sunk into the ground about three feet deep. The tops of the lodges reached about three feet above ground, giving a low-slung appearance but allowing adequate head room inside.*

*Captain Clark described the construction of the lodges as a framework of poles overlaid with cedar planks secured by leather thongs. A small, oval shaped opening, just large enough for a person to enter by bending over, served as a door and was covered by a suspended plank to keep out the weather. Inside, a firepit about eight feet by six feet was dug a foot deep in the floor. The natives slept on beds constructed four-and-a-half feet above the floor and reached by ladders. Dried fish was stored under the bunks, and other provisions—such as roots, nuts and berries— were spread on mats along the walls. Captain Clark noted carved and painted images of men in all of the houses, situated where they could best be seen.*

*The natives gave the travelers nuts, berries and dried fish to eat, but demanded a high price for everything. The natives were very proud of the copper tea kettles, brass armbands, scarlet and blue robes and articles of European clothing they had received from trading, but they had little direct knowledge of whites coming into the river. Clark surmised that these tribes had an intermediate trade with others who had traded at the mouth of the river. Above all else, these natives coveted blue and white beads, and Captain Clark discovered that they would sacrifice their last article of clothing or mouthful of food in order to procure them.*

*The Corps of Discovery stayed another day at the cascades to study the method used by the natives to negotiate the rapids. On November 1, Lewis and Clark used the same techniques to bring their boats safely through the cascades. The following day, after passing some islands, the party came to an unusually high perpendicular rock on the north shore of the river, estimated to be eight hundred feet high and about four hundred yards around at its base. They named this monolith "Beacon Rock." Along the south side of the river, a series of sentinel lava formations extended fourteen or fifteen miles below Beacon Rock. Near one of these large rocks, the party made camp for the night.*

Late that night, a messenger arrived at the Quathlahpottle village. Cassino was awakened and informed of the exact location of the white men's camp. He also learned that a group of natives was staying the night with the traveling party. Cassino sent word that he wished to see the white men the next day and then went back to sleep.

A heavy fog blanketed Wappato the next morning and word soon came that the white man's party had been delayed. The fog did not deter the natives who had camped with the explorers and they arrived that evening. Before they continued downriver to trade, Cassino wisely paid generously for some of their goods and invited them to linger and tell about the strangers.

When all the villagers had gathered, Cassino started the conversation with a question. "Tell us first about the black person."

"York," replied the leader of the trading party. "He is most mysterious. His skin is black all over. He is always smiling and his gleaming white teeth are like the inside of a shell from the ocean."

"Best of all is his magic singing and dancing," added another. Each member of the native party added details about the black man and the others in the white man's party.

"The native woman is from the Snake tribe and is called Sacajawea. She is the wife of one called Charbonneau. She helps to speak with the natives."

Finally, Cassino broke in. "Tell me about the chiefs." He knew they were the ones he must deal with.

"Both Captain Lewis and Captain Clark are friendly and anxious to meet with our people. They have many questions about us, how we live, and about the land. The other men are quick to do their bidding. They are eager to reach the mouth of the Great River and want to know how many white men's ships have come to the river, and how long they have stayed."

"Did they know that the ships come in the summer?" asked Cassino.

"We did not tell them that," came the reply.

The conversation continued and Cassino sat back, allowing others to ask questions while he gleaned the information that was important to him. He knew that Monsoe and his family had gone to stay with the white travelers, pretending to be from an upriver tribe, and that he would report in the next morning. Cassino sent a message to Tanohah, inviting him to go out on the river the next day to look the strangers over.

*In the evening, one of the captains wrote in his journal that a native and his wife and three children arrived at the camp to visit. They said they came from the village near the last rapids and had with them a Snake woman who had been taken prisoner. They introduced her to Sacajawea in the hopes that the two women could converse, but they were unable to communicate beyond a few words. The native was obviously proud of his musket, with brass barrel and lock, and considered it of great value.*

Monsoe was disappointed that the slave woman sent along by Cassino was unable to speak with Sacajawea, but his small band was invited to stay the night in the white man's camp. Monsoe carefully observed the activities of the white explorers in order to give an accurate report to Cassino.

*The next morning, Lewis and Clark set off again. After passing two smaller islands, the party put ashore on the south side of the river near a village of twenty-five houses. The men were impressed by the large number of canoes and their excellent construction. Captain Clark made several sketches of these boats in his journal. The natives introduced the explorers to one of the staple foods of the area, the wappato root. Discovering that it was a good substitute for bread when roasted, the party purchased a supply for their journey. On an open, grassy prairie rising gradually from the river on the north shore, the party met with other natives, many of whom had guns with tin flasks of powder.*

When Cassino arose in the morning, he clothed himself in his finest native garments. Selecting his most ornate canoe and his strongest slaves for paddlers, he set out for the Multnomah village. He and Tanohah smoked and talked for some time. They planned to go upriver behind the long, slim island across from Skit-so-to-ho, the place of the turtle.

*After lunch, the Corps of Discovery saw two canoes emerge from behind an island on the south shore. One canoe was very ornate and held two finely dressed individuals wearing round hats. This was the party's first opportunity to see how prominent natives traveled on the river, and Lewis and Clark were so impressed that they named the larger island "Hidden Canoe Island," and the smaller one, "Tomahawk Island."*

Cassino and Tanohah succeeded in their attempt to impress the explorers as they passed majestically upriver. The natives appeared to take little notice of the white man's party, but in reality were studying them with great care. A short distance beyond Skit-so-to-ho, they ordered the slaves to turn the canoes around and returned to their respective camps by paddling behind the island. Cassino had determined that the white travelers would pass directly by the Quathlahpottle village, and he made plans to receive them there.

The next day, Cassino dispatched ambassadors in seven canoes to ask Lewis and Clark to visit. But the explorers were intent on reaching the ocean quickly and declined the invitation. The stormy weather, rough water and unfamiliar country were wearing on the party. They were unable to handle their river boats with anything approaching the skill of the natives. As they neared the mouth of the river, they were often trapped by the swirling waters and mountainous waves caused by the tides and had to camp in desperate locations.

A few days later, Cassino received word that the white men had established a camp just off the beach on the north side of the river. He decided that the time had come to see the strangers for himself. He set off to visit Chief Comcomly and meet the two captains, Lewis and Clark.

*November 20, 1805. Captain Clark returned to camp and found Captain Lewis entertaining a number of Chinook visitors. Among these were two chiefs, "Com-com-ly" and "Chil-lar-la-wil." The chiefs were given medals by the captains, and one was also given a flag. The next day, more natives arrived, including a chief from the Grand Rapid, who was also given a medal.*

Cassino was impressed by the white chiefs, but because so many other native visitors were in the camp, he had little time to talk to the two men.

They had little knowledge of Chinook jargon and Cassino knew only a few words of English, which he had learned from his fur trading enterprise, so communication relied on sign language, gestures and pantomime. Cassino was gratified to be recognized as sufficiently important to receive a medal, and he was able to arrange for the two captains to visit the village of the Quathlahpottle on their return journey.

That night, Cassino sat with Comcomly in the great chief's lodge. The two men discussed what they had seen and heard, and tried to put the information into perspective.

"They have come a long way," said Cassino, "over great mountains and through the lands of many people. They have seen no other white men since crossing the mountains and reaching the Great River."

"This will be the second winter they will see since they departed," added Comcomly. "The land of the white man is far away toward the rising sun—a distance so great that none have reached our river until now."

"What of the Boston Men and King George Men? Do they come from another place?" asked Cassino.

"The King George Men and Boston Men come only on ships. But that is hard to understand. Surely these men have a home on land," said Comcomly.

"I cannot understand the reason for the white man's journey," said Cassino. "Although they trade with us, they are not interested in gaining riches like the King George Men. They say that they want to see the river for their Great Father, but what is their purpose? More ships have come into the river each year. Will more white men come down the river from above the Cascades? This is my concern."

Comcomly frowned. "I am also concerned and I am certain that more will come, because their magic is great. They are like gods and our people cannot oppose them. These men seem fair and I don't think we will have any problems. We will get to know these men better. One of the chiefs has taken six young girls over to the camp to sleep with the white men."

Cassino smiled and nodded. "Where do you think these men will make their camp? They can't stay where they are."

Comcomly hesitated before replying. "Probably somewhere on the south shore, among the Clatsops," he said thoughtfully. "The hunting is best over there. These men have strange tastes and seem to prefer fresh meat over fish. They are out hunting all the time. When they discover the plentiful elk in the lowlands below the south shore, my guess is they'll establish their winter camp there."

"Have you suggested this?" asked Cassino.

"No," Comcomly replied, "although perhaps I should. There is no purpose in keeping them on this side of the river. They will stay near the water in hopes of seeing a ship, which is unlikely at this time of year. But if a ship does arrive and does not stay long, perhaps we could keep this information from the white men."

Cassino looked at the great chief with surprise. "Why would you want to do that?"

"These are the first white men to come down the river and the first to stay with us. If a ship comes into the river, these men might leave. But if they stay, we can learn more about the white man's magic from them. Eventually, the white men will want to establish a village here. Some on the ships have already mentioned this."

This news about a white man's village came as a surprise to Cassino, especially the information that Comcomly was expecting it. He wondered how such a village would affect the tribes in the Wappato area.

The winter days were not as cold as in previous years—just the usual rain and winds, and Cassino kept his tribes consolidated by regular visits. Pilmowitsh turned fifty and began to pass more responsibility for making the canoes along to Sohowitsh, who had established his own reputation for fine craftsmanship. The Multnomah were saddened when Lopahtah's father, Chief Taneeho, died, but his place as the most prominent chief was quickly taken by Tanohah. As was the custom, the body of Taneeho was placed in his favorite canoe along with his most cherished possessions. The canoe was hoisted into a huge tree overlooking Wappato and pointed northwest to send the old chief on his last spirit journey down the river and into the ocean to the great spirit world of the Chinook.

*December 7, 1805. Upon the advice of the natives, Lewis and Clark moved to the south shore of the river and established their winter quarters alongside a small creek. The fort was completed by January 1, 1806. Their nearest neighbors were members of the Clatsop tribe, and the settlement was named Fort Clatsop accordingly. The log stockade was located in a thick grove of timber on a knoll about thirty feet above high tide. The fort was fifty feet square, with a row of four cabins along one side facing a row of three cabins on the other. Parade grounds twenty feet wide separated the rows of cabins. The quarters were snug and comfortable, but the men soon tired of the monotonous diet.*

*The men of the Corps of Discovery found the natives to be friendly and peaceable, and were most favorably impressed by the Clatsops. Their conversations with the natives centered on trading, smoking, eating, and women. Captain Lewis observed that in speaking of their women, the natives "speak without reserve in their presents, of their every part, and of the most formiliar connection. They do not hold the virtue of their women in high estimation."*

*Both captains were amazed with the memories of the natives, especially with regard to various ships, their sizes and cargoes, and the nature of their captains and crews. Lewis and Clark appreciated many qualities of the Chinook, and in particular, the role of the women in Chinook life and the care of the aged and infirm.*

After the white men had settled in their new camp, Cassino decided it was time to visit again. This time, he stayed eleven days, spending considerable time at the fort, learning more of the white man's language, and gleaning information from the native women who were intimate with the white men. He watched the men's daily routines, their hunting and marksmanship, and their use of unusual tools. He heard about the party who had gone to the ocean beach to make salt, and he took note of the many visitors to the fort. Each day brought a new wonder, filling his head so full that returning home was a welcome change.

Shortly after his visit to Fort Clatsop, Cassino called together several of his closest friends and associates for a feast. Shanum was called back to the Cathlahminnamin village after an incident with a band of Tualitis, but Monsoe, Tanohah, Concomsin, Sohowitsh, Laquano, Asotan, Kinsenitsh and Pilmowitsh stayed for the feast.

In the evening, after the group had settled around the fire, Cassino revealed his true purpose for the gathering. "I want to talk to you about many things. I have learned much at the mouth of the river from Chief Comcomly and from the white chiefs, Lewis and Clark. One thing is certain: More white men will be coming to the Great River—both by ship and over the mountains from the east. It may take some time, but they will come."

Cassino looked at the men assembled around the fire. Everyone remained silent, waiting for him to continue.

"Comcomly thinks that a village will soon be established at the mouth of the river. Several men from the ships have spoken of this."

Concomsin spoke up. "Could this mean more trading for us?"

"I suppose," said Cassino, "but a white man's village on the river could create problems for us. Will the ships trade only with their white brothers? Will the white men come up the river to trade with us and at the Cascades? We must consider all the possibilities."

"Perhaps we should oppose this new village," Monsoe suggested.

"No, no," Cassino said quickly. "That is not our intention. Comcomly has said, and I agree, that we must learn to live and work with the white men. They are like gods and their magic is great. We must study them, learn from them, and make our plans. As you know, Monsoe, I have believed this way for a long time. Captain Lewis and Captain Clark told me that they made this great journey to learn about us and the Great River and our land. They will return to their people and tell them what they have seen."

Tanohah was the next to speak. "What can we do, Cassino? We have seen that there are both good and bad men among the King George Men. When the bad ones come, there is much trouble."

"We must not fear the coming of the white men," answered Cassino, "but we must control our own people. The Wappato tribes are united and we must continue our plans to bring together the mid-river tribes. Already there is talk among the Kalama of making me a chief. We will favor them in trade and help them in their troubles with the Cowlitch."

"Chief Soleutu has told me he would like to settle his differences with the Kalama," said Pilmowitsh.

"Yes, my father, and I think that you can help to bring that about. The Cowlitch have great respect for you as a canoe builder and as a mediator. Perhaps then the Cowlitch can concentrate on strengthening their ties with the Cathlamet."

*March 23, 1806. Lewis and Clark's Corps of Discovery left Fort Clatsop on their homeward journey. The waters of the Columbia were rough and the group had great difficulty as they hugged the south shore. When they reached Wappato Island, they visited the Quathlahpottle village and explored the mid-river region. Captain Clark went in search of the Multnomah River and the rest of the party visited the large Multnomah village, which they had missed on the way downriver. Captain Clark explored a short distance up the Multnomah and the expedition left the Wappato area on Sunday, April 6.*

*April 8, 1806. The explorers were hampered by violent winds blowing down the gorge and had difficulty keeping their boats secured. They did not pass by Beacon Rock until about two o'clock on the afternoon of April 9.*

Cassino was sorry to see the captains and their men leave Wappato. The expedition had passed through the area at the worst possible time of year, and Cassino wondered if the explorers had any idea of the pleasant springtime, summer and early autumn weather enjoyed by the tribes along the Great River.

# CHIEF
# OF THE
# KALAMA

It was not uncommon for the tribes around Wappato to relocate their homes whenever the accumulation of refuse or the infestation of fleas became unpleasant. When it was time to move again, Cassino decided to establish his headquarters near the Kalama. The planks for the longhouse were easily transported and the new camp was soon ready to occupy. The Kalama territory was downriver from the Quathlahpottle, where the Great River runs north before its final turn westward toward the sea, and another river pours in from the east.

Cassino ingratiated himself with the Kalama by inviting their chiefs to visit him and his tribes and encouraging the Quathlahpottle and Clackstar tribes to increase their trade with the Kalama. He also took a wife from the Kalama and encouraged several of his allied chiefs to do the same.

Early in the fall, a dispute arose between the Kalama and the Cowlitch over a large canoe. The Kalama maintained that the canoe belonged to them and that the Cowlitch had stolen it and injured a Kalama warrior in the process. Cassino secretly dispatched a message to Soleutu, asking for his help in consolidating the two tribes through the reconciliation of this matter. He then counseled the Kalama to demand restitution or go to war, and promised to help them if they chose to fight.

Pilmowitsh the Canoe Builder was called upon to mediate the dispute and the disagreement was settled amicably. In the process, the Kalama and Cowlitch discovered that they could negotiate with each other.

Four years passed with little contact with white traders, even though Cassino had moved downstream to be closer to the mouth of the river and any new settlement. During these years, he became chief of the Kalama and moved his extensive household to the tribe's main village. His most vigorous supporter among the Kalama was young Lamkos, who had been among the first to rally around Cassino.

*May 26, 1810. Sailing from Boston, the* Albatross *reached the mouth of the Columbia River, with Captain Nathan Winship in command, along with assistant captain William Gale, first mate William Smith, and twenty-two crew members. Well provisioned with tools, stores and ammunition, their purpose was to establish a permanent trading post on the river. The ship crossed the bar at high water and proceeded upstream approximately forty-five miles to a place subsequently named Oak Point. On June 4, they moored their ship to the bank and began clearing a site for constructing a fort.*

Monsoe brought word to Cassino about the new arrivals. He had been trading downriver and had seen the ship cross the bar. On his return trip, he saw where the *Albatross* had put in to shore.

"The time has come," said Cassino. "If the white man's ship has traveled upriver, they will establish a permanent settlement."

"They are cutting down trees and beginning to build a fort like that of Captain Lewis and Captain Clark," Monsoe reported.

"Where have they decided to build this fort?" Cassino inquired.

Monsoe told him and then added with a smile, "They do not know the river and have selected a site that may soon be under water. Some Chinook and Chehalis are joining together to try to stop them."

"That is foolish and will only bring trouble," said Cassino, shaking his head.

"What are you going to do?" Monsoe said quietly. He knew his friend well.

With a smile, Cassino replied, "The river will soon be rising. Let us see what these white men do then. Until then, I will not get involved. That is Cathlamet territory and I will not go looking for trouble. My scouting parties will keep us informed. Lamkos will contact the Chinook in that area, and Sohowitsh will observe the building of the fort."

As predicted, the river began to rise within four days, and Captain Winship's men were forced to tear down their construction and float the logs downriver about a quarter of a mile to a more suitable location. Soon after, disturbing reports began filtering in to Cassino's camp. News came that a war party had surrounded the white settlement in preparation for an attack. Word soon followed that cooler heads had prevailed and a large powwow was held instead. When he heard that the Chinook had offered to help the white men settle lower on the river, Cassino recognized the influence of Comcomly. A few days later, a scouting party came in with a report that the settlers had abandoned their site and had left on their ship, promising to return the following summer.

Later that spring, Chief Comcomly led a party of Chinook upriver to the Cascades. The great chief accepted Cassino's invitation to spend the night with the Kalama. While discussing the recent attempt by the white settlers to build at Oak Point, Comcomly said, "These white men were good men, but because their party was not large, some young hotheads from the Chehalis planned to steal their ship. I was able to stop the attack and the white men soon sailed away. It would have been bad to have a permanent white settlement in that area, because it would disrupt the usual trading among the Chinook. Trading with ships should be done at my village."

"Do you think the white men will return?" asked Cassino.

Comcomly looked into the fire and sighed, "It is only a matter of time. They will soon return, and next time they will not leave. We must convince them to settle downriver or we will be cut off from the trading."

Cassino took a few moments before asking his next question. He didn't want to offend the great chief of the Chinook. "Don't you think that they will send parties up the river to trade? And what if more white men come down the river, like the chiefs Lewis and Clark?"

Comcomly shook his head. "They will come also. How many will come and how soon, who can say? But they will come."

The two chiefs sat for a long time lost in their own thoughts. Comcomly finally broke the silence. "Cassino, you must consolidate your power in the mid-river area. Contact with the white men will weaken your tribes. I have seen this happen in my own village and with other tribes near the mouth of the river. It is hard to describe and it makes me very sad, but perhaps if you are prepared..." his voice trailed away.

Cassino slowly nodded his head. "I think I understand what you are saying." He also knew that Comcomly was admitting that he could not control the balance of trade.

That summer, Tanohah decided it was time for Cassino to become a chief of the Multnomah, but the other chiefs would not acknowledge him. Wise in the ways of the Wappato tribe, Cassino did not press the issue. When the time was right, it would happen.

As the warm days began to fade into the crispness of autumn, the time came for the return of the salmon to the falls at Wallamt. But before Cassino could gather his family for the annual fishing trip upriver, word came of trouble between the Clannaquah and the Quathlahpottle.

While Laquano and Concomsin were away on trading business, an ambitious young Clannaquah chief had slipped across the river and stolen two attractive, young slave girls belonging to the Quathlahpottle. Notwithstanding the alliance between Laquano and Concomsin, which had preserved peace between the two tribes, resentment between the groups had been festering for a long time. To make matters worse, the Clannaquah quietly moved the girls downriver and sold them to the Cowlitch.

When the news reached Cassino, he went immediately to the Quathlahpottle camp and called for a council. The tribe was reluctant to listen to Cassino, and some warriors began preparing to pursue the culprits. Across the river, a canoe was launched from the Clannaquah camp and began to make its way toward the Quathlahpottle village. As the canoe neared the east side of the river, Cassino was relieved to see that the Multnomah chief, his friend Tanohah, was leading the party, followed by several Clannaquah men bearing gifts. When the canoe had been pulled ashore, Chief Tanohah assured the Quathlahpottle that the slave girls would be returned. Chief Cassino solemnly thanked Chief Tanohah, but the two exchanged a knowing glance.

On his way back to his own camp, Cassino stopped to see Pilmowitsh. "Come into my house," said the older man, "and let us smoke and you can tell me the latest happenings. We seldom have time to talk and I am often busy with my canoes."

As Cassino discussed recent events and explained the problems he was facing, he found Pilmowitsh's calming wisdom to be a great help and encouragement. Finally he got around to the main reason he had stopped. "My father," he said, "Sohowitsh tells me you are finishing a very fine canoe—perhaps the most beautiful you have done. Is this new canoe special in some way?"

"Yes, my son, it is special," Pilmowitsh replied.

"I would like to buy this canoe," Cassino said firmly.

"It is not for sale."

Cassino looked into the fire for a long time before asking, "Can you build another one as fine and beautiful? I want to give a gift to Tanohah, a gift that will express my greatest appreciation and affection. He has prevented war between the Clannaquah and the Quathlahpottle. Tanohah understands that the tribes along the river must never again fight against each other. We must be united. Nothing would please him more than to own the finest canoe made by Pilmowitsh the Canoe Maker. Can you think of a more magnificent gift for this occasion, my father?"

Pilmowitsh sat quietly and considered his next words carefully. "This canoe was the one I was building for the long journey, but do not tell this to Tanohah. You may have this canoe and I will begin another. My heart is full with gratitude for two fine sons, two great chiefs."

Lop came to the fire and gently touched Pilmowitsh's face. "There will be time to build another."

The next day, Pilmowitsh put the finishing touches on the resplendent canoe and sent Cassino on his way. As the sun was slipping below the crest of the Scappoose Hills, Cassino beached the canoe on the southeast shore of Wappato and summoned Tanohah. When the chief of the Multnomah came down to the river, Cassino said, "This canoe is for you, my brother, for keeping peace between our tribes."

Word soon spread about the significance of the intricately carved canoe, and all the tribes along the river learned the legend of Chief Tanohah and his magnificent "peace canoe."

# THE
# FIRST WHITE
# SETTLEMENT

*arch 22, 1811. Amid strong winds and heavy seas, the* Tonquin *sailed toward the mouth of the Columbia River, with Captain Thorn in command. The ship carried a crew of twenty-one, along with thirty-three members of a fur trading and settlement group and twenty-four natives from the Hawaiian Islands. In preparation for crossing the bar, a boat with five men aboard was lowered into the churning waters to attempt to sound the channel. The small boat was caught in a squall and capsized and the five men were lost.*

*Two days later, the seas had quieted enough for a second attempt to enter the Columbia. Although the ship's pinnance and three more men were lost, this time the* Tonquin *made it inside the river before grounding on a sandbar. The incoming tide finally freed the ship and carried her up the channel to a small bay just inside Cape Disappointment.*

*Eventually, a site at Point George, named by Lieutenant Broughton in 1792, was selected for the establishment of a permanent trading post for the Astor Company. The fort, on the south side of the river mouth, was named Astoria and became the first permanent white settlement on the Columbia.*

The long-awaited news finally came. The white settlers had sailed into the Great River and put down anchor near the Chinook village. Cassino sent word to all the Wappato tribes and asked Tanohah and Monsoe to meet him at Comcomly's lodge. Quickly assembling a large party, with enough supplies to make camp if the Chinook village was full, Cassino settled into one canoe, while Sohowitsh and Lamkos took charge of the other two for the trip downriver. They lost no time in departing and soon met a number of canoes from other tribes and villages, all making the journey to see the new group of settlers.

When they arrived at the mouth of the river, Monsoe and Tanohah set up camp, but Cassino was invited into Comcomly's house as his guest. The great chief convened a meeting of leading Chinook chiefs, which lasted far into the night. Comcomly reviewed the events of the past few days for the benefit of the newly arrived chiefs from upriver. "The new ship is called *Tonquin*, and it has been in the river for several days. The ship carries natives of an unknown tribe in addition to many white men. Some of these men died when the ship was entering the river, but the men still plan to build their village here."

"How did the men fall off the big ship?" asked one chief.

"They didn't," replied Comcomly. "The ocean was very angry and the waves were large, but the white men sent small boats into the river and it was these that were lost. Every day now, men come ashore to look for a place to build their village."

"Have you met their chief?" asked Cassino.

Comcomly nodded and said, "He is a man called McDougal. He says that they will build their village and then there will be much trade. Soon the ship will go north to trade with the Nootkas, but it will return. He also asked us about the white men from the east."

The chiefs had many questions for Comcomly and then debated matters of trade. Finally, Monsoe asked, "Have they decided where they will build this village?"

"Chief McDougal has assured me that they will build their village near the mouth of the river, so our trading arrangements will remain the same. Do not worry. You may return to your villages and I will send word when the time has come for trading."

Several of the chiefs returned home, but Cassino decided to stay at the mouth of the river to watch the developments for himself. Shannaway, chief of the Cowlitch, also decided to stay, and he and Cassino spent time discussing their mutual interests. Shannaway was well on his way to becoming a powerful chief in the Cathlamet group of tribes.

The next morning, Cassino met with his chiefs and told them of his decision to stay downriver for a while. He suggested that they return to their tribes and said he would relay any news through Lamkos and the Kalama.

Cassino visited the site of the white village regularly and soon became known as a young chief of unusual intelligence. He talked with the settlers and fur traders at every opportunity and studied their organization and methods of work. Along with Chief Comcomly and Chief Shannaway, Cassino spent many evenings analyzing the latest developments and contemplating their implications for the Chinook.

Cassino was careful not to take the other two wily chiefs completely into his confidence, and he suspected that they were hedging their positions as well. Comcomly liked to pit Cassino and Shannaway against each other, and it was obvious that he considered them both as rivals. Cassino began to realize the strategic importance of his neck of the river as the ultimate trade center for furs, but he never discussed this idea with the other two chiefs.

As Fort Astoria took shape, Cassino decided that it was time to return to Wappato. Sohowitsh gathered the group and they headed upriver early one morning. When they reached a secluded spot along the south shore, Cassino pointed toward the beach and the canoes turned in to shore. Cassino instructed Sohowitsh to select a few men to form a surveillance party. "Find a spot along this side of the river near the point of land that juts out into the water," he said. "Scout the area every day, but let no one see that you have remained behind, not even Comcomly. Watch the Chinook village and send word when Shannaway leaves. It will probably be soon. Report any unusual developments from the white man's village, especially if they send a party upriver. I must know as soon as they leave. The rest of us will go to our village, but Lamkos will return soon with fast canoes, young men to serve as messengers, and further instructions. Do you understand the importance of secrecy?"

Sohowitsh nodded. "We will remain concealed. Tell Lamkos that we will watch for him on the upriver side of the point. He will not need to search for us. We will contact him."

The trip back to the Kalama village seemed short, because Cassino was busy making plans while the others paddled upstream. After a dry winter, the river was not as high as normal and the current was not as strong. The travelers stopped only for food and rest along the way.

Lamkos was on shore to greet them. "The landing of the white men has caused a lot of excitement along the river," he said. "Tanohah says that the Multnomah are no longer feeling invincible. They are speaking to their brothers on Wappato and Tanohah thinks that they will turn to you, Cassino, at the first sign of white traders coming upriver."

Cassino nodded and raised his hand to silence Lamkos. "Do not mention this to anyone else. We have other matters that must be taken care of first." Cassino then gave Lamkos full instructions for the upcoming journey, adding, "Tomorrow you must leave early and move quickly downriver. Tell Sohowitsh to return here when the white traders depart. You will stay behind and continue to scout. If you are discovered, tell anyone who asks that you were simply curious about the white village and came to see for yourself."

Cassino entered his lodge and sat down on a mat near the firepit. As soon as he was seated, his wives brought steaming hot food to serve him. After he had eaten, he lit a pipe and enjoyed a smoke, while his wives crowded around to hear the news about the new fort and his trip downriver.

When he had finished his pipe, his wives quietly returned to their evening chores and Cassino stood up and went outside. He had much to think about and the fresh air was invigorating. He began to plan for his trip the next day to visit Tanohah and the Multnomah, and he rehashed in his mind a conversation he'd had with Chief Coalpo of the Clatsops.

While watching the building of the new fort, Cassino had quietly gone about renewing his ties with Coalpo, who was a blood relative through the family of his real father, the late chief of the Chinook. Next to Comcomly, Coalpo was the leading chief on the lower river, and he and Cassino agreed that strengthening their alliance would be beneficial to both men. No longer would Cassino have to rely solely on Comcomly or his own scouts for information about the white settlement, and Cassino agreed to provide Coalpo with information from further upriver, which could become important if more white men came into the area from the east.

Cassino slept late the next morning, then arose and dressed with care. Calmly and deliberately, he directed the select cadre of slaves who would accompany him to the Multnomah village. Each man was dressed in a blue sailor's jacket and armed with a musket, and Cassino issued precise instructions for their arrival upriver. When the sun was nearing its apex, the small party pushed off into the Great River.

A single musket shot announced their arrival to the Multnomah. Reaching the shallow water, four of Cassino's men jumped out of the canoe and hauled it straight up onto the beach. As Cassino solemnly stepped ashore, his men stacked their muskets at the bow of the canoe and formed a brigade for the march up to the village. When the men were assembled, Cassino strode ceremoniously toward the village between two lines of smartly dressed bodyguards.

When the parade of warriors reached the cluster of houses at the edge of the Multnomah village, Tanohah greeted Cassino and the two men went inside Tanohah's lodge, where Cassino was free to speak openly. "I received your message from Lamkos," he said. "My plan was to send for you, but it seemed more appropriate for me to visit you instead. A group of white settlers will come upriver soon, but Sohowitsh will give us advance warning. Would it be wise for me to pledge an alliance to the Multnomah now on behalf of all my Wappato tribes?"

"There has been talk of joining with you," Tanohah replied, "and pledging your support would be the first step. When the white men arrive, even those among us who drag their feet will know that the time has come to make you chief of the Multnomah and all Wappato. I will call a tribal council immediately."

Cassino joined the distinguished leaders entering the longhouse where the meeting would be held. With a mixture of pride and humility, he seated himself to the right of Tanohah. He wished that Sohowitsh and Monsoe could have been there, because this meeting was vitally important to their futures as well. Cassino acknowledged Tanohah's introduction and began to speak.

"My brothers of the greatest of all Wappato tribes—the proud and strong Multnomah—I bring you greetings from the tribes at the mouth of the Great River. Chief Tanohah has invited me to report to you about my observations of the new white settlement. This is the first report I have given to any Wappato tribe. I am here to strengthen the alliance between the Multnomah and all of my tribes, great and small: the Clackstar, the Quathlahpottle, the Kalama, the Niakowkow, Cathlahminnamin, and the Shoto.

"My brothers, the white men are here to stay. They are building a strong village at the mouth of the river on the south shore. They will soon send a trading party to establish agreements with the tribes up the river. Never before has there been such a need for all of our tribes to stand together. My tribes need the Multnomah, the Clannaquah, and the

Wakanasisi to stand with us. We must work together and trade together as the brothers we truly are. Chief Comcomly wants the old Chinook trading agreements to prevail, but I do not think this is possible. Chief Coalpo and Chief Shannaway agree with me, although they may not say so. We must be alert for more white men coming from the east. The white men at the settlement are expecting this, and so am I.

"Our interests are the same, and I pledge my support to you. I have scouts at the mouth of the Great River and they are led by Sohowitsh, the blood brother of Chief Tanohah, the grandson of old Chief Taneeho who has gone on the long journey. Sohowitsh will inform all of us.

"Remember Chief Tanohah's 'peace canoe,' for it is the symbol of the brotherhood of all Wappato tribes. My brothers, I speak from my heart. We must preserve peace among all of our brothers."

When he had finished speaking, Cassino rose and left the longhouse to allow the Multnomah leaders to confer. With his contingent of slaves, Cassino walked back to the beach and climbed into the canoe for the journey home.

Back at his Kalama house, a messenger from the Multnomah was awaiting him with startling news: A large canoe with a single white man was coming downriver from the east after wintering on the headwaters of the Great River. A second messenger soon brought news that the canoe was very near and "Thompson" was proceeding to the mouth of the river.

Cassino hurried out onto the river in time to see the white man's canoe. The huge flag at the stern was different from the one at the fort, and Cassino knew that Thompson was a King George Man rather than a Boston Man. He ordered his paddlers to pull in close to the other boat, and engaged the white explorer in a brief conversation. He was impressed by the man's attire and his businesslike, yet friendly, manner.

Cassino sensed that the stranger had not been aware of the new settlement until he had spoken with the Multnomah. The man questioned Cassino eagerly about the situation at the fort and appeared disappointed by the information. Cassino was puzzled by Thompson's response and decided that the men at the fort were expecting different white men to come from the east. After a while, Thompson continued downriver and Cassino returned to the Kalama village.

The next morning brought Sohowitsh with a report that a party from the fort was on its way upriver, with Coalpo serving as guide. A message from Coalpo assured Cassino that the group would visit the Kalama, but they would spend the first night at Coalpo's village. As the traders worked their way upriver, Cassino received daily reports, which he passed along to the other Wappato tribes.

On the fourth morning, a large canoe turned in from the Great River and glided up the small stream leading to the Kalama village. Cassino was on the beach to greet Coalpo and the four traders: McKay, the leader; Stuart, Montigny, and Franchere. Coalpo told the white men that Cassino was his relative and chief of the Kalama, but after a look from Cassino, he went no further in his explanation. There was much talk of trade and the visitors were obviously impressed by the location of the village and its setting amid brightly blooming spring flowers and groves of stately oak trees.

As the traders continued to look around the village, Cassino pulled Coalpo aside and said, "Do not tell them that I am the chief of other tribes. It might cause problems when we're making trade agreements."

Coalpo nodded. "These men want to work with small groups."

"When you visit the Quathlahpottle," Cassino continued, "speak to Concomsin. He is in charge of all Wappato trade on my behalf. But avoid the Multnomah so they cannot make any agreements. If we are to unite the Wappato tribes, the Multnomah must join with us. If we have established trade agreements and they do not, this will strengthen our position in dealing with them."

Again Coalpo nodded his agreement. "We will stay across the river from Wappato and avoid the Multnomah village. Did you know that McKay has established a trade agreement with Chief Shannaway and the Cowlitch?"

Cassino was instantly alert. "So, Shannaway is the first to break away from the old Chinook agreements. We will watch carefully to see what Comcomly will do. Meanwhile, tell Concomsin to make no definite commitments, but leave the way open for later agreements."

# 14 CHIEF OF THE MULTNOMAH

The proud Multnomah did not respond to Cassino's visit the way he had hoped, but his disappointment was tempered by Coalpo's successful circumvention of their village with McKay's party. The Multnomah were very angry that the white traders had totally ignored them, but were impressed by Cassino's obvious influence. Cassino had seen to it that word filtered back to the Multnomah about McKay's visit to the Kalama village on both the upriver and downriver legs of his journey.

Summer was fast approaching, and Cassino's other concerns left him little time to worry about developments at Fort Astoria, until one evening when an urgent message arrived from Coalpo. The white man's ship had left the river, but another trading party was heading upriver. This time they planned to travel above the Cascades to establish a settlement east of the mountains. Cassino was stunned. The trade aspirations of the white settlers were far beyond what he had imagined. He could foresee trouble, because the tribes above the Cascades were unreliable.

Cassino sent word to the other Wappato tribes and summoned Tanohah, Asotan, Monsoe, and Concomsin to meet him at the Quathlahpottle village the next day. He knew that the best way to reach a consensus was to ask for everyone's input. He also recalled Lamkos from his downriver scouting mission and sent Sohowitsh to stay with Coalpo and keep an eye on developments at the fort.

As soon as the group had gathered at Concomsin's house, Cassino got right to the point. "Time is running out," he said. "The white men will be above us and below us on the river before we know it. Tanohah, the Multnomah must gain stronger control of the tribes above Wappato as far as the Cascades. The traders who are coming upriver will spend the winter east of the mountains. They have no interest in stopping to talk trading with us. We must gain solidarity among the mid-river tribes or it will be too late. The Multnomah have become the problem—a log in our path—but Tanohah cannot do the job alone.

"Asotan, you must use your influence with the other medicine men to strengthen alliances. Concomsin, find new ways to gather furs. The gathering and storing of furs is important. We will trade them to the white men in so many ways, our operation will not be known. Monsoe, your tribe is the largest, and you must provide assistance in gathering furs and trading. Do you have any questions?"

The men offered their suggestions and decisions were made about how to proceed. Tanohah, who had been unusually quiet, finally spoke up. "One of the troubles with the Multnomah is old Chief Posen. After his return from downriver, he insists that Comcomly wants to oppose the white settlers. Now the ship is gone and some of the settlers have gone east of the mountains. There will be few remaining at the fort. No matter what I say, the idea persists in my village that the white man can be opposed."

Cassino spoke sharply. "Tell them that other ships may appear at any time, and more white men will come from the east. Your people must understand that it is foolish to oppose the white man's magic."

Tanohah nodded in agreement and Cassino continued, "As for the rumors about Comcomly, he is getting desperate and afraid of losing his power. He knows he cannot maintain the old Chinook trading agreements. He knows that Shannaway has made his own agreements with the white traders. Comcomly also fears Coalpo and his influence at the fort. He is wary of me, but he does not fear my influence as he would if I were chief of the Multnomah. Perhaps this explains Posen's efforts, Tanohah."

Asotan spoke up before Tanohah could answer. "Posen's influence is growing weaker. Most Multnomah now follow Tanohah. I believe that I can undermine Posen's influence."

The planning continued into the afternoon until Cassino began to make preparations to depart. Before he left, he said to Tanohah, "You are wise not to push your brothers. You are their chief and you know them better than anyone. When the time is right, you will know it, and they will follow you."

The second party of white traders passed Wappato two days later. As Cassino had predicted, they avoided the native settlements and camped on a sheltered beach along the river. Cassino met them out on the river and spoke a few words to Stuart, who was in charge. He wished them a good journey and the settlers continued upstream. Some scouts from the Multnomah followed the boat upriver as far as the Cascades, and watched as Stuart's expedition made the portage without difficulty. Passing through the gorge, the party made its way into the territory of the eastern tribes. Much later, Cassino heard that they had established their fort, a fur trading post, at the mouth of the Okanogan River where it meets the Great River far to the northeast.

When Lamkos returned from his time with the Clatsops, he brought back some unusual information. The men at the fort were building a small ship, called a "schooner," in the bay southwest of the fort. Cassino immediately sent word to Pilmowitsh about this new kind of boat.

Pilmowitsh was enthusiastic about the opportunity to observe the details of shipbuilding, and he hoped he might even join in doing some of the work. He and Lopahtah and several of his best artisan slaves paddled downriver to join Sohowitsh near the white man's settlement.

When Pilmowitsh arrived near the mouth of the river, he was surprised to learn that Sohowitsh had gone upriver to see Cassino. Cassino, who was spending a few nights in the Clackstar village, was equally surprised to see Sohowitsh arrive. Food was hastily set out and the men sat down to eat and discuss the latest developments.

"Five days ago, with so few white men at the fort, suddenly all the Chinook disappeared," Sohowitsh said excitedly. "Then a message came from Chief Comcomly asking for Stuart and Franchere to bring medicine to the village, because Comcomly was very sick. Stuart is the one who is going to the east side of the mountains, so he was not there, but the other traders were wary because there were not the usual Chinook visiting at the fort. They decided to wait until the next day.

"That evening, the sister of Coalpo came to the fort and said that the message from Comcomly was a trap. The Chinook planned to take Stuart and Franchere prisoner. So the white men did not go."

"What did they do?" asked Cassino.

Pausing to swallow some of his food, Sohowitsh continued, "The white chief, McDougal, called all the native chiefs to a meeting the next day—including Comcomly. When all the chiefs were there, McDougal held up a small bottle and said, 'Remember the smallpox that killed many of your people a few winters ago?' He shook the bottle for all the chiefs to see. Then he said, 'I am the Great Smallpox Chief and I have the smallpox in this bottle. If I let it out, it will kill all of your men, women and children.' Then he told the chiefs to go in peace. If they make war on the white man, he will let the smallpox out of the bottle and everyone will die."

"The white man's medicine is great," Monsoe said in a subdued voice.

Angrily, Cassino responded, "This is what I have been saying all along! We must live with the white man in peace."

"But that is not all," Sohowitsh continued. "McDougal is taking a daughter of Comcomly as his wife. A great feast will be held at the fort to celebrate the marriage of the white chief and the Chinook princess."

Cassino laughed, "That sly old, one-eyed Comcomly."

An invitation soon arrived from Comcomly, and Cassino took several members of his family with him to the wedding celebration at the fort. The princess had been scrubbed clean in the white fashion and was radiant in her colorful costume. The old Chinook chief was proud and pleased with himself and McDougal did all he could to emphasize his father-in-law's importance. The men at the fort were given a day off from work and joined with Comcomly's guests in singing, dancing, demonstrations of marksmanship, and general merrymaking. Most of the Wappato chiefs were in attendance, Asotan accompanied Tanohah, and Sohowitsh had come with Cassino and Monsoe. The feast and celebration lasted all day and Cassino used the opportunity to visit old friends and make some new acquaintances.

Pilmowitsh and Lopahtah had made the short journey from their camp near where the little schooner was under construction. Pilmowitsh was determined to stay to see the ship finished and his eyes sparkled with renewed energy as he talked about the white man's tools and skills. When he had a few moments alone with Cassino, the older man was pleased to announce, "The small ship will sail soon, and the white chief plans to bring it up the river."

Even though Cassino stayed two nights as Comcomly's guest, the two men found little time to talk; but it was evident that the Chinook chief planned to work closely with the white traders at the fort. Cassino knew that it was time to make new arrangements, and he went across the river to confer with Coalpo.

The hottest summer days passed and the time came for the annual gathering at Wallamt. Cassino was reunited with his mother, and had an opportunity to discuss the arrival of the white traders with her husband, Olahno, chief of the Calapooya. Both men expected the white men to go above Wallamt Falls to trade, and Olahno said, "The organization of trade between my tribe and the other valley tribes is going well but we are not consolidated. I'm afraid that when these new traders arrive, we will not get the good prices we have received by trading with you."

"You can continue to trade through the Wappato tribes instead of directly with the white men. If you hold back enough good furs for me, then I can demand a higher price."

"Then we have an agreement," said Olahno. "In the meantime, I will work to establish a better system of communication between the valley tribes."

During the fall and early winter, as more and more white settlers were seen along the river, it became more difficult for Cassino and Concomsin to keep abreast of the trading arrangements. Pilmowitsh and Lopahtah returned to Wappato and the canoe builder brought word that the schooner, dubbed "Dolly," was finished and sailing around the lower river. Pilmowitsh expected to see the boat in the Wappato area by spring.

Cassino had been hard at work learning the white man's language, and often surprised the traders with his proficiency. Every chance he had, he picked up new words and practiced speaking with the white traders and settlers. He began to understand the seasons of the year, and how the traders marked time in months from winter to winter, and he struggled to understand how the white man's "month" changed from thirty days to thirty-one and back again.

One day in the month called "November," Franchere and three other traders stopped at the Kalama village to say they were looking for three white men who had left the fort without permission. They offered rewards for information or capture of these men, but they found no trace of them all the way upriver to the Cascades. Cassino learned that the three deserters had fallen into the hands of the Cathlahminnamin, and that Shanum was the one holding them prisoner. Cassino was especially angry because Shanum withheld this information from him and he found out about the three men from Monsoe and the Clackstar.

Cassino passed the word to the search party and they went to Shanum's house to barter for the return of the runaways. Shanum received them in an insolent manner and extorted a ransom of blankets, a copper kettle, a hatchet, a small pistol, a powder horn, and some musket balls. Cassino was furious and left immediately for the Cathlahminnamin village.

Cassino had always had reservations about Shanum. The young chief had always been loyal when it counted most and carried out orders faithfully, but Cassino rarely approved his actions when Shanum acted on his own. Cassino knew he must act quickly and decisively to establish that no Wappato chief was to take action with the white traders without his prior approval. He stopped at the Clackstar village to pick up Monsoe and outlined his plan to his friend as they completed the journey to the Cathlahminnamin village.

Shanum was clearly uneasy as Cassino and Monsoe seated themselves by the fire. He knew that Cassino was angry and the presence of Monsoe only emphasized the seriousness of the situation. Cassino wasted no time getting to the point. "You took three white men prisoner without a word to me. You know that I am working to establish a good relationship with the white traders, yet you did this."

Shanum shifted uneasily. "They are roundheads and never before has a chief been questioned for taking roundheads as slaves. As for the ransom, the white men paid well. It was good business."

Cassino shook his head. "No, Shanum, it was not good business. The white men are here to trade for many seasons. What will they think of you and your tribe? Will they trust you and want to trade with you? Or have you traded that trust for a few blankets and some powder?

"And what about the Multnomah?" Cassino continued. "You are very close to them and the white men may think that they cannot trust the Multnomah because they cannot trust you."

"Who cares about the Multnomah?" came Shanum's sullen reply.

Cassino's anger was unconcealed. "I instructed you to do everything to establish good relations with the Multnomah. You must make amends. We will go together to the Multnomah village and you will give them the full ransom."

Blood rushed to Shanum's cheeks. "I will not do that. It will bring disgrace to me."

Cassino's words were carefully measured and the message was crystal clear. "You will do this, or I will bring disgrace to you."

The news of the chastisement of Shanum soon spread among the tribes. Again, the Multnomah were impressed by Cassino's wisdom and influence, and old Chief Posen was so delighted to receive the small pistol that he ceased his opposition to Cassino.

Winter blew in stormy and wet, but not too cold. A single white trader established a trading station above the falls on the Multnomah River, and Olahno assigned scouts to keep Cassino informed. The men from the fort also set up a station at Oak Point for fishing and trading and white traders moved about on the river as the weather permitted.

Just after the celebration of the new year at the fort, two canoes with eleven white men came down the river from the east. They had suffered many hardships of winter and told Cassino that a larger party would soon follow. A month later, the second group, with thirty men, came by. The village at the mouth of the river was considerably reinforced. It was obvious the white men were here to stay.

Not long after the reinforcements arrived at the fort, the call came to Cassino from the Multnomah. He felt the power of his *tamanowos*. Ever since his boyhood he had looked forward to this time, forever planning and thinking about what must be done. The proud Multnomah had taken their time before naming him chief, but once it was done, the Clannaquah and Wakanasisi soon followed and the alliances along the mid-river were completed. Cassino was now the primary chief of every Wappato tribe, an awesome responsibility. No other chief on the river had more power, including Comcomly. Cassino was still a young man; at thirty-five years old, he was still strong and vigorous.

Cassino immediately moved his base of operations to the large village of the Multnomah. His new house was built at the front of the village on the east side, overlooking the river and beach. From his doorway, the view was magnificent. He could see the bend in the river where it turned east past the Multnomah, and on the horizon was the towering, snow-capped Wyeast. In front of his door, the river was smooth and wide and he could seen downstream for quite a distance. The lovely, rounded contours of Loowit, her white shoulders reflecting the moods of the setting sun, loomed over the country across the wide expanse of water. On clear nights, with the moon on the mountains and the water, and the stars sparkling overhead, Cassino was caught in a spell of enchantment. He enjoyed the ever-changing panorama.

Cassino's headquarters and the Multnomah village became the key stopping place for all travelers. With its strategic location at the confluence of the Great River and the Multnomah—which the white traders had begun to call the Willamette after the native name, Wallamt, for the meeting place at the falls—the Multnomah village was at the very center of native life and commerce along the river. Horses, a new means of transportation for the natives, were now used for rapid communication across and around the island. Across the river, the Wakanasisi also kept a few horses.

Cassino's foresight and wisdom in consolidating the Wappato tribes was soon put to the test by the rapid influx of white traders. In late spring, the men at the fort sent two more parties upriver. The larger party continued east beyond the mountains, but the smaller band, led by men named McKenzie and Matthews, turned up the Willamette. Cassino sent word ahead to Olahno and the other valley tribes. As spring stretched toward summer, Sohowitsh sent word that another ship, the *Beaver*, had arrived at Astoria. He also reported that the *Tonquin* had been destroyed at Nootka, with only one survivor, a Chehalis native.

Trouble occurred at the Cascades, just as Cassino had feared. The large party traveling upriver from the fort had been attacked by natives on horseback near the narrowest part of the falls. The expedition had made it safely through the battle and on to Fort Okanogan, returning back downriver later. The natives in the attack were from east of the Cascades, not Chinook, but Cassino sent scouts anyway to investigate. They kept a close watch throughout the summer as groups of white settlers moved up and down the river.

It was time to recall Sohowitsh from the mouth of the river. Tanohah invited him to come live with the Multnomah. A new house was built and Sohowitsh's family moved from their quarters in Pilmowitsh's camp. When Sohowitsh arrived with a new Clatsop wife, a feast was held in his honor and all of his friends and relatives attended the joyous homecoming.

The first evening in his new house, Sohowitsh gave his report to Cassino. "When the ship called *Beaver* arrived at the Astoria village, Chief Comcomly was the first to greet the newcomers before the ship crossed the bar. His canoe was followed by a boat that the white men call a "barge," and they anchored on the north side of the river in the area known as Baker Bay. Thirty-six more men came to live in the village, so the fort now holds one hundred and forty white settlers. This is according to the white man's numbers that you taught us, Cassino."

"It is wise to understand their numbers and words, especially when trading." Cassino replied.

Sohowitsh continued, "The fort is now a large village, with houses for the white leaders they call 'proprietors' and 'clerks.' There are large houses for many purposes. The men eat in a large house called a 'dining hall,' and another house for trading they call a 'store.' They have another house for making iron, and they call the ironmaker 'smith.' There is also a place for men who work with wood, and they are called 'carpenters.' The entire village is surrounded by a wall of thick logs, about as high as three men. They call these walls 'stockade,' and the natives must go outside the walls at night. The white men have many muskets and they are very careful since the news of the *Tonquin*."

Cassino listened closely, saying the new words to himself, and tried to imagine this large stockade. "How do they feed so many men?" he asked.

Food is abundant and much is stored, Sohowitsh replied. "They bring in many supplies and also trade for food with the surrounding tribes. They gather fish at Oak Point and hunters are always bringing in fresh meat. From the wall of the stockade to the edge of the river, they grow many plants in what they call a 'garden.' They eat well and never want for food."

Early that summer, a large contingent from the fort traversed the Wappato area. Cassino was astounded by its size and provisions: some ninety men, in a great number of boats packed with bales, boxes, and kegs. The natives could see a tremendous amount of goods for trade: guns and ammunition, spears, hatchets, knives, beaver traps, copper and brass kettles, white and green blankets, dyed wool cloth, calico, beads, rings, thimbles, hawk bells, and abundant food supplies.

The size of the group removed all thoughts of plunder from the minds of Cassino and the natives. The well-armed and vigilant traders passed beyond Wappato without a single incident.

# FORT GEORGE AND THE HMS *RACCOON*

Cassino was surprised to hear that the Boston Men and the King George Men were at war. He had always been careful to address each group with the proper term, but to him they were all white men.

The Boston Men had been the first to arrive at the mouth of the river, and they were also the first white men to come down the river from the Cascades. As a boy, Cassino had been impressed by Lieutenant Broughton, a King George Man, and most of his early trading had been with King George Men. He respected Lewis and Clark, who were Boston Men, as were the settlers of Fort Astoria.

At first, Cassino heard that Chief Comcomly was urging the Boston Men to drive the King George Men out of the country. It was not long, however, before Comcomly reversed himself and professed to be a King George Man. Cassino was amused when he learned that the men in Fort Astoria had sold out and the village had been renamed Fort George, with the King George flag flying over the stockade.

On a dreary rainy day, Cassino beached his canoe near Pilmowitsh's camp and made his way up to the house. His old friend and father-figure waved to him from the front of his house. The two men hastily entered the house and slid the cedar plank over the opening to keep out the wind and rain. Thankful for the fire, they sat down on mats and shook the rainwater off their faces.

After enjoying a smoke, Cassino remarked, "Another ship has come into the river, my father. It is a ship of the King George Men and different from any we have seen. Would you like to go with your sons to see it?"

Pilmowitsh's face lit up. "It would be good to go with my sons, though the weather will be bad and the river rough. I would like to see this ship.

117

What can you tell me about it, my son?"

"Not much," replied Cassino. "I have not yet seen it myself. It is not large, yet carries many men. It is called *Raccoon* and 'sloop of war,' and is not used for trading. That is all I know."

Later that evening, Cassino cautioned Tanohah and Sohowitsh. "We must remember that Pilmowitsh is no longer a young man. We must take care to keep him from becoming too wet, cold or weary."

"We will take a large canoe," said Tanohah, "so it will be comfortable. Do not worry, Cassino. We will make all the arrangements."

"And I will tell Monsoe," added Sohowitsh.

The rain persisted for three more days, but the dawn of the fourth day was clear. It was mild for winter and the rain had washed the sky to a brilliant blue. Soon father and sons, along with six of Cassino's finest slaves, were propelling their handsome canoe down the fast moving river. Tanohah was wary, sensing the strong, rushing current, watching carefully for any disturbance on the surface that would indicate danger below, and feeling the force and direction of the wind as it blew across the channel. Life would be short in the cold waters of the swelling river, and Tanohah was not about to risk a capsize.

As the sun rose higher, the wind died down to a gentle breeze. They stopped at the Kalama village just long enough to pick up two additional paddlers, and then they were off. Gliding through the water in one of Pilmowitsh's finest canoes, with Cassino's slaves decked out in their matching blue sailor's jackets and the chiefs resplendent in their finest furs, the group made an impressive sight.

When they reached the mouth of the river, Coalpo greeted them warmly and quickly accommodated the whole party for the night. The exciting trip had taken its toll on Pilmowitsh and he retired early, but the rest of the group sat around the fire with Coalpo, smoking and talking.

The conversation soon turned to the affairs of the fort, and Coalpo commented, "Cassino, do you remember awhile back, when the white party came down the river in two birch bark canoes? There were two chiefs, one named Henry and the other was Stewart, and they had sixteen men along?"

"Yes, they were anxious to reach the fort," Cassino said, nodding to invite Coalpo to continue.

"Henry and Stewart are the new chiefs in charge of trading at the fort. They call themselves 'partners.' They are planning many changes and have spoken of building bigger houses. They also talk about many trading trips and many more trading posts."

"These men, are they good and fair?" Cassino inquired.

"It is too soon to tell. They have welcomed me into the fort and traded fairly. The trader named Henry seems especially friendly. He often asks for me, Comcomly, and the other chiefs to visit the fort. He asks us questions and listens carefully to our answers. I think he is the top chief."

Monsoe took advantage of Cassino's silence to ask Coalpo, "Are there many more men at the fort?"

"Yes, many more," the Clatsop chief said. "And the new ship is full of them. This ship has nothing but men in it, but the rumor is they will not stay."

"Then they are not settlers," said Tanohah.

"This ship is for making war against the enemies of the King George Men," said Coalpo. "Because we are friends, there is no reason for the ship to stay."

"What have you seen of this ship," Cassino interjected. "Have you visited it yet?"

Coalpo shook his head. "They will not let us near it. They have a small boat, like a canoe, that goes round and round the ship, day and night. The men in this boat have guns and they will not let our canoes come close. Only a few of the men from the ship have come ashore, and then only to go to the fort."

The others continued in conversation, but Cassino sat quietly, deep in thought. Before retiring, he arranged for Coalpo to go to the fort the next day to tell the King George Men of his visit with Comcomly. Cassino knew that the white men would be anxious to meet him and his chiefs from the Wappato area.

The next morning, after a rough crossing, Cassino and the other men arrived wet and cold at the Chinook village. Comcomly was delighted to see them and housed the entire party, including slaves.

Once the chiefs and Pilmowitsh were settled around the fire, Cassino explained his plan to Comcomly. The great chief was aghast. "We dare not ask this," he said warily. "They have let no natives near the ship since it arrived. Captain Black—the great one in the blue coat with the shiny ornaments on his shoulder—will not allow it."

Calmly, Cassino replied, "Are we not the friends of the King George Men? Are we not their helpers in trading? Why should the chief of the Chinook and the chief of the Multnomah and all Wappato tribes not visit the warship? When you introduce me to Henry and Stewart at the fort tomorrow, I will ask them this favor."

Comcomly shook his head and stared into the fire. He was tempted to assist Cassino in his plan, but he did not want to risk angering the white traders at the fort.

Cassino smiled to himself. *It is done*, he thought. *The idea has been placed into the mind of Comcomly. He will be no problem from here on.*

The next day, when Comcomly presented him at the fort, Cassino did not hesitate to let the partners know of his desire to visit the ship. However, he cleverly made his request in a such a way that the traders were not forced to make an immediate commitment. Alexander Henry was no stranger to dealing with natives. He had gained extensive experience trading with the Canadian Northwest tribes. Coalpo had make it clear that Cassino controlled the most strategic fur trading territory on the entire river.

Henry recognized the superior intelligence of Cassino among the other Chinook chiefs, and decided to do everything he could to ally him with the interests of the fort and its enterprises. As soon as Comcomly and Cassino left the stockade, Henry sent for Captain Black of HMS *Raccoon.*

Some time later, Captain Black stood before Henry's desk in the partners' quarters—and he was visibly upset. "Your request is out of the question, sir, and contrary to my orders from the Admiralty. It has been difficult enough to keep my men away from these savages, especially the women, and now you want me to bring them aboard?"

Henry pulled on his pipe, and in a quiet and persuasive voice replied, "Sit down, Captain, have a smoke and let us look at this situation in a different light. Captain Black, I am a trader, a man who has spent most of his life in the wilderness. I know the Indians; sometimes, what seems a matter of little consequence to us may be of great importance to them. If we are to be successful in our enterprise here, we must maintain the friendliest relationship possible with the natives. To do this, one must continually strive to make friends with their chiefs and to cooperate with them."

Henry stood up and walked over to the fireplace to tap out his pipe, then returned to his desk to refill it. He fussed with it for a minute or two, and when he at last had it drawing well, he leaned back in his chair and continued, "This has been a disappointing voyage for you and your men, Captain. The Admiralty sent you this great distance to take the fort from the Americans. You arrived only to find that the Americans had sold out to the British subjects of the Northwest Company. Now there is nothing for you to do but return to your home port, having accomplished a long and arduous journey of little consequence."

"I have carried out my orders," Captain Black said stiffly.

"So you have. But suppose you were to carry back reports from the partners at Fort George that your timely arrival and assistance was of great use in re-establishing British control at the mouth of the mighty Columbia River?"

Black considered Henry's words for a moment before he replied. "Perhaps some good can come from this voyage after all," he mused. Although he had command of a sloop of war, the smallest three-masted warship in the navy list, a young commander could hardly hope to attain post rank of captain if he returned from such a long voyage with nothing to show for it. His feat of seamanship would be taken for granted, but securing Fort George would be another matter. He looked back at Henry and said, "Sir, I am beginning to see the situation in a new light."

The two men continued their discussion for some time. Henry explained Cassino's importance to the British and reiterated his request to see the ship. Finally, Black stood up to go, saying, "It's settled then; either tomorrow or the first day of opportune weather."

Alexander Henry dispatched a messenger to Cassino at Comcomly's village, inviting him not only to tour the ship, but to take a short sail upriver as well.

The next morning, two hours before slack tide, a singular procession was seen going up the side of HMS *Raccoon*. Alexander Henry was in the lead, followed closely by Comcomly, Cassino, Coalpo, Pilmowitsh, Tanohah, Monsoe, and Sohowitsh. The chiefs were arrayed in their finest furs and ornaments. As Henry set foot on deck, the commander barked an order and a saluting cannon was fired. Comcomly was so frightened he nearly fell off the ladder. Henry quickly shouted down to Cassino, "Tell your men not to be afraid. The firing of the cannon is in honor of your visit!"

As Cassino stepped onto the spotless deck, he noted how different this ship was from the others he had seen. Everything was in perfect order. The sailors on deck were standing at attention, clothed in beautiful red coats—the handsomest coats Cassino had ever seen—and each man held a "firestick." Captain Black greeted the visitors dressed in a crisp blue coat, with gold buttons and a large gold decoration on one shoulder. A magnificent tricorn hat, bright white breeches, white stockings and black shoes with large brass buckles completed his impressive attire. Behind the captain stood three other men in similar uniforms, lacking only the shoulder ornament. The entire display was magnificent.

As the last of the chiefs stepped aboard, the firing of the cannon ceased. Captain Black took one step forward, saluted, and said something to Henry before the two men shook hands. Next, each of three men behind Black stepped forward in turn and saluted Henry. Henry then turned to Cassino and explained that Captain Black was the officer in charge, and the other three men were subordinate officers. He now wished to present each of the chiefs to Captain Black. As each chief stepped forward, Captain Black saluted him. Cassino was surprised by how well he could understand the English spoken by the sailors. He was able to follow most of the conversation, though only Henry seemed to be aware of this.

As they toured the ship, Cassino was astounded by the number of men aboard and how efficiently they were housed and fed. The chiefs watched the food preparation in the galley and were shown how the hammocks were used and stowed. The chiefs responded with delight to each new surprise and the sailors outdid each other performing for them. The huge iron guns provoked the greatest wonder. Pilmowitsh's eyes were wide as the sailors demonstrated the loading and firing process.

Cassino had learned to count in English and he understood the relationship between tens, hundreds, and thousands. He was impressed to learn that the *Raccoon* carried a contingent of one hundred and fifty men. He shook his head when Henry told him that this was the smallest of King George's warships—rating only twenty cannon—and that many of the larger ships had seventy-four of the big guns on board. Cassino found it almost impossible to visualize such a large ship, but he knew that the King George Men did not tend to exaggerate facts.

When the visitors had returned to the quarterdeck, Henry explained that Captain Black was about to take the ship for a short cruise up the river. Captain Black turned to his first lieutenant and gave the order: "Prepare to get underway, if you please."

"Aye, aye, sir," replied the first lieutenant. He turned crisply and bellowed to the men, "Stand by at the capstan. Loose the heads'ls. Hands aloft to loose the tops'ls."

The crew sprang to action. The first lieutenant watched the men scramble up the yards, then shouted, "Haul anchor!" The men at the capstan threw themselves to the task and the anchor was soon hauled and broken out. The ship slowly began to make sternway.

"Wheel hard over! Hands at the fo'castle—'aul in on the heads'l." The head of the ship gradually came about and they were off.

Feeling the motion of the ship, Pilmowitsh was overjoyed. Not only was he now able to experience the sensation of moving across the water in this great vessel, but he could observe the actions of the men that brought about this magic. He understood how the wind moved the ship and he watched as the helmsman turned the wheel, and felt the response of the ship beneath his feet. As the bow of the ship pulled in the appropriate direction, Pilmowitsh thought how wonderful it would be to turn the great wheel. Cassino saw the look on the older man's face and read his desire.

Well out into the river and heading upstream, the sailors on the yardarms released the braces to lower more sails as needed. Combined with the last of the incoming tide, the crisp breeze moved the ship quickly along. Cassino watched as Captain Black peered repeatedly at a very thin skin with pictures on it. Cassino nodded to Henry and pointed toward the captain. Henry took Cassino over to see the captain's charts and explained how to read them. Cassino told the men about Lieutenant Broughton's expedition and his memories of watching the lieutenant making his charts. Cassino was pleased that his acquaintance with Broughton seemed to make a strong impression on the two white men. Captain Black remarked to Henry, "He couldn't have been much more than a boy when Broughton was here, yet he remembers details of the expedition remarkably well. You were right, Henry. He is very intelligent."

Captain Black again consulted his charts and ordered a man to take soundings with a lead and chain. Henry explained the need to keep a careful watch on the depth of the water beneath the ship, and Cassino immediately asked Comcomly and Coalpo to warn the captain of shallow spots in the channel. As the soundings were reported back to him, Captain Black seemed pleased with the accuracy of Broughton's charts.

Past Comcomly's village and well upstream, the captain ordered a gun drill. Henry explained the procedure to Cassino and asked him to reassure the other chiefs.

Near the south shore, a massive pile of driftwood, brush, and tree trunks had accumulated on a narrow sandbar. Captain Black ordered the sailors to man the guns on the starboard side, then turned to Henry and said, "We will fire a broadside as we bear on that mass of debris at the head of the island. It will make a suitable target. Tell the chiefs to watch the island as soon as the guns fire."

Approaching the upper end of the island, the lieutenant sang out, "Sponge!" The gun crews sprang to the cannon and sponged them out.

"Load!" bellowed the lieutenant, and the crews responded.

"Take aim!" he ordered. "Ready—fire!" A tremendous explosion rocked the ship, and smoked billowed up and away from the guns. The captain and Henry pointed toward the small island. A second, lesser, explosion soon followed and the men on board saw the mass of timber blown apart. Sand and splinters were thrown up into the air and rained down on the river. It was a sight that none of the chiefs would forget.

The first lieutenant broke the silence and startled the spellbound chiefs by shouting, "Run in your guns…. Secure!" After a moment, he turned to the captain, saluted, and announced, "Guns secured, sir."

"Well done, lieutenant," came the reply.

The chiefs had never seen such havoc and destruction, and they would never have believed it if they hadn't seen it with their own eyes. The magic of the gun drill was sobering.

The ship continued upriver until the tide had reached full flood. Soon the ebb would begin and it was time to bring the ship around for the return trip. Orders were given, the wheel spun, and the ship came smartly about. Pilmowitsh stood as near to the helmsman as he could, delighted with each maneuver and the response of the great ship.

Observing Pilmowitsh, Cassino turned to Henry. "The King George Men are good and I will be their friend always. You have done much to honor us today and we will never forget our friends. One further honor would fill my heart, if I could see my father, Pilmowitsh—the finest builder of canoes on the Great River—steer this great ship."

Henry spoke briefly to Captain Black. A short time later, the sailor at the helm stepped aside and motioned for Pilmowitsh to take the wheel. As he grasped the spokes of the wheel firmly in his hands, the old canoe builder's dream became a reality. Pilmowitsh was a natural helmsman, and as he felt the great ship respond to his will, it was if he and the ship were one. He finally relinquished the wheel at they approached Fort George, and stood proudly near the helm for the rest of the trip. As the sailors swarmed out on the yards and the canvas was taken in, Pilmowitsh imagined himself bringing the ship in to port and dropping anchor at the precise point it had been before.

The chiefs were impressed by everything they saw during their visit and journey, and Henry knew he had pulled off a major stroke of diplomacy by convincing Captain Black to break protocol and allow the natives on board the ship.

Before going over the side, Cassino paused, removed his beautiful fur coat, and asked Henry to give it to Captain Black as a gift. "Chief Cassino knows the value of this coat, captain," Henry said to Black as he made the presentation. "When you return to London, it will be worth a fortune to you. These magnificent matched furs are rare and virtually priceless. I suggest you give him one of your scarlet marine coats in return. To him, this will be as rare and valuable as the gift he has given you."

And so it was that Cassino acquired his famous scarlet coat from the captain of the *Raccoon*. For many years, it was the only coat of its kind anywhere on the river. Cassino knew that his red "chief's coat" would have commanded scores of the finest furs, but he enjoyed the prestige that the coat brought to him, and it was not for sale at any price.

The journey back to Wappato was delayed by bad weather, so Cassino used the time to become better acquainted with Stewart, Henry, and the others at the fort. The men discussed business matters, and the various river tribes and their areas. Cassino told the traders about the natural boundary at the mountains between the Chinook and the "horse tribes" of the east, and warned them to be wary of marauding tribes in the area of the Cascades.

When weather broke, the Wappato chiefs bid farewell to Comcomly and Coalpo and headed upriver. It was very cold by the time they reached the Kalama village, so the warmth, comfort, and hot food was a welcome relief. After telling all about their exciting trip on the warship, Cassino emphasized the importance of friendship with the new traders. Then, he asked Lamkos, "How are relations with the Cowlitch?"

"Everything is peaceful," Lamkos replied. "At this time of year, they stay close to their houses, and we stay close to ours. We will continue to do everything we can to avoid incidents, just as you have said. The Cowlitch rarely come upriver these days, and those who do are friendly."

The next morning brought a miserable freezing rain, sometimes mixed with a wet, slushy snow. The Kalama stayed indoors and there was no activity on the river, until a canoe came unexpectedly out of the mist and headed in to shore. Asotan jumped out and raced up to the village, looking for Cassino.

When he reached Cassino's lodge, he said breathlessly, "There is trouble with the Tualitis. Shanum and his warriors have given offense and the Tualitis are threatening war. They sent a messenger to seek redress from you, but Shanum has taken the young brave captive. Some have said that the Tualiti messenger was killed."

"We will leave at once," Cassino ordered. "Tanohah, wait with Pilmowitsh for better weather before you return home. Monsoe, you come with me and Asotan." He quickly removed his ceremonial red coat and handed it to a slave to bundle in waterproof skins.

The trip to the Multnomah village was cold and miserable, but Cassino was seething inside at Shanum's stupidity. Something would have to be done to remove the chief of the Cathlahminnamin.

# 16 THE MULTNOMAH YEARS

I t was necessary for Cassino to move quickly to avert war between the tribes. Drawing on all of his persuasive abilities, he was able to appease the Tualitis and broker compensation from the Cathlahminnamin. Fortunately, the Tualiti messenger had not been killed, and he was returned to his village. A few weeks later, a suspicious hunting accident took Shanum's life. The other men in his hunting party all denied responsibility and no charges were ever proved.

It grieved Cassino to lose the first member of his original trading group, but Shanum had been a weak chief and had nearly caused the Multnomah to lose control of the lower Willamette basin. Shanum was given a chief's funeral, and immediately afterward, Monsoe was named chief of the Cathlahminnamin. A rumor began to circulate that the new chief had earned his position by taking care of Shanum, but no one could substantiate the allegations and the whispering soon died down.

During the winter of 1814, by the white man's calendar, Cassino received word of an attack on an English trading party at the Cascades. A large force was dispatched from the fort in early January—with Henry in command—to recover the goods. Coalpo served as a guide for the group and recommended to Henry that Cassino's help be solicited when they reached Wappato. Cassino used his contacts among the upper river tribes to identify the marauders and recover much of the plunder.

By the end of the month, Henry's party was able to return to Fort George with most of the stolen goods. Cassino was invited to accompany the group downriver, and when he reached the fort, the Northwest Company rewarded him for his assistance. They gave him a flag and awarded him an annuity as a "loyal chief."

The partners wanted to discuss the possibility of relocating the fort to the mouth of the Willamette, but they were concerned about creating trouble with the Wappato tribes and asked for Cassino's advice. He was pleased to hear about their plans. He didn't tell the partners that he was chief of the entire region, but he assured them he would do all he could to keep all the tribes in order. In early February, Henry left the fort to survey sites around Wappato. Cassino traveled along as Henry's aide-de-camp. Later, when Cassino heard that the King George Men had decided against the move, he could not understand their reasoning.

With the spring came new tensions between the Kalama and the Cowlitch. Lamkos kept Cassino apprised of the difficulties, so the chief of the Multnomah was not surprised when Lamkos and three large canoes of warriors came racing up the river early in April. As soon as the canoes hit the beach, Lamkos ran up the embankment to Cassino's house. "The Cowlitch are coming!" he shouted. "About forty canoes and three hundred warriors. They have their allies along with them!"

Cassino immediately sounded the alarm to all of the Wappato tribes and as far up the Willamette as the Calapooya.

By mid-morning, the impressive fleet of Cowlitch war canoes appeared around the bend in the river. They kept to the middle of the channel until they had passed the Quathlahpottle and Clannaquah villages, then swung over to the eastern shore to stage their attack from the far side. They set up their war camp directly opposite the Multnomah village and soon three canoes were launched toward Wappato.

Shannaway stepped from the first canoe to land and approached Cassino, who stood at the top of the rise. There was not a sound until Shannaway spoke.

"We are tired of the lies that Cassino is telling the King George Men to entice them to trade only with the Wappato tribes," he began. "We must have a fair trade agreement and compensation for the trade we lost this winter, or we will make war."

"My Chinook brother and chief of the Cowlitch," Cassino replied, "you speak harsh words. Were you not the first of all the Chinook chiefs to break the old trade agreements?"

When Shannaway merely grunted in response, Cassino continued. "You are the one who lies," he said contemptuously. "The King George Men trade with those who are their friends. They make trades with those they can trust. They know that I am their friend and I do not lie to them. What do have to say for yourself, Chief Shannaway?"

The Cowlitch chief knew he was no match for Cassino in parley. He cried out, "Enough with words. The Cowlitch will attack. When you have been disgraced in your village, then we will talk about compensation."

It was apparent that Shannaway was becoming desperate, and Cassino knew he must delay him from launching an attack. "Wait," he said. "It is not good for Chinook brothers to fight. We are honorable men and we must try to settle this dispute without resorting to war. What compensation do you want?"

Shannaway began to list a multitude of grievances and demanded outrageous payments. Cassino led him on, pretending to negotiate a reasonable settlement. It was difficult for him to conceal his contempt for the Cowlitch chief, but he was careful not to underestimate his treacherous adversary. Shannaway had not become a powerful chief without being cunning and strong.

Before the two men could reach an agreement, Shannaway proposed to break off the parley in order to return to his camp and consult with his warriors. He promised to return soon.

As soon as the three canoes reached a safe distance from the shore, the Cowlitch paddlers began to yell and jeer. There was a commotion in one of the canoes, and a captive, who had been hidden in the bottom of the boat, was suddenly thrust into full view. Cassino recognized one of his household slaves. After further taunts and insults, the Cowlitch paddled quickly across the river to their camp.

Cassino was furious, but his anger knew no bounds when a messenger from Shannaway arrived with an offer to return the kidnaped slave for the paltry price of two blankets. To put such a trivial price on the slave of a great chief was a calculated insult of the highest magnitude to a Chinook. Cassino refused to answer the messenger, who was only too happy to return safely to the Cowlitch camp.

Cassino knew that he must act quickly to gain the upper hand, but he also knew he could only put out about twenty canoes and one hundred and fifty warriors. Before he could solve his dilemma, an excited cry went up along the beach. He looked downriver and saw a large group of canoes paddling upstream toward the village. When the lead canoe came into range, Cassino recognized Monsoe and several of his top Clackstar chiefs. As the fleet drew nearer, he counted at least thirty canoes including several from the Clannaquah and Cathlahminnamin.

When a contingent of Quathlahpottle and Shoto also arrived, Cassino saw that he now commanded a superior force. He instructed the newcomers to make camp directly below the Cowlitch, and sent Monsoe and his Clackstar group to establish a position above the Cowlitch camp. Still, he wondered, "What will that fool, Shannaway, do next?"

Another large canoe soon put out from the Cowlitch side of the river. When Cassino saw Soleutu in the bow of the boat, he knew that Shannaway was having second thoughts about the dispute.

"This is not my doing," Soleutu said after he came ashore, "but Shannaway is determined to make war. He says he will attack and burn your village unless his demands are met. He says you have not been honorable—you would not meet the Cowlitch with equal force. My tribe and our allies will follow him, Cassino."

Cassino studied Soleutu's face. He respected him and liked him but he could not let his personal feelings influence his decision.

"Tell Shannaway that before the sun sets he will slink down the river with his tail between his legs like the cowardly, lying cur he is," Cassino said dismissively. "Use my exact words. Before you can cross the river, the Wakanasisi will have joined the camp above you and the Kalama will arrive below you. I have only begun to marshal my forces."

Soleutu nodded, but before he turned away, he said, "Our friendship remains, Cassino."

As the sun began its daily descent over the Scappoose Hills, Cassino decided it was time to be rid of the Cowlitch. He summoned several of his best Multnomah marksmen and ordered them to begin firing musket shots across the river. He was fairly certain that the Cowlitch did not have any muskets and he wanted to underscore the superiority of his forces by giving a demonstration of their firepower. He had learned from his experience aboard the *Raccoon* the value of an impressive show of force.

Before long, the Cowlitch began scurrying along the opposite shore. Just as the sun touched the tops of the hills, the war party paddled their canoes downriver and out of the Wappato territory. Cassino was certain he would have no more difficulty with Shannaway for a long time.

As spring turned into summer, Cassino led a large party of Multnomah up the Willamette. He had never extensively surveyed the rich valley above the falls, and he wanted to establish his connections with the valley tribes and their chiefs on their home grounds. He visited the Calapooya, staying for several days with Olahno and Tenastsil, and Cassino's mother gave him many important insights into the customs and traditions of the neighboring tribes. When the journey continued, Olahno joined the party as a guide. Together, he and Cassino negotiated mutually advantageous trade agreements with other chiefs along the Willamette. Everywhere they went, the group was treated with honor and respect.

When Cassino returned to Wappato, Tanohah reported that Pilmowitsh was failing fast. "Lopahtah says my father no longer takes interest in building canoes. He sits by himself and dreams about the great ship we visited. In his dreams, he steers the ship more and more."

At Pilmowitsh's house, the old canoe builder was gazing dreamily into the fire, looking very frail and weak. Lopahtah sat quietly beside him and stroked his hand with hers.

"My husband," she whispered softly, "we must speak again of the long journey. It is my wish to make the voyage with you. Many times we have spoken of this, and always we have agreed to go together. The time is near and we must make our plans."

Pilmowitsh turned his face toward his beloved wife and placed his worn hand on her still beautiful face. "My life has been good," he said, "and the time for the long journey draws near. My canoe is ready and many times, lately, I have dreamed about this journey. In every dream, I paddle my canoe downriver a short way and then turn and wait for you, but we do not travel together."

Lopahtah gave a helpless little cry. "No! We must go together. You promised me. We must find a way."

Pilmowitsh held her gently as she began to cry. He stroked her hair and felt the long, anguished sobs that shook her delicate body. The pain cut through him like a knife. Holding her close, he finally said, "There is a way. We will go together in each other's arms."

The next morning, Cassino paddled downriver to visit the old canoe builder. When he arrived, he saw Pilmowitsh's slaves constructing a new sweat hut on the crest of the hill overlooking the river. He was puzzled by the large size of the hut and its odd location. Walking up to inspect the new building, Cassino was surprised to see that the entire structure was coated with a layer of river mud, and the door was too small to be of any practical use. Shaking his head, Cassino walked down to the house to see Pilmowitsh.

When he ducked inside the lodge, he was shocked to see how frail Pilmowitsh had become. Even though he had been warned by Tanohah, Cassino had not expected such a drastic change since the last time he had visited.

Pilmowitsh looked up from his place near the fire and smiled wanly. "It is good to see you, my son. I am weary, but I must speak to you about matters of great importance. I ask that you listen to me and ask no questions."

Cassino frowned but nodded his head.

Pilmowitsh continued, "The time for the long journey is near. I have chosen you, of all my sons, to hear my last wishes. What you do not understand now, you will understand soon, so listen carefully. Lopahtah desires to go on the long journey with me, and this is my greatest wish. We will go together."

Cassino started to protest, but Pilmowitsh held up a gnarled hand to silence him.

"Please. Just listen and you will soon understand. My house will go to Tsultsis, and thus to Monsoe. He is to care for his mother. Half of my slaves, the furs, the stored food and other wealth will go to Nanalla and the younger children. Find a good husband for her from among her people, the Shoto.

"Tanohah will have his choice of my canoes and he may distribute the rest as he sees fit. My tools go to Sohowitsh, along with all of the artisan slaves. My carvings belong to you, and you may divide my remaining slaves with Tanohah. No slaves are to be put to death at my funeral. My weapons, fishing nets and other such articles belong to Monsoe. My first iron knife, the gift from Shenshina—my greatest treasure—is yours my son, to remember your father. See that all is well taken care of, my son."

When Pilmowitsh had finished, he coughed hoarsely and bowed his head. Cassino remained quiet for a long time, then said softly, "I will do exactly as you have said, my father."

Cassino returned home and summoned Monsoe, Tanohah, and Sohowitsh to tell them their father's wishes, but he did not mention Lopahtah.

After Cassino had departed, Pilmowitsh walked slowly up the hill to inspect the sweat hut. Everything had been done to his satisfaction. Returning to his house, he extended his hand to Lopahtah and said, "Come my dear wife. It is time to go. Are you ready?"

Taking Pilmowitsh's hand in hers, Lopahtah said gently, "I am ready, my husband."

A nearly full moon brightened the night sky as Pilmowitsh and Lop walked hand in hand to the sweat hut. They were dressed in their finest clothes: Pilmowitsh in his blue coat and Lop in fur-trimmed doeskin. When they reached the crest of the hill, they paused to enjoy the view of the magnificent silvery ribbon of water—the Great River—then crawled silently into the hut. Pilmowitsh kindled a fire, and when the flames were well established in the pitch-soaked wood, he secured the skin tightly over the small door of the hut.

"Remember," he said, "we stay in each other's arms no matter how hard the beginning of the journey."

While Lopahtah settled down on a soft bed of fir boughs and mats off to one side of the interior, Pilmowitsh reached for a basket filled with wet leaves. Taking enough leaves from the basket to partially smother the fire, he spread them over the flames. Smoke began to fill the hut as Pilmowitsh lowered himself onto the fir boughs and reached for Lopahtah. Pressing his face to hers, he whispered, "We will travel together forever, my dear wife." They embraced, holding each other tightly as the smoke swirled around them.

The next morning dawned bright and clear. The sun stretched above the horizon, turning the cloudless heavens into an azure jewel from the mountains to the sea. The wildflowers along the shores of Wappato exploded in a riot of cheerful colors, and not a ripple disturbed the shimmering surface of the Great River, which stretched like an endless mirror reflecting the deep blue of the skies above.

Tsultsis found Pilmowitsh and Lopahtah, still locked in their eternal embrace long after the smoky flames had died away. Stricken with grief, she sent word to Pilmowitsh's sons to come at once. Cassino arrived first and immediately took charge. He ordered the slaves to wrap the bodies in the finest robes and skins. He found the iron Shenshina knife and pressed it into Pilmowitsh's lifeless hand. He would have the carvings to remind him of his father, but the treasured knife belonged with Pilmowitsh on the long journey.

Two days later, the large Clackstar village on Scappoose Bay overflowed with mourners. Tanohah brought his prized "peace canoe" and arranged the exquisitely adorned craft on the beach. The wrapped bodies of Pilmowitsh and Lop were placed in the canoe, along with their most prized possessions and provisions for the long journey. Each member of the family chose a special article and placed it in the canoe. According to custom, all members of the family, including Cassino, had shorn their hair. The mourners wailed, but the names of the departed were never mentioned.

Comcomly arrived with a large retinue of Chinook, and Coalpo soon followed, bringing several of his wives along. Soleutu and Shenshina represented the Cowlitch, and Pilmowitsh's wives embraced Shenshina with tears. Tanohah said to Soleutu, "Of all the Chinook, our father thought of you as his brother." Cassino clasped hands with the Cowlitch chief and Sohowitsh made a place of honor for him. Just before midday, Olahno and Tenastsil arrived after their long journey, along with several Willamette chiefs who had joined them along the way.

At high noon, the four great chiefs of Wappato—Cassino and Monsoe at the bow and Tanohah and Sohowitsh at the stern—gently lifted the peace canoe and carried it to the water. Wailing loudly, they set it in the water and tethered it to a larger canoe, where Tsultsis and Nanalla sat with their children. The four sons climbed into the family canoe and paddled slowly out into the channel with the small canoe trailing behind. The other mourners climbed into their own canoes and joined the procession, which made its way down the bay to a beach at the northern tip of Wappato. Gently lifting the peace canoe from the water, the sons carried it to the base of a huge cedar tree close to Warrior Rock. The site overlooked the island, the channel, and the river. Several slaves stepped forward to hoist the canoe onto its platform high up in the branches of the massive tree.

The canoe was pointed toward the northwest, so the departing spirits might more easily find their way to Memaloose Illahee.

As the years went by, the great cedar became a special place for Pilmowitsh's sons and their families. In good weather, the chiefs often convened there to discuss the worries, concerns, and problems that faced their tribes, guarded over by the spirits of their beloved parents.

# PEE-KIN, THE GREAT WHITE-HEADED EAGLE

**F**our years after the departure of the *Raccoon*, a warship belonging to the Boston Men appeared at the mouth of the Great River, causing a brief flurry of excitement. Comcomly saw the ship and was prepared to meet it, but the Boston Men anchored in the ocean outside the river and sent three small boats over the bar, and across Baker's Bay to the north shore. The Chinook chief watched as some kind of ceremony was held. The Boston Men hoisted their flag and then nailed a piece of metal to a tree. Comcomly greeted the men and invited them to his village, but they insisted on visiting Fort George first.

At the fort, Captain Biddle and his party from the *Ontario* received a chilly reception. They returned to the north side of the river and stayed the night as Comcomly's guests. The next day, the men returned to the ship and sailed away. After they were gone, some King George Men from the fort crossed the river and found the metal sign on the tree. They explained that the Americans, as they called the Boston Men, were claiming the lands north of the river as their own. This announcement made no sense to Comcomly and seemed of little consequence, because the only ones living in this territory were the Chinook.

About a month after the *Ontario*'s departure, a King George warship, HMS *Blossom*, arrived. Cassino was visiting Comcomly at the time and the two chiefs decided to visit the fort to gain a better understanding of what was happening. They were confused because Captain Hickey of the *Blossom* was a King George Man, yet he had an American aboard named Prevost. Cassino knew that the Americans and the King George Men, or the British as they called themselves, were rivals, but they seemed to alternate between antagonism and cooperation.

Five days later, a ceremony was held at the fort and the American flag was raised above the stockade. By this time, Cassino had returned to Wappato, but he shook his head in confusion when he later heard that as soon as the American, Prevost, left the river, the British flag was again hoisted above the fort.

Though he continued to emulate the white men as much as possible, Cassino's life was still drawn largely along Chinook lines. Like the trappers, he had come to prefer fresh meat to fish, but fish was still a staple part of his diet. He enjoyed wearing at least some of the white men's clothing all the time, and he always donned trousers in their presence once he learned their queer prejudice against going bare below the waist.  Cassino sensed the importance that others placed on appearance and he often displayed a flair for dramatic impressions. He was a good showman and he had an eye for the nuances of gesture and expression that the white men used. Though he continued to live in the traditional Chinook style of house, the furniture and interior appointments were copied from what he had seen at the fort. He had a profusion of metal pots and kettles, blankets, trinkets and other articles of comfort and luxury from his successful trading.

The next year, he added a most prestigious wife, Princess Ilchee, and Comcomly became his father-in-law. Ilchee had been married to the trader McDougal at Astoria, but he had left the fort and returned home without her. Ilchee bore Cassino a son and soon became his most favored wife. He doted on his young son, who had the distinction of being the son of the chief of all the Wappato tribes and the grandson of Comcomly, the chief of all the Chinook.

Early in November of 1824, Cassino paddled downriver to visit Comcomly and the white men at the fort. The British at Fort George had recently become a part of the Hudson's Bay Company after many years with the Northwest Company. The current white chief, Alexander Kennedy, announced that a new leader, Dr. John McLoughlin, was on his way downriver from the east to take charge of the fort. As soon as Cassino heard the news, he left immediately. He wanted his first meeting with the new white chief to be in his own home territory.

When the McLoughlin party reached the Cascades, and paid the toll to the natives for portage, Cassino received a report about the new chief. His scouts also said that a single explorer was preceding the group to announce their imminent arrival at Fort George. Cassino was able to intercept the advance scout and learned that the McLoughlin party would stop somewhere in the vicinity of Wappato. At dusk, the report came that the travelers were making camp on the north side of the river at Skit-so-to-ho, the same place where Lewis and Clark had stopped on their way downriver years before. The Place of the Turtle was a natural campsite because of its lush prairie sloping down to the Great River.

Cassino quickly donned his scarlet chief's coat, blue trousers, finely beaded moccasins of soft doeskin, and a lone eagle feather in his hair. His necklace of matched white dentalium shells was accentuated by the richness of the scarlet coat. The chief selected his most ornate canoe and embarked upriver. The slaves rowing his canoe wore their matching blue sailors' jackets and another canoe followed carrying freshly caught salmon. They were an impressive sight.

Skit-so-to-ho was only a short distance upstream from Wappato, across from Hidden Canoe and Tomahawk Islands. Cassino and his group beached the canoes and approached the camp. A giant of a man with white flowing hair arose from near the fire and came to meet them. Cassino could not take his eyes off the tall stranger. *So this is the one they call Pee-Kin, the Great White-Headed Eagle!*

As soon as the man approached, Cassino began the speech in English he had carefully rehearsed:

"Cassino, chief of the Multnomah and all Wappato tribes, welcomes the new white chief to Fort George. I come as a friend and subject of King George and Hudson's Bay Company. My people bring fresh fish for you and your men." He motioned for the slaves to bring the salmon forward.

Dr. McLoughlin was quick to reply. "We have heard good things concerning Chief Cassino and know him to be a loyal subject of King George. We accept the gift of salmon and in return, please accept our gift of tobacco for you and your people." One of his men stepped forward and handed out twists of tobacco.

"Come to our fire," McLoughlin continued, "and let us talk. I would like for you to meet the deputy governor of the Hudson's Bay Company, Mr. George Simpson. He is my chief."

Simpson was short and stocky, not quite as tall as Cassino, and the giant McLoughlin towered over both of them. Simpson began to explain some of the changes planned by the company, while McLoughlin listened politely. He was studying Cassino as carefully as Cassino was studying the two white strangers. Cassino indicated to Simpson that he understood and approved of the new changes.

Simpson and McLoughlin then questioned Cassino about the location of different tribes and the leading chiefs in the area. McLoughlin was curious about the furs from the Willamette Valley: were they traded principally through Cassino? Cassino responded cautiously, because he sensed that he could not easily fool the new chief. He explained his control of the area around Wappato and mentioned Olahno and the Calapooya. He made casual references to some trade agreements, adding that eventually all furs went to Fort George. McLoughlin acknowledged the inference with a twinkle in his eye. Cassino noticed and thought, *Pee-Kin is a strong one in every way.* The questions from Simpson and McLoughlin indicated they were both well acquainted with the Fort George fur operation.

Food was served and Cassino was invited to stay. He ate carefully, trying to do just as his hosts did. After dinner, the men shaved and dressed in their best clothes. Cassino was surprised to learn that they planned to continue downriver that evening.

"I will be at the fort to meet you when you arrive tomorrow," he told them.

Cassino stopped at the Multnomah village only long enough to pick up Tanohah. He wanted him to meet the new white chief. Both men knew they would have no difficulty staying ahead of the heavy boats of the British. Paddling through the dark night, Cassino told Tanohah his impressions of McLoughlin and Simpson. "That Pee-Kin, he has a way about him," Cassino concluded. "There is much greatness in him."

The two Multnomah chiefs arrived at Fort George before midday and went to the nearby Clatsop village to rest. By the middle of the afternoon, the fort was engulfed in a state of feverish anticipation, and Cassino and Tanohah joined Comcomly, Coalpo and several other chiefs to await the imminent arrival of the newcomers. Kennedy and McDonald, the chief clerk, had gone upriver to Tongue Point to accompany the party into port.

As the sun began to set, the sound of singing carried faintly over the water, and then around the point came the gaily decorated boats in which Simpson and McLoughlin were seated. The sentry at the fort fired the signal gun and the clear, piercing sound of the bugle answered from the water. Just then, the sound of bagpipes burst over the river as a piper in full Highland regalia stood in another boat and played a lively march of the clans. It was a stirring sight!

The cannon at the fort began its slow, measured, seven volley salute as the gentlemen of the fort advanced to the landing, followed by the chiefs and other natives. The salute was answered by another blast from the bugle and the voyageurs again burst into song as they expertly turned the boats to shore.

The cheering and enthusiastic greetings amused the chiefs and natives, who stayed in the background of the celebration. Cassino noticed that many of the old-time residents of the fort knew McLoughlin—greeting him warmly and calling him "Doctor" with genuine respect. It pleased Cassino when Dr. McLoughlin spotted him and said quietly, "Chief Cassino, it is good to see you again. You did arrive first as you said you would."

After introductions and greetings were extended all around, the group started for the fort behind a voyageur carrying the standard of the Hudson's Bay Company and the kilted piper playing a spirited march. Governor Simpson headed the main procession, followed by the two chief factors, Kennedy and McLoughlin. The gentlemen and others from the Company followed in rank order, all marching to the tune from the pipes. As the sun hit the water on the western horizon, Simpson and McLoughlin joined Kennedy in his office, the stockade flag was lowered and the gates locked. The chiefs and other natives were sorry to see the spectacle end and returned reluctantly to their villages.

Cassino and Tanohah were invited to Comcomly's lodge for the evening meal, a smoke, and serious discussion. Comcomly broached the subject that had been occupying his mind. "The old chief, Kennedy, told me that the white men may change their headquarters and this fort will be only a trading post. He is not concerned, because he is leaving. It will be the business of the new chief, Pee-Kin. They have talked of moving before, but this time I am concerned."

Cassino remembered the surveying trip when he had accompanied Alexander Henry ten years before. He had always believed that Henry decided against moving to the Wappato area based on advice from Comcomly. Henry had been fearful of opposition from the mid-river tribes, and Comcomly would have done nothing to allay those fears.

Cassino asked cautiously, "Did Kennedy say they would move upriver?"

"No, he said he did not know," replied Comcomly. "Only that it must be someplace where the ships could go. He mentioned the great island far to the north, and Nootka.

This news was not what Cassino wanted to hear, but he saw an opportunity to gain Comcomly's support. "Such a move would be very bad for your people," he pointed out, "but if we could convince them to move the fort up the river, it would still be in Chinook territory and under your influence."

Comcomly nodded thoughtfully. "Yes, it would be better to move upriver than out of the river altogether. Kennedy said the place must be easily reached from all their trading posts, and the Great River serves that purpose."

Cassino breathed easier and decided it was time to change the subject. "The Company chief, Simpson, explained the new policies of the Company to me, and I agree with most of their ideas. He says no firewater will be traded and he discourages the exchange of presents, but he says they will guarantee the best prices for furs. He says the company will give us clothing before we give them some of the furs. He told me this when we talked at Skit-so-to-ho."

Comcomly was annoyed that Cassino had spoken to the new chiefs first, but he tried not to show it. "The policies will be good for our people," he said, "and the reasoning is sound." Turning to Tanohah, he asked, "Will you be moving your village this spring?"

Tanohah had been listening quietly and he knew Comcomly's question was only out of courtesy. "If the river goes very high, we will move," he said, "but we have chosen our location carefully and I do not think a move will be necessary. Sometimes the water covers the island; then we all move."

Comcomly turned back to Cassino. "In late summer, when the water is low, could the white man's ship reach Wappato?"

"If they know where to go—where the water is deepest—it could be done. But no one knows the river better than Tanohah. What is your opinion, my brother?"

Tanohah pursed his lips and looked upward as he pictured the Great River in his mind. "If the ships stay where the current is strong, there should be no trouble, even in late summer. The water is deep from the Cascades to Wappato, and even deeper below where the Willamette comes in. The great sandbars shift each spring and care must be taken to avoid them, but it could be done. When the white men become familiar with the river, they can bring their ships to Wappato."

Comcomly sat silently for some time, then sighed and said, "If the new white chief asks me, I will say they should move upriver to Wappato. It is better for us than Nootka."

Cassino was ecstatic, but dared not show his feelings to the other chiefs. He turned the conversation back to events at the fort.

After a few more visits to Fort George, it was time to head back upriver before the weather turned bad. Before the two men reached home, Cassino cautioned Tanohah, "Say nothing about moving the fort to the Wappato area. It is sure to happen, because it is by far the best place on the river, but we must wait until Pee-Kin makes his decision. When he does, we will be ready."

"Is Comcomly ready for this move?" asked Tanohah.

"You heard him speak. He is saddened by the changes that are coming, but he will make the changes. We must all do the same, because the white man will not leave. Already the Chinook life is different. We have traded well and learned many of the white man's ways. Some of that is good, but I am not certain that everything is good."

"Perhaps Comcomly can persuade them to stay at the mouth of the river and life will stay the same in our villages," Tanohah said hopefully.

"It makes no difference," said Cassino with a tinge of regret in his voice. "The white man cannot be stopped. Pee-Kin will become the great white chief and he will be a good chief. We must work with him to control our people. Then he will value our trading agreements."

Tanohah felt his heart grow heavy as the men paddled hard upstream to reach the warm fires of Wappato. An icy cold rain began, drenching their canoe and dampening their spirits.

When Cassino had been home for a few days, a troubling message arrived from Comcomly. A surveying party of forty men had left the fort, heading north, under the command of a man named McMillan. Several Chinook women who were sleeping with men from Fort George reported that the explorers were going to a place called Fraser River to see about moving the fort there. They had departed ten days after the arrival of Simpson and McLoughlin, and Comcomly had dispatched scouts to follow the group and report on its progress. After crossing Baker's Bay, they had portaged to Shoalwater Bay, crossed it, then portaged to Gray's Harbor. From there, they had gone up the Chehalis River and proceeded overland to Puget Sound. This news was not what Cassino wanted to hear, but there was nothing he could do.

During the winter a silver thaw settled on Wappato . After a week of cold weather and a little bit of snow, the weather warmed enough to bring on freezing rain. A layer of cold air trapped near the ground kept everything frigid, while an overriding layer of warmer air poured on the moisture, which froze as soon as it hit the ground. Everything turned to beautiful but treacherous ice. Every blade of grass, each leaf and limb was sheathed in a coating of ice, and bushes and trees bent to the ground under the weight. The trails around the island were sheets of ice, making even short trips slippery and dangerous. Overburdened tree limbs snapped off and fell.

When the sun came out after a few days, it transformed the landscape into a crystal wonderland of sparkling lights. The children quickly grabbed mats and held contests to see who could slide the farthest and the fastest on the icy slopes around the village. By the end of the week, a warmer storm blew in over the western hills, freeing the area from winter's icy grip. Intermittent explosions—the sounds of ice falling from the trees—broke the stillness of the day.

Well into the new year of 1825, McLoughlin sent a message to Cassino, summoning him to the fort on urgent business. Cassino felt a vague uneasiness about the invitation, but he had no reason not to trust Pee-Kin, so he made hurried preparations for the trip downriver.

The weather had warmed somewhat, but the wind along the river was still bitingly brisk, so Cassino and his small party wasted no time making the journey to Fort George. Cassino wisely decided not to bypass Comcomly and was rewarded with news of McMillan's return from the Fraser River.

At the fort the next day, Cassino was received with honor. One of the native women was instructed to prepare a small room for him to stay while he was downriver. He sent his slaves to find accommodations at the nearest Clatsop village, and prepared for his audience with Simpson and McLoughlin.

When Cassino was seated with the two white leaders, Simpson opened the conversation with a question. "The place you call Skit-so-to-ho impressed us both when we stopped there on our way downriver," he said, indicating himself and McLoughlin with a small wave of his hand. "Can you tell us which tribes live in that area and who the chiefs are?"

"The land is shared by the Wakanasisi and the Shoto," Cassino replied, "and I am the chief of both tribes."

"It seems the south valley along the Willamette River is very fertile," said McLoughlin. "Do you think the soil of the prairie around Skit-so-to-ho will also be good for growing things?"

"The grass grows green and thick above Skit-so-to-ho," Cassino said with a shrug, "and other plants grow in abundance as well."

"Skit-so-to-ho seems to be a central location for all fur trading routes in the area," continued McLoughlin. "For the Columbia, the Willamette, and the Cowlitz, which is our inland route to the north. Do you think large ships can sail that far upriver?"

The two men seemed pleased when Cassino nodded and confirmed Tanohah's opinion of the river channel near Wappato.

"Rarely have I seen such a place in England, with a combination of natural advantages and so much beauty," said Simpson. "No wonder hardened voyageurs refer to the area as 'Jolie Prairie.'"

The traders continued to talk about the great stands of timber close at hand, and the plentiful fish and game in the area. Cassino could tell by their enthusiasm that the new fort would be built near Skit-so-to-ho. He was curious about their insistence on finding a suitable location on the *north* side of the river, until they explained that the Americans wanted to control the south side of the river and the British the north. Cassino now understood why they wanted to move Fort George from its present location on the south shore. *How can the white men talk of dividing Chinook land?* he wondered, but he said nothing.

Cassino slept fitfully that night. Though he was proud and honored to be the first native chief ever invited to spend the night at Fort George, he knew it was only because they needed him. He also suspected that the unusual hospitality was a means of preventing him from communicating openly with the other Chinook chiefs. Cassino could foresee the end of his power and influence—and that of every other Chinook chief along the river. Still, he reminded himself, *I must think*

*of what is best for my people, and that is to cooperate with the white man*
*and their new chief.*

The next morning, Dr. McLoughlin broached the subject of moving
the fort to Skit-so-to-ho. "Chief Cassino," he said, "we are asking for
your permission and support to make this move possible. We promise to
be fair and pay for the land, including benefits for your people. We will
consult with you and work through you in all matters pertaining to your
people. I want to you to always feel free to discuss any concerns you may
have with me—and we should start right now."

Cassino was surprised to feel a closeness developing between himself
and Pee-Kin. He believed he could trust the Great White-Headed Eagle,
because he observed that the white leader truly listened. He told
McLoughlin about his fears and doubts for his people. With the coming
of white settlers to Wappato, he knew that control of his people would be
difficult and he needed Pee-Kin's help.

Dr. McLoughlin assured him he would have his help, and the matter
was settled. Work on the new fort would begin as soon as the weather
allowed. "Chief Cassino," McLoughlin added, "the new fort will always
be open to you whenever you wish to visit and stay."

When Cassino brought the news back to Wappato, tremendous
excitement engulfed the longhouses, leading to many parleys and
conversations around the campfire. True to Pee-Kin's word, forty men,
under the leadership of company clerk Donald Manson, soon came to
Skit-so-to-ho and began to build the new fort. Natives swarmed the work
site, and Cassino was kept well informed of practically every move made
by the workmen.

The chosen site was well back from the river on a high rise in the
prairie that afforded a long view in every direction. Much like Fort
George, a large stockade—well over the height of two men—was erected
of strong split logs. Higher lookout areas were built on the two corners
facing the river and four cannon were mounted, one in each corner of the
stockade. The placement of the guns ensured that the entire area
surrounding the fort could be covered by cannon fire. The main stockade
entrance was a large gate, with smaller entrances secured by solid doors.
The natives were astounded by the speed of construction and they were
fascinated by the tools the workmen used. The whipsawing of boards for
floors and interior finishing of the buildings particularly impressed them,

because the planks used in Chinook houses were laboriously split from logs by use of stone tools and hard knot wedges. Only recently had the natives learned to use iron hatchets.

Cassino visited the site frequently to keep track of the progress of the work. He sent messages to Olahno and other valley chiefs, and as the news of the new white village spread, many visitors came to Cassino's house to meet with him. Comcomly stayed for several days, and Coalpo also came to take a look. Olahno and Tenastsil led a large party of Calapooya down the Willamette to see the new fort, and Shannaway and Soleutu brought several Cowlitch warriors—although their group camped away from the Multnomah village and the two chiefs avoided contact with Cassino. It was a busy and exciting time for all the tribes along the river.

During the late winter and early spring, Cassino traveled from tribe to tribe, emphasizing with each chief the importance of maintaining strong control over his people, and trying to foresee any difficulties that might arise. He and Concomsin set up new trading patterns and tried to think of ways to serve as trading intermediaries for the chiefs downriver—especially Comcomly, Coalpo, and Shannaway.

One evening, Cassino said to Tanohah, "What happens at the new fort will depend on Pee-Kin. He will consult with me on matters dealing with our people, but can he control his own people? I have confidence in Pee-Kin, for he is like no other white man I have met. The white chiefs who have come before—Broughton, Lewis, and Clark—have dealt honorably with our people, but they were not interested in trading furs. Pee-Kin has a great vision for trading furs. He has not told me, but I know. Pee-Kin has a *tamanowos* that is great and noble and strong. I am certain that Pee-Kin will be a strong leader.

# 18 FORT VANCOUVER

At sunrise on the nineteenth day of March, the British held a ceremony to name the new fort. McLoughlin and Simpson had arrived from Fort George along with other gentlemen of the Hudson's Bay Company. In the presence of many chiefs and tribesmen, Governor Simpson ordered the British colors raised over the stockade. Breaking a bottle of brandy on the flagpost, he loudly proclaimed, "I hereby christen this new establishment, Fort Vancouver." When he completed his dedication by saying, "God save King George the Fourth!" three cheers rang out and the celebration began.

Although many buildings were yet to be completed at the new fort, the move from Fort George began at once. A barge with sails was built to ferry livestock upriver, and only a few men were left in charge of Fort George under a clerk's supervision. Their main duty was to aid ships coming into the river on their way to Fort Vancouver. By April 11, the entire relocation had been accomplished, and Governor Simpson soon departed, leaving Dr. McLoughlin in complete charge of the affairs of the Company.

Cassino quickly learned that he and Pee-Kin would have disagreements, but they could discuss them freely. McLoughlin admired Cassino's ability to maintain peace among the Wappato tribes, and supported his efforts whenever possible. One especially troubling thorn was the matter of slaves. Cassino explained at great length the need for slaves and the Chinook tradition, but Pee-Kin made it clear he thought the practice was wrong. The issue would continue to be a sore point between them for a long time.

It wasn't long before many of the natives wanted to deal directly with

147

the white traders, ignoring their chiefs and tribal authorities. Although Cassino recognized Pee-Kin as a chief above him, he still exercised his own power over his tribes. In order not to jeopardize his standing at the fort, Cassino often acted quickly and decisively to keep his tribesmen in order. When the old means of persuasion through wealth and wives no longer sufficed, he resorted to ruthless intimidation and occasional assassinations.

As the old fur trading practices became inoperable, Cassino and Concomsin developed a scheme to exact tribute from Comcomly, Shannaway, and other chiefs from downriver when they brought their furs through Wappato territory. Comcomly was enraged by what he viewed as extortion. The dispute accelerated, jeopardizing all trade along the river. McLoughlin sent for Cassino.

Courteous as always, Pee-Kin made the proper acknowledgments, then quickly got down to business. "Chief Cassino," he said solemnly, "anyone who brings furs to the fort cannot be taxed. This is a rule that must not be broken. As you have seen, it has caused many problems and much unrest. I know we both agree that we must maintain peace. Because of my trust in you, I have given you special privileges and your tribe is paid well as the only supplier of fish and game for the fort. You must see that this policy is carried out and that all the other chiefs know about it."

Cassino was disappointed by McLoughlin's words, but he knew better than to make an issue of the new policy. "I do not want any trouble," he said. "We will do as you say. It is an honor to be welcome at the fort at all times and I know that it is a privilege to have a table in the gentlemen's dining hall."

"Thank you, Chief Cassino," said the Great White-Headed Eagle. "I know that I can count on you. I hope that you will dine often with the Company officers, and I would like to extend to you the honor of firing the signal cannon whenever a ship comes in sight of Fort Vancouver."

With his vanity appeased, Cassino made peace with Comcomly, and it wasn't long before the great Chinook chief arrived at the fort with his canoes piled high with furs. Attired in his blue captain's coat and tricorn hat, Comcomly strode regally across the parade grounds to meet Dr. McLoughlin, who received him with proper ceremony. That evening, Comcomly was Cassino's guest at the "chief's table" in the dining hall. The dinner was a grand occasion, and Cassino was pleased at the profound impression he had made on his father-in-law.

Not long after Comcomly returned to his village, Cassino's scouts brought word of a ship making its way up the river. Dressing carefully in his scarlet coat, blue trousers and priceless chief's necklace, Cassino hurried to the fort, where he found everything in readiness. Even Pee-Kin, dressed in his formal finery, had come to the corner of the stockade where the downriver cannon faced the river. Cassino stood proudly, with a smoldering matchstick in his hand. He watched vigilantly for any sign of the approaching ship. He wanted to carry out his responsibility in the exact, prescribed manner.

As the ship came into view around the bend and pulled even with the downstream tip of Hidden Canoe Island, Cassino took a deep breath and touched the match to the hole in the top of the cannon. A tremendous explosion rocked the platform. A moment later, from across the water, came the answering salute. Everyone in the fort stopped working and headed to the water's edge.

"You timed the salute perfectly, Chief Cassino," said Dr. McLoughlin. "Well done!" Swinging his ever-present cane, McLoughlin turned and set out toward the dock to welcome the new arrivals. Word soon spread about the latest honor accorded to Cassino, and he became known as the chief who fires the white man's cannon.

By now, Cassino had ten wives, four children, and nearly one hundred slaves in his Multnomah household. Princess Ilchee, Comcomly's daughter, was still Cassino's favorite wife, by virtue of being the only one to bear him a legitimate son. Several of his female slaves had sons whom they claimed were Cassino's, but paternity could not be reliably established. In any case, the boys were roundheads and not recognized within the tribe. Though Cassino was proud of his flathead son, he was preoccupied with the responsibilities of leadership and had little time for fatherhood while his children were small.

The days were fast approaching for the fishing and trading time at Willamette Falls, but Cassino was reluctant to go. He invited several chiefs and other friends to a feast at his Multnomah house and asked their advice.

"If a new ship arrives while I am away, who will fire the cannon?" he said.

"Your scouts will keep you informed," said Monsoe, "and you would have time to return. As the chief of all the Wappato tribes, you should be at Wallamt. It is expected."

"You are right," Cassino conceded, "and it is also a good time to renew our agreements with Olahno and the other valley tribes. But I am worried. Pee-Kin might need my help or need to speak with me. Every day, something new happens at the fort—more building, more planting of food, new traders arriving or leaving, and new trading posts are planned. Something is always new, and I need to know about such things."

Cassino paused to choose his next words carefully. "There is another matter we must discuss. It should not come as a surprise to Tanohah, because he understands the situation." Again, he hesitated before continuing, "I need to be closer to the fort. I am considering a move to the Wakanasisi village."

The assembled chiefs and leaders reacted with shock and dismay, then lapsed into sullen silence to underscore their displeasure. Cassino was about to speak, when Sohowitsh angrily proclaimed, "Chief Cassino's place is with the Multnomah!"

An immediate outburst of approval followed. Before Cassino could respond, Tanohah silenced the others, "No one wishes to see Chief Cassino leave the Multnomah village—least of all me, his brother. But Cassino is also chief of the Wakanasisi and all other Wappato tribes. He must go where he is most needed and where it is best for everyone. Remember, he has lived with all our tribes at one time or another, and always when that tribe's location was most strategic. At one time, it was with the Clackstar; when the white men came down the river from the Cascades, it was with the Quathlahpottle; when the ships came into the river and the fort was built, his place was with the Kalama; and for a long time, the Multnomah were central to all Wappato affairs and he was here with us. Now it is time for a move to the Wakanasisi, because they are closest to Fort Vancouver."

The assembled chiefs looked at one another and slowly nodded. Cassino seized the opportunity to deliver a heartfelt message to his friends:

"I am no longer the single all-powerful chief of Wappato. There is another, the Great White-Headed Eagle, Pee-Kin. He is good, fair, and just. I will follow his judgment, because it is best for our people. You must follow me as I follow Pee-Kin. We are brothers, and we must remain as brothers. Any chief or tribesman who departs from this path must deal with me. The consequences will be harsh, and the action will be swift and final. The old ways no longer work as they once did. We must change to do what is best for all of our people. I will go to live with the Wakanasisi, because it is the best thing."

Cassino's speech was met with silence. Knowing that this dispute marked an important turning point in his leadership of the Wappato, Cassino sat stoically until each chief expressed support for his move. Although many of the chiefs had misgivings, all of them remained loyal to Cassino.

After telling McLoughlin of his plans and receiving assurances from the white chief that no ships were expected, Cassino went to Wallamt. At the falls, the atmosphere was festive, as always, but unlike in years past, very few furs were traded. The old trading patterns had forever been altered, and the natives spent most of their time gambling, feasting, visiting and, of course, fishing. The salmon run was as yet unaffected by the presence of the white settlers along the river, and the year's catch was plentiful. Cassino spent most of his time briefing Olahno on developments at the fort.

The Wakanasisi village was located on the north shore of the Great River, directly opposite the mouth of the Willamette and the lower tip of Hidden Canoe Island. The fine house built by Cassino's slaves was not as large as his Multnomah house, but it was sufficient for his wives and children. Cassino's ideas about holding slaves had not changed, but in deference to Pee-Kin's continuing disapproval, he decided to bring along only twenty select slaves, leaving the other eighty with Tanohah, along with the understanding that they would be at his disposal if needed. His house in the Multnomah village was preserved for his use when visiting Wappato Island. As soon as Cassino was settled with the Wakanasisi, Dr. McLoughlin stationed some Hudson's Bay Company horses with him, which he used for riding the short distance to the fort.

Allying himself with a new leader—and submitting to authority—was not easy for Cassino, but he knew it was necessary in order to preserve his own power. The wisdom he had observed in his first father-in-law, Kinsenitsh of the Clackstar, had made a strong impression. He remembered how Kinsenitsh had thought at first that taking the young

Niakowkow chief as a son-in-law would reinforce his strength, but it soon
became apparent that his son-in-law, Cassino, who had the ultimate
power. Kinsenitsh was quick to ally himself with Cassino and promoted
the younger man's power. Now many of the Wappato chiefs thought
Cassino was giving in to the rule of the white traders, and they couldn't
understand his seeming eagerness to become an underling to the great
white chief, Pee-Kin. The new trends in life along the Columbia were still
a mystery to most of the natives. Even Comcomly, a powerful and
perceptive leader who had lived alongside the white settlers much longer
than Cassino had, did not see and interpret events according to their
long-range significance. Cassino had learned a lot from Kinsenitsh, and it
was time to test the value of some of those lessons.

Three winters passed at Fort Vancouver, and Cassino's fascination
with everything inside the stockade was unabated. To avoid the
temptation of over-involvement in the mundane details of life inside the
fort, he forced himself to concentrate on the affairs of his tribes; but the
more he tried, the harder it became to resist the lure of the white man's
business. He began to spend even more time at the fort, working closely
with the men of the Hudson's Bay Company, and he frequently took his
place at the chief's table in the dining hall.

On any given day, countless natives were milling around outside the
stockade gates seeking admittance, but only Cassino could come and go
as he pleased. McLoughlin frequently consulted with him and always
answered his questions directly and honestly. Cassino was a trusted
"insider," and McLoughlin's confidence in him was not misplaced.

The incident that cemented Cassino's loyalty to Pee-Kin involved
justice and punishment. One day, a native committed an offense and was
tied to a cannon and given five lashes. The very next day, a white man
committed the same offense. Without hesitation, McLoughlin ordered
him bound to the cannon and he also received five lashes. Word of this
incident spread quickly; the law was the same for everyone, native or
white, and Pee-Kin kept his promises. Cassino knew that he could trust
the white leader not to permit invasion of native hunting and fishing
grounds without compensation, and that native lands would not be seized.

Although he was reluctant to admit it, Cassino realized that, in many
ways, he was beginning to think more like the white traders. Not that he

was ashamed of his Chinook heritage, but he had to admit that the native ways were simple and naive compared to the complex traditions and beliefs of the white men. He began to see more and more disparity between the ways of his people and the ways of Pee-Kin and the white traders.

One warm summer day, an urgent message from McLoughlin arrived at the Wakanasisi village. Cassino immediately mounted his horse and set off at a full gallop. At the fort, a sentry led him directly to Pee-Kin's office. One of Cassino's scouts from the area around the Cascades was already in the room.

"Thank you for coming so quickly, Chief Cassino," said McLoughlin. "Your man has disturbing news." He turned to the scout and motioned for him to speak.

"Chief Cassino, a Wasco war party is coming downriver to attack the fort. They are angry that Pee-Kin closed their trading post at The Dalles. They say they will burn the fort to the ground. It is a large force, with many canoes, and they are moving fast."

"How many canoes? How many warriors?" Cassino asked.

"There was no time to see, but their canoes filled the river."

Cassino turned quickly to McLoughlin and said quietly, "We have little time. These warriors are not Chinook. They will attack without warning. If we can show a large enough force, perhaps we can convince them to parley instead. I will call for all of the war canoes around Wappato."

"We must do everything we can to avoid bloodshed," cautioned McLoughlin.

Cassino turned to the scout. "Run to the Multnomah and tell Chief Tanohah to rally the Clackstar, Clannaquah and Quathlahpottle. Tell him to send every available warrior and canoe to the Wakanasisi village—and hurry! GO!"

As they watched the departing messenger, McLoughlin said to Cassino, "My policy has always been to avoid harm to the natives. How do you propose we avoid a battle?"

"We are not dealing with Chinook, Pee-Kin. The tribes in the east are more dangerous and warlike. But if they can see that an attack will not be successful, they will parley. Then you can talk to them and satisfy them. But first we must impress them with our force and let them know we are ready to do battle. I have a plan."

Cassino outlined his ideas carefully, and McLoughlin agreed, adding, "I will order everyone into the fort at once, and we will send muskets to your men at the river. Will you need anything else?"

"It will do no harm to send extra tobacco for my warriors, if you can spare it," Cassino replied. "I must go; there is little time to prepare."

By the time Cassino returned to his village, most of the Wakanasisi had gathered to see what was happening. They had seen him leave in haste and they anticipated trouble. He quickly explained the situation and ordered, "Ready the war canoes and prepare for battle. We will soon be joined by our Wappato brothers."

A shout went up from the bluff above the river. "Here come the Multnomah canoes!"

By the time the five Wakanasisi canoes were ready, Tanohah had arrived with ten canoes, followed closely by Laquano and fifteen Clannaquah warriors in five canoes. The chiefs quickly agreed to gather their forces at the inlet below the fort. Scouts were stationed at the upper end of Tomahawk Island, which offered an unobstructed view upriver for quite a distance.

A contingent from the fort soon arrived with muskets and tobacco. Several of the warriors had their own muskets, but most were armed with bow and arrows, so the muskets from the fort were distributed evenly among the canoes. Cassino knew that the Wasco war party would have very few firearms, and he knew the chilling effect that several well-timed volleys could have on the enemy's willingness to fight. But he also knew that a strong showing of warriors and canoes was vital to his strategy. He watched anxiously for the rest of his forces to arrive.

More muskets arrived from the fort, along with a message from McLoughlin that food would be provided if needed. The lookout on Tomahawk reported no sign of the Wasco war party, and a scout from downriver came with news that the Clackstar and Quathlahpottle canoes would soon arrive. When the warriors arrived, Cassino reviewed his strategy with the leader of each canoe and distributed more muskets.

The time seemed to drag by and Cassino began to feel anxious when the Wasco still did not appear.

"More canoes from downriver," came the call, and Cassino breathed a sigh of relief when seventeen more canoes came pouring into the inlet from the north. Concomsin brought six canoes from the Quathlahpottle, and Monsoe headed a large fleet of eleven Clackstar crews. By now, the inlet was so crowded that all Cassino could see in every direction was canoes and warriors.

Just then, a scout from Tomahawk Island raced into the inlet to announce the arrival of the Wasco. "They are spread out in a single line stretching clear across the river," he reported breathlessly.

Cassino had expected the Wasco to present a formidable front. "Have all the muskets been distributed?" he asked Tanohah. "Be sure to keep the guns hidden. We do not want the Wasco to know our strength until it is time."

From his vantage point atop the stockade, Dr. McLoughlin concealed his uneasiness as he watched the unfolding drama on the river. He wondered whether all his work and effort would be destroyed by a single Indian attack. Standing by the signal cannon, McLoughlin waited until the line of Wasco canoes reached a point about a mile above the fort, then ordered the cannon fired. The stillness of the summer day was shattered by the loud report from the fort's big gun. As the echo died away and the smoke began to clear, McLoughlin saw a steady stream of Chinook canoes streaming out of the inlet and fanning across the main channel. Through his spyglass he saw the Wasco chief signal from a middle canoe and immediately the advancing line of war canoes stopped and began maintaining its position against the strong downstream current.

Cassino ordered his canoe to be paddled out ahead of the line of Chinooks. It was time to put his plan into action. He stood up in the canoe and his scarlet coat was the center of attention. At his signal, every canoe turned into the current and moved in a precise line upriver toward the Wasco boats. When he determined that his forces had drawn close enough to be clearly seen, he signaled for his troops to turn their canoes broadside and show the hidden muskets.

The Wasco had seen enough. Their chief gave the command, their line turned toward the south shore and they headed for the beach to make camp. As the last Wasco warrior went ashore, Cassino motioned for the Chinook paddlers to return to the inlet, where they would keep a vigil until the Wasco chief called for a parley.

The next morning, five Wasco canoes crossed the river and the chiefs asked to meet with Pee-Kin. They were taken to the dining hall inside the stockade, where they were entertained by the Highland Guard and its bagpipe player.

Following Cassino's advice, McLoughlin kept the chiefs waiting for nearly three hours before he went to meet them. He explained to them why the trading post at The Dalles was being closed and told them, "If you bring your furs to Fort Vancouver, you will receive a better price and we will show you a greater variety of goods for trade. And there are more traders here." He assured them that they were always welcome at the fort, and the appeased chiefs returned to their camp laden with gifts. Before long, the Wasco canoes were launched back into the river and paddled upstream toward the Cascades.

Later, McLoughlin told Cassino, "Once again you have proven your loyalty to King George and the Hudson's Bay Company, and once again you have demonstrated your ability to keep the peace. I am very grateful and I shall not forget what you have done for us on this occasion."

# 19 THE SICKNESS BEGINS

O ne night later that summer, a party of natives arrived in the Wakanasisi village. Cassino was quickly summoned to meet with the strangers. He quickly learned that they were Tillamook from the coast. They had with them an exhausted white man, whom they had rescued along their ocean beach. They were bringing him to Pee-Kin and Cassino was quick to escort them to the fort.

The next morning, Dr. McLoughlin told Cassino that the man, named Black, was a survivor of a white party that had been attacked by the Umpqua. "I need runners to go to the chiefs of the Willamette tribes with orders to search for any white men who may have survived the attack," said McLoughlin. "We will send gifts of tobacco and I have ordered a relief party dispatched from the fort to help in the search."

Before the messengers could leave the next day, three more whites in starving condition, were brought to the fort by valley natives. Jedediah Smith, the leader of the group, and two of his men, Turner and Leland, were Americans who were coming from far south. This news was unsettling to Cassino, because these were the first white men he had seen come north by land from the south.

The Americans recuperated at the fort as guests of McLoughlin and Cassino was able to learn about their fur trapping enterprise in the great mountains to the east. He asked many questions and heard about many strange new places. The men told of a giant salt lake far inland to the southeast, and spoke of white men called "Spanish" from a place called "California." Cassino had heard Pee-Kin mention California before and hearing about it again gave him an uneasy feeling. White men were beginning to come from every direction. Cassino knew from experience

157

that once they appeared, more were sure to follow.

As Cassino's role as emissary to the Great White-Headed Eagle continued to increase, it divorced him from the ordinary pursuits of his people. When Pee-Kin brought twenty Klickitat warriors to the fort to serve as hunters, Cassino became their honorary chief—which was unheard of for a Chinook. His reputation spread along with McLoughlin's, and he became known as a great chief far beyond the land of the Chinook. He saw his old friends less frequently, and he knew that he was losing touch when he could not break down the reticence, suspicion, and in some cases fear, that his fame and connection to Pee-Kin brought him.

One evening, in the gentlemen's dining hall, an unusual tension hung in the air. Dinner was normally a congenial time at the fort, and but tonight Cassino sensed that something was seriously wrong. He went quietly to his table and listened carefully while he ate.

When McLoughlin entered the room, accompanied by several gentlemen from the Company, and strode to the head of the great table, he appeared angry and preoccupied. A few days before, word had reached Fort Vancouver that a British ship, the *William and Ann* had been wrecked off Clatsop Spit on the south side of the Columbia River bar. The *William and Ann* had been enroute to the fort, heavily laden with supplies and trading goods. There were no survivors and it was believed the crew had been murdered by Clatsop natives when they reached shore. McLoughlin dispatched a party, under the leadership of a man named Connolly, to ask the Clatsop to restore the goods.

After an abnormally quiet meal, the food was cleared and the gentlemen lit their cigars. McLoughlin stood and broke the silence. "Gentlemen, I have just received a reply from the Clatsop regarding the *William and Ann*. They sent an old broom and a rusty dipper to Mr. Connolly and said we are welcome to have them, but as for the ship's cargo, they intend to keep it."

Angry shouts erupted around the table and Cassino's heart sank. He knew Pee-Kin would not abide such an affront.

"Tomorrow, I am sending a schooner with a howitzer and fifty men," McLoughlin continued. "We'll teach the Clatsops a lesson they won't soon forget. I want as much of that cargo reclaimed as possible. We will fire upon their village, knock down a few houses, and when they run off, we'll raid the village. If possible, we will avoid bloodshed, but these deeds must be punished, or there's no telling how this insurrection might spread."

By early morning, a crowd had gathered at the dock to see the schooner off. The crew on board was heavily armed and Cassino knew that the Clatsops would pay dearly for what they had done. He was glad he would not have to witness the destruction. He remembered the gun drill aboard HMS *Raccoon* years before. He felt sorry for his people. It was the fall fishing season and he knew the village would be crowded. He noticed Pee-Kin looking at him.

"I'm truly sorry, Chief Cassino," McLoughlin said, "but it must be done." The two men walked slowly back to the fort.

The schooner returned a week later with most of the salvaged cargo from the William and Ann aboard. The bombardment and ransacking of the Clatsop village had gone as planned and the British forces suffered no casualties. Several natives had been killed in the initial attack, and a few more died in an ill-fated counterattack after the goods had been recovered. McLoughlin sent Celiast, a daughter of one of the Clatsop chiefs, who had been staying at the fort, to make peace. Order was restored and the Clatsop village was soon rebuilt near the original site.

The warm, golden days of autumn enveloped the country and the salmon run at Wallamt was about to begin. The lazy atmosphere lay heavy on Cassino as he sat outside his house in the Wakanasisi village. He knew how deceptive this season could be. If he wasn't diligent about preparing for winter, the first frost would come before he knew it, and winter would soon follow. Cassino leaned against a tree at the top of the embankment overlooking the river. He was watching his son and the other boys from the village playing with a canoe in an eddy just off the beach. They had divided into two war parties, each trying to take and hold the canoe. No sooner would one group take possession than the other group would capsize the craft and take over. Amid shouts and laughter, the game went back and forth in the shallow waters. Cassino sighed as he watched his eleven-year-old son romping with the other boys. *With all the changes coming so fast*, he wondered, *how can he be prepared to grow up and become a leader?* "It is time that he and I go off together," Cassino said out loud to himself. "The women and slaves can go ahead to Wallamt and set up the chief's lodge. Little Cassino and I will take a few days to camp, just the two of us, along the way up the river."

Little Cassino was slight of build and not as strong as some of the other boys, but he was right in the thick of the action as the Chinook youngsters whooped and hollered throughout the village and up and down the nearby waterways. He was well-liked for his gentle and patient disposition—so different from both his mother and father. Even though the other boys knew that Little Cassino was "royalty," the son of the great chief of the Wappato and his princess bride, the daughter of Comcomly, they treated him as "one of the boys" and genuinely respected him.

Little Cassino was overjoyed at the opportunity to spend a few days alone with his father. During most of his son's growing up years, the great chief had spared little time apart from his duties, travels and other responsibilities. The night before their departure, the boy hardly slept, and he was up at first light feverishly preparing the canoe. Before they could leave, Cassino had to go to the fort for one last conference with Pee-Kin. Back at the camp little Cassino thought the time to shove off would never come. Finally, he heard the galloping of hooves and knew his father was returning.

Father and son pushed their canoe out into the lazy current of the late summer river. Hardly a ripple cut the surface as they paddled into the mainstream. It was a glorious day, cloudless and warm, and Cassino decided to take the long way to the Willamette, around Wappato, in order to share memories of his own boyhood with his son and to give him some idea of how things had been before the white men had arrived. Little Cassino paddled in rapt silence as he listened to his father's story.

Waving his arm toward Wappato, Cassino said, "This is the country where I grew from boyhood to manhood. Many times, I paddled around this part of the river. Our first camp will be in the place where I grew up, and when we get there, I have something important to tell you. But that can wait. There is much to see and talk about before then." For the next hour, as their canoe drifted lazily downstream, Cassino told his son stories of growing up on the Great River.

As they paddled past the Clannaquah village and came into sight of Warrior Rock, Cassino steered in to the shore and they pulled the canoe up on the beach. Cassino looked around then walked a short distance back upriver until he found a place where they could easily climb the bank. When they reached the top of the rise, they had a clear view up the river and they could see the houses at the edge of the Clannaquah village. "When I was not much older than you are now," Cassino said, "this is the place where I watched the last battle between Wappato tribes, along with my friends."

While Little Cassino gazed out across the water and tried to imagine what his father was describing, Cassino told the story of the skirmish between the Clannaquah and the Quathlahpottle. "It was here," he concluded, "where Chief Monsoe and I vowed to each other there would be no more war between brothers." He paused, then added, "We will see many of these places on our trip. It is important for you to know the story of your people and your place of honor among them."

When the two had rested and eaten a small meal of dried fish and berries, they pushed the canoe back into the river to continue to the site Cassino had chosen for their first camp. A short while later, they pulled the canoe out of the water below Pilmowitsh's old camp. The house had been removed long ago and little remained of the place that had been such an important part of Cassino's boyhood. The site seemed so desolate, but father and son carried their gear as near to the location of the old house as Cassino could remember. They set up their campsite for the evening, and Cassino kindled a fire and crafted a small spit to roast a fresh salmon they had brought along with them for dinner. While they worked, Cassino continued to talk about his youth and his rise to power as the leading chief. Little was said about the coming of the white men, but Cassino did mention trip to see the first ship in the Great River.

As dusk began to settle along the river, Cassino and his son settled around the fire and continued their conversation. Cassino could feel the spirit of Pilmowitsh around them as they ate their meal, and he told Little Cassino about the great canoe builder's artistry. "The beauty of his carvings and the magnificence of his canoes was legendary. No one could match his work." He went on to describe how a canoe was built and the tools they used before there were iron knives and hatchets. Little Cassino especially liked the story of the little canoe that his father and Monsoe had built under Pilmowitsh's direction.

"Pilmowitsh was a father to me," Cassino continued, "but he was not your real grandfather. I am going to tell you a secret, one that not even your mother knows, but first you must promise me that you will tell no one else. This secret is just between you and me." Little Cassino nodded solemnly and Cassino continued, "Your grandmother, Tenastsil is the only other person who knows. My father was the great chief of all the Chinook before Chief Comcomly, your mother's father. So you are the grandson of two all-powerful Chinook chiefs. But remember, everyone thinks that I am the son of Pilmowitsh, because it was important for all the people of Wappato to think of me as a son of Wappato. While I smoke my pipe I will tell you the story of how your grandmother and I came to the Niakowkow."

They talked long into the night, until the fire burned down and they were stretched out on their mats. Before long, father and son had drifted off to sleep.

When they awoke the next day, the sun was already high in the sky. It was another lazy, warm afternoon before they finally pushed off and paddled at a leisurely pace up the channel and into the bay of the Clackstar.

Chief Monsoe greeted them warmly and Little Cassino ran off to play with his cousins. Once the boy was gone, Cassino sensed immediately that Monsoe was preoccupied and worried. Since Cassino's move to the Wakanasisi village, the two old friends had seldom seen each other, and Cassino was anxious to catch up on events. Before the two men had even walked the short distance to Monsoe's house, the Clackstar chief began to pour out his troubles to Cassino.

"Cassino, my brother, it is good that you have come," Monsoe began. "Our people need you and your wisdom. I have great concerns about a problem that has struck our village. Have you heard about the sickness?"

Cassino felt a chill run down his back. "No, you are the first one to speak of it. What sickness?"

"It is like nothing we have known, my brother, and it is spreading from village to village. Those who have the sickness grow very hot.

When they go to the sweat hut and then plunge into the river, instead of getting better, they have more pains and soon die. The sickness is in our village now. No one who gets the sickness lives. All die."

"You say it is also in other villages," Cassino said with a cold fear growing in his heart. "Which ones?"

"The Cowlitch, the Kalama, the Quathlahpottle, the Multnomah—all have reported it. The sickness is the same in every place and it is growing worse. Everyone dies."

"Has Pee-Kin been told?" Cassino asked.

Monsoe was silent as he looked at his lifelong friend. Cassino was dismayed and finally asked the Clackstar chief, "Monsoe, we are brothers. We have trusted each other since we were little boys. What are you not telling me?"

Monsoe looked away, then turned back with a renewed resolve. "Our medicine men blame Pee-Kin and the white men for this sickness. They say it is caused by evil spirits who have come up from the ground where it has been broken by the white man when he does his planting. These evil spirits also come in the white men's ships. We are afraid of what Pee-Kin and his people will do if we tell them."

Cassino was angry that he had not been told sooner about the sickness. "Monsoe, do not believe the stories told by the medicine men. We must tell Pee-Kin; he will know what to do. The white man's magic is strong. I will go to tell him. Do nothing until you hear from me."

Cassino called for his son to join him. He started to run down to the beach, but he felt uneasy and turned back to talk to Monsoe once again. "My brother, it is not easy for me to leave. We have seen and done so much together and my heart goes with you forever. The old days were good, but they are gone. I wish it were not so. Now we must trust the white man and learn from his magic. I must tell Pee-Kin about this sickness, or else everyone may die. Farewell, my brother. Take care of our people. I will send word when I have spoken to Pee-Kin."

The two men clasped hands and Cassino turned and walked quickly down to his canoe. As he and Little Cassino paddled down the bay, the chief did not look back. He had a strong premonition that he would never see Monsoe again.

After rounding the tip of Wappato back into the Columbia, Cassino told his son that they must go to the fort immediately. Little Cassino could hear the anxiety in his father's voice and tried to conceal his disappointment about cutting short their trip. It was early evening before they reached the Wakanasisi village. It was nearly deserted, because most of the tribe had left already for Wallamt. Cassino told the boy to wait for him at their house, then mounted a horse and set off at a full gallop for the fort.

After gaining admittance at the gate, Cassino went straight to see Dr. McLoughlin. The white chief looked up from his books when he heard Cassino's knock and immediately ushered him in to his office. "Come in, Cassino. I thought you had left for Wallamt."

"We went to Wappato first, my son and I," Cassino said. "Pee-Kin, there is great trouble among my people. A strange new sickness is in the villages and many people are dying. I first heard of it from Chief Monsoe of the Clackstar. Have you heard of this sickness?"

The doctor looked grave and shook his head. "What are the symptoms, Cassino? That is, what happens to these people when they get sick? How do they look? How do they feel?"

"I did not see any of these sick people, but Monsoe says they grow very hot and soon die. Even when they go to the sweat hut and plunge themselves in the river, it does no good. They still die. No one gets well. Monsoe says that all the Wappato tribes have spoken of this sickness."

McLoughlin was clearly upset by Cassino's report. "With certain kinds of illness, Cassino, the sweat hut is not good. I have told you this before. With this kind of fever, the sweat hut could be deadly."

"The sweat hut is the Chinook way," Cassino replied with a shrug. "Our people have always done this. They do not know that they must change their ways."

"I know. I know," murmured Dr. McLoughlin. "Some of our people have had a strange kind of fever. It must have come in on one of the ships. I must see some of the sick ones at once."

"No, no, Pee-Kin. You cannot. Monsoe says the medicine men blame you and the other white men for letting the evil spirits out of the ground when you break it to plant your food."

"You mean where we have plowed?"

"Yes, that is it. And they blame the ships for bringing in the evil spirits from across the water. What can we do, Pee-Kin?"

"First I must find out what the sickness is, Cassino, before I can know how to treat it. If it is the same illness that some have here at the fort, I have a medicine called 'quinine' that helps. If many of your people are sick, we will need much more quinine than we have and it takes a long time for the medicine to arrive by ship. If someone who is sick in your tribes will come to see me, then I can find out. Meanwhile, go on to Wallamt and find out all you can about the sickness and whether it has spread to the Willamette tribes. Cassino, do not go near to anyone who is sick. Stay away from them! Report back as soon as you can."

Riding back to his village, Cassino thought about everything Pee-Kin had said, and weariness spread over him like a blanket. He told Little Cassino that they would be going to Wallamt after all, but all the joy and anticipation was gone.

# THE DEATH OF THE MULTNOMAH

At Wallamt, Cassino found widespread fear and suspicion. The sickness had reached the Willamette tribes, with devastating results. Because of his closeness to the white traders at the fort, Cassino was met with sullen reserve by the other chiefs. His recommendation to isolate the sick and avoid use of the sweat hut were ignored or openly derided. The medicine men had warned the people not to listen to advice from the white man, and even some of Cassino's closest friends were inclined to mistrust him. He could not consult with Asotan, because the Shoto medicine man had not made the trip to Wallamt. Tanohah was cordial but distant with Cassino, and when more Multnomah fell sick at Wallamt, he refused to quarantine them, deciding instead to return immediately to Wappato.

Olahno was friendly to Cassino, but reticent about the white traders at the fort. "Since they have come into the country, all has gone wrong. We used to trade furs here at Wallamt and it was an important time," he said, "but everything has changed." When Olahno said he wasn't planning to bring the Calapooya to Wallamt the following year, Cassino believed he was seeing his mother for perhaps the last time. With each day at the falls, his heart grew heavier.

Following Pee-Kin's advice, Cassino learned everything he could about the sickness, but he was in no position to help. With reluctance, he designated a few fishing parties to stay behind to net salmon for the winter and ordered the rest of the Wakanasisi to return home.

When Cassino reached the Wakanasisi village, he immediately grabbed a horse and rode up to the fort. Dr. McLoughlin reported that an epidemic of "intermittent fever" was moving quickly among the

167

natives and he warned Cassino to stay away from the infected villages. "A few of the sick have come to the fort for treatment," McLoughlin said, "and the quinine seems to help. But the sweat hut remedy makes the fever worse and death comes more quickly."

Other issues were also of pressing concern to Dr. McLoughlin, including plans to move the fort closer to the river for easier access to drinking water. The matter of Americans trading along the river was also a constant worry. About the time the William and Ann had been lost, an American ship called the *Owhyhee* had crossed the bar and anchored opposite Fort George. The Americans traded with the natives all summer and moved upriver as far as Deer Island. The competition forced McLoughlin and the British traders to pay higher prices for furs, and the fort was running low on goods for barter. Despite his concerns when they found out it wasn't a King George ship, McLoughlin would not allow the Chinook to attack the *Owhyhee*. Cassino did not understand Pee-Kin's logic. A few days before, the White Headed Eagle had refused to stop a party of Americans from going upriver to trade at The Dalles.

Cassino knew that dealing with the sickness among the tribes was his responsibility. He sent word to all of his chiefs that he would survey the situation from Wappato to the mouth of the river. He asked the chiefs to meet him out on the river as he came by and not to bring any of the sick along.

Cassino was determined to camp away from the villages, and he instructed his wives and slaves to equip the canoe with the necessary supplies. Gathering the Wakanasisi tribe together, he gave them strict orders: "Because of the sickness, everyone must do as I say. Stay away from the other villages; do not use the sweat huts; swimming and bathing in the river is for healthy ones only. If anyone becomes sick, isolate them and send someone to the fort immediately for help. Pee-Kin has some medicine and his instructions must be followed faithfully." Then, with his select group of bodyguards, dressed in their blue jackets and armed with the best muskets, Cassino set out.

Off the shore of the Multnomah village, one of Cassino's paddlers fired his musket and soon a lone canoe put off from the beach. It was Tanohah, and Cassino was startled at his brother's haggard appearance. The two chiefs talked as their canoes drifted side by side. Tanohah would not leave his village and his people, but he was willing to try anything to treat the terrible sickness, which seemed worse with the women and children. He agreed to stay away from the sick and to try to convince them to quit using the sweat huts. Many had already died, including Asotan. Tanohah reported that all the medicine men had already died.

As Cassino's party pushed on through Wappato territory, he became increasingly appalled by what he saw. The sickness was everywhere, and the reports from every village were the same. When he reached Warrior Rock and rounded the tip of Wappato, a Clackstar canoe pulled up nearby. The news was worse than Cassino had anticipated. His dear brother Monsoe was dead and many more in the village were dying. Cassino was overcome with grief. Two of his closest friends were gone and nothing could be done to save dozens of others who were suffering from this terrible sickness. He sat stoically as his slaves continued to paddle downstream. He thoughts were consumed with memories of Monsoe—his oldest and most dear friend.

When the expedition reached the area of the Kalama, Lamkos was waiting out in the river. "My heart is full at seeing you well and free of the sickness, Lamkos," Cassino said when the canoes had met in the slackwater near the mouth of the Kalama's stream. "Tell me, how are the Kalama?"

"We have lost many, Cassino, but we have stopped using the sweat hut since receiving your message. A brew made from the bark of the dogwood tree helps the sick and we have not had any new ones catch the sickness for several days. None of our people are allowed to visit other villages."

This report was the first good news Cassino had heard, and he said, "This confirms the soundness of Pee-Kin's advice." He then passed along the sad news of the death of Monsoe, and Asotan, but added, "Continue what you are doing, and I will speak with you again on my way back up the river. We will tell the other tribes to try the dogwood bark remedy."

Cassino soon learned that the Cowlitch had been hit hardest of all. The two boys who met Cassino out on the river reported that their tribe had been devastated by the sickness, and that more were dead than alive in the village. Cassino was worried about Soleutu and Shenshina but he didn't dare go near the village. As they passed the *Owhyhee*, they paddled to the far side of the river to avoid the Americans.

The lower river tribes had been only mildly affected by the sickness, which they blamed on the Americans on the *Owhyhee*. Deep in his heart, Cassino knew that the illness must have started in the Wappato area, possibly at Fort Vancouver. A stop at Fort George turned up nothing new, but some Clatsop women living there reported that their village was free of the disease. Comcomly also said that his villages were unscathed, but Cassino tried to explain the dangers and precautions that Pee-Kin had advised. He soon realized his entreaties were falling on deaf ears. He was disgusted with Comcomly, whom he believed saw the sickness in the mid-river area as an opportunity to reinforce his power. Cassino wondered whether the old man and his tribe would survive the winter.

On his return trip upriver, Cassino was pleased to find Lamkos and the Kalama still holding their own. In the Wappato area, the situation was still desperate, but hadn't worsened. The number of deaths was diminishing, but the toll on the women and children was frightful. Concomsin was dead, along with most of his household, and the Quathlahpottle were in disarray without strong leadership. The same was true of the Clannaquah. Laquano had become ill and had isolated himself somewhere on the island. No one knew whether he was alive or dead. Lohtahsen, Cassino's younger sister, had died, along with her two children. With a heart heavy with sorrow and bitterness, Cassino returned to the Wakanasisi village. The sickness had struck the Wakanasisi, but was being controlled with the help of medicine from the fort.

The Princess and Little Cassino were at the fort when Cassino arrived, and McLoughlin insisted that Cassino and his family move into one of the small cabins just outside the stockade walls and close to the river. Though Ilchee complained about having no slaves nearby to help her with the work, the cabin was comfortable and she was delighted to be living alongside families who were employees of the Hudson's Bay Company.

Winter took its toll on the Wappato tribes. Splinter groups—mostly bedraggled young men who had fled the sickness—were living away from the villages and having a hard time staying warm and dry through the damp winter days. The villages housed mostly the sick and others too lethargic to be of any help. Cassino agonized over his inability to help his people. He himself was vigorous and strong as he faced his fifty-second winter. He did not fear the sickness, because he took every precaution and he still had the strong sense of his own destiny that he'd had since his youth. He was at last beginning to understand the fullness of the *tamanowos*.

He remembered the vision as if it had happened yesterday. He had seen a young chief from a small tribe rise to a position of great leadership as the chief of many tribes. He knew that he was the young chief. In the last part of the vision, a greater chief had come, but he had appeared blurry and indistinct—and Cassino could not make him out. When he was younger, Cassino had assumed that the stronger chief was the spirit of his father—or perhaps it was Comcomly. But now he understood that the vision was blurry because he had never seen this kind of chief before. He knew without a doubt that the great chief was Pee-Kin, the Great White-Headed Eagle. He marveled at how precise his *tamanowos* vision had been.

Then fear clutched his heart as the end of the vision—which had always been puzzling—finally became clear. The great chief, Cassino, was in his village. It was a large village, even larger than the Clackstar village, and the chief came out of his house and looked around. Everywhere, his people were lying still on the ground. He had always interpreted this scene as confirmation of his strength and power, but he suddenly understood that it was a sure sign of his ultimate weakness: his inability to protect his people from the sickness. The people in his vision were not prostrate in honor of him, they were dead.

Spring and summer finally arrived, and with them came a respite from the devastating disease. All winter the building had continued, and the new fort had taken shape along the lines of all Hudson's Bay Company stockades. It was positioned close to the river, where the water level in the large, deep well in the northeast corner rose and fell with the height of the river. Two large gates in the wall facing the river were entrances for wagons and carts. Near the center of the back wall, a smaller gate led to the granary, garden, orchard and fields. A small door built into this gate allowed individuals to come and go without having to open the gate. Inside the stockade, various buildings surrounded two courts. Dr. McLoughlin's quarters and the bachelors' dining hall sat in the east center near the large flagpole. All buildings were constructed of logs, with sawn plank roofing, except for the McLoughlin home, which was clapboard and painted white. The new fort was much more comfortable than the old and better suited to the ever growing business of the Company.

Cassino and his family now lived in one of about sixty houses near the new stockade. The new quarters were large enough to accommodate Cassino, Ilchee, two of his other wives—Sateena and Poleetah, the mothers of his daughters—Little Cassino, and Cassino's three girls. His other wives remained in the Wakanasisi village. The houses around Cassino's were occupied by employees of the Hudson's Bay Company and their families. The houses were built in rows up from the river, with streets running in between, where the children played, and the little neighborhood was near the wharves, the salmon curing house, and the hospital.

Traveling from the fort to the sea many times that summer, Cassino saw fear, confusion and disarray everywhere. Many leaders had died, leaving no one to replace them. The Cowlitch were in the worst shape of all. All of their leading chiefs were dead, including Shannaway and Soleutu. The large village was abandoned and all that remained were empty, desolate houses strewn with decaying corpses. The stench was so great and the fear of sickness so real that no one would go near. The few remaining Cowlitch were scattered in small groups up and down the river. Cassino assumed that Shenshina and her children had also died in the epidemic, and he grieved for them.

The lower river tribes had survived the winter pretty much intact and many were convinced they were immune to the "white man's sickness." Chief Comcomly could hardly hide his conviction that his power was greater than ever. He even went so far as to suggest to Cassino, "Perhaps Pee-Kin would prefer to deal directly with Comcomly. Your *tamanowos* is at last failing you, Cassino."

With bitterness, Cassino turned away from Comcomly for the last time. "Farewell," he said with resignation in his voice. He was again struck by a strong premonition: Comcomly would not be around long. The old chief simply did not have the insight to realize what was happening to his people.

On the return trip, Cassino was plagued by many black thoughts. Comcomly's mention of his *tamanowos* had bothered him greatly. One should not speak of such things. Was this "superstition," as Pee-Kin would say? Should he dismiss it? No, one must be Chinook in order to understand the *tamanowos*. It was not superstition. His vision had been the guiding spirit in his life. It had been good and it had been accurate. He had followed his tamanowos and had come to power. Pee-Kin was part of his vision and had appeared in his time. But where did it lead? What of the rest of the vision?—the part where the chief came out of his house and saw his people scattered on the ground. One thing was clear: the chief was there; he had remained. Cassino was certain that no matter what happened, he was destined to survive.

By late summer, Cassino had restored some measure of order and organization among the mid-river tribes, often compromising his terms to assure the best leadership. Many splinter groups of young men, with a few women along, roved along the river, stirring up trouble and defying external control.

Laquano had survived his bout with the sickness, and he had returned to lead the Clannaquah. He came to see Cassino, determined to leave the Wappato area with his people. Cassino was surprised to learn that it was Sohowitsh who had convinced Laquano to leave. The two chiefs asked to meet with Cassino and Tanohah the next day. Sohowitsh suggested that they meet at the site of their old boyhood home across from the tip of Wappato.

With the bright sun overhead and the smooth, placid water under his trim canoe, Cassino paddled slowly downriver. The vivid golds and greens of the trees lining the river were of little consolation as he thought about his destination and the reason for his journey. He had wanted to bring along Little Cassino, but this would hardly be a happy occasion to share with his son. More likely, he would meeting with his friends and brothers for the last time.

He thought about Monsoe and an involuntary sigh escaped his lips. How he wished his friend and brother were still alive, so they could all—Pilmowitsh's sons—be together again. But it was not to be, just as so many other things had forever changed. Cassino felt very much alone and increased the pace of his paddle to reach his brothers sooner.

As he rounded the bend of the island out of the main current of the river, he saw two canoes pulled up on Pilmowitsh's beach. His brothers were already there! As he put ashore, he saw Tanohah walking down the bank to greet him. "Chief Cassino, my brother, it is so good you came. Sohowitsh and Laquano are up at the old campsite."

Cassino seized Tanohah's arm and said earnestly, "It is like old times, my brother. Of course I would come."

Tanohah's drawn face and evident thinness emphasized his distinguished bearing. *Of all our chiefs*, Cassino thought, *he is the most faithful, the most noble of our people.* He represents the best devotion to his Chinook brothers. As he followed Tanohah up the beach, a quick pain stabbed Cassino's heart over the unfair burden his faithful brother had endured.

For awhile, the chiefs forgot their troubles and worries as the sun warmed their bodies and they talked and reminisced about their boyhood. Wonderful memories, the old familiar scenes they had shared, the joys and sorrows, all filled their hearts—but it was the absence of Monsoe that brought them back to the present reality.

"Wappato has become an accursed land," said Sohowitsh sadly. "You have made your place with the white men, Cassino, but there is no such place for us. Our people are dying—we all know that. But what happened to Monsoe will not happen to me or my family. There was much sickness among the Cathlahminnamin, but we survived. Many times I have thought about taking my wives and children and making our way through the land of the Tualitis, up and over the great hills to the land of the Tillamook. Twice, we were prepared to go, but always my Clatsop wife pleaded to return to her people. 'We are Chinook,' she said, 'and we should remain with our people.' Now I see that she is right. We are leaving Wappato and will live with the Clatsops. Laquano and what is left of his family will go with us."

"You are chiefs," Tanohah said calmly when his brother had finished. "You are needed here. You cannot leave your people. Are you taking your tribes with you?"

Sohowitsh looked at Tanohah in anguish. "There is no one I respect more than you, my brother. It has been this way since we were small boys playing on Wappato, and never have I questioned your word. You are brave and faithful and noble, but you cannot help our people.

Cassino cannot help our people. They have the fear of death in them and no one can lead them. To stay means death, and I will not stay to die."

"Tanohah," pleaded Laquano, "come with us. We have followed you faithfully until today, but no one knows better than I do the futility of staying to die of the sickness. I am still alive after the sickness has passed through our village once. I will not be there to see it again." He looked at Tanohah with imploring eyes. "Come with us, my brother. You cannot help the Multnomah. They will die no matter what you do."

Tanohah could not look at his brothers. He scratched at the ground with a stick and shook his head. "The chief of the Multnomah will stay with his people."

Sohowitsh and Laquano turned to Cassino, hoping that his wisdom would prevail upon Tanohah and settle this conflict. With a deep sadness in his eyes, he looked at the two chiefs. Finally, he said, "Not long ago, Chief Comcomly told me that he thought my *tamanowos* was failing, but he was wrong. What is happening to our people I have seen for some time, but I am powerless to stop it. You have all been loyal to me ever since we were boys, and this must not change, but the time has come for each of you to follow your own *tamanowos*, just as every good Chinook has always done. Each of you is right to do what you see in your heart. None of us should judge the other. Tanohah is right when he says that our tribes need us. Sohowitsh and Laquano are right when they say that our people are too frightened to follow their chiefs. Whatever you decide, take the advice of Pee-Kin in dealing with the sickness. His word is good and to do otherwise is certain death."

Cassino looked at each of the other chiefs before continuing, "I made my choice long ago. I have not left my people in favor of the white men, although it may appear so. My people have left me. From the time of the very first ship, anyone could see that Chinook magic could never match the white man's magic. There was only one path to take: learn the white man's magic and use it to survive. Few Chinook have understood this truth, and now you are seeing the result."

Tanohah turned to Sohowitsh and Laquano and smiled sadly. "Go then, my brothers, if in your hearts it seems the right thing to do. I have never known Cassino to be wrong about the important things. Sohowitsh, my little brother, it is hard to see you go, but I must stay. Let us say our farewells under the great cedar where our father and mother left us to take the long journey. Cassino, my brother, will you join us?"

At the beach, Laquano said good-bye to Cassino and Tanohah and headed upriver toward the Clannaquah village. The three brothers paddled across the channel to Warrior Rock, pulled up their canoes and walked silently to the giant cedar. High in the giant tree, the little peace canoe still rested, weather-beaten and covered by the bright green foliage of the sweet-smelling cedar. The silence was broken from time to time as the brothers spoke softly. As Sohowitsh clasped Tanohah in his arms for the last time, a stifled sob escaped his throat. Cassino had to turn away. The sudden memory of Monsoe was too much to bear.

Wearily, Casino propelled his canoe back toward the fort. A black cloud of discouragement dogged his every stroke. He had said good-bye to two of his best chiefs and a gnawing sense of impending disaster haunted him. He wished Tanohah was leaving too—he wanted him to be safe—but he knew the winter would be chaos without him.

Alone on the beach, Tanohah watched Sohowitsh's canoe grow smaller in the distance. Just before he rounded a bend in the river and glided out of sight, Sohowitsh turned and waved. There was a sense of finality and futility in the gesture—the end to a long and wonderful relationship, the ultimate separation. When his brother was no longer in sight, Tanohah gazed across the magnificent river to where Loowit raised her head—her soft shoulders blanketed in the pinks and golds of the fading day.

The last days of summer gave way to the crisp mornings of fall, and the dreaded winter moved inexorably closer. Tanohah rallied his tribesmen to lay in an abundant supply of food. He knew that if the sickness returned, the people would be too few or too weak to care for one another. Only the best fishermen—and no women and children—went to Wallamt to fish for salmon. What had once been a joyful gathering of the tribes was now all business, and very little trading was done.

When the cold and rain of winter set in, the sickness reappeared. Cassino begged Tanohah to stay with him, but the chief of the Multnomah refused. His place was with his people, he said, and leaving them would be the final blow. The sickness soon spread into every house in the village. Day and night there was wailing and the stench of death. Before long, most of the women and children were gone, but the sickness continued. At first, Tanohah tried to have the bodies removed, but panic-stricken surviving family members would not allow it. Ultimately, no one would help to move the dead and all order broke down.

After losing every member of his own family, the brave and valiant chief of the Multnomah was struck down by a grieving father who thought Tanohah was trying to take his son—who was deathly ill but still clinging to life—away. Weakened by fever and exertion, Tanohah died from a stone blow to the head. The next morning, the deranged father and his small son died in each other's arms.

A few days later, a heavy snow blanketed the Multnomah village. Under the carpet of pure, glistening white, all was quiet. Not a sound broke the silence of the cold winter morning. The great tribe that had lived on the island for nearly one thousand years was gone.

# 21 LITTLE CASSINO

The winter of 1830 marked the end of a life that the Wappato tribes had known for centuries. Except for a few individuals who had fled the village before the last epidemic, the Multnomah and Clannaquah were completely wiped out by the sickness. The Cathlahminnamin village was deserted. Only a few Shoto, Quathlahpottle and Clackstar survived. The Kalama suffered greatly, but remained together as a tribe under the brave leadership of Chief Lamkos. The Cowlitch had finally succumbed as the disease spread downriver, and up near the fort, only a few Wakanasisi survived. Among those who died were all of Cassino's wives died whom he left in the village when he moved to the fort.

Dr. McLoughlin was exhausted by his never-ending duties and the additional burden of treating the sick. Conditions at the fort became desperate and much of the work came to a standstill. The "intermittent fever" also struck the white settlers, but they seemed to be able to throw it off and recover. Only Big Pierre Karaganyate died as a result of the sickness.

Early in the fall, Poleetah and Cassino's youngest daughter had gone to visit Poleetah's family in the Multnomah village. Both came down with the fever and died on Wappato before they could return to the fort. Soon afterward, Sateena's two daughters were taken to the hospital. Although Dr. McLoughlin treated them with medicine, both girls died. By spring of Cassino's immediate family, only Little Cassino, Ilchee, and Sateena were left.

Late that winter, McLoughlin came to see Cassino. "My friend," he said, "several natives have come to the fort seeking our protection. They say we must bury them when they die. For the safety of the others, I must turn them away, Cassino. I hate to do it, but I must. I thought I should tell you."

Cassino did not hesitate. "Pee-Kin, it is not for you to do; it is for me, their chief."

With great dignity, Cassino talked to his people and persuaded them to leave. McLoughlin was amazed at how it was accomplished without force and asked, "What reasoning did you use to convince them, Cassino?"

"I told them the truth. I said, 'You are Chinook. Though you are dying, you must follow your *tamanowos* as all good Chinook do. Nobody's *tamanowos* leads them to beg the white man to bury them.'"

Comcomly died that winter and Cassino became chief of all the remaining Chinook, thus fulfilling his tamanowos.

The coming of summer made the desolation brutally apparent, and it was overwhelming. Up and down the river, unburied corpses lay rotting in deserted villages, and small bands of frightened, desperate Chinook roved the area in search of food and shelter. Cassino did what he could to rally and solidify his remaining people. He went to the Clatsops and prevailed upon Sohowitsh to move across the Great River to the Chinook village to be with his people and serve as Cassino's representative in the area. Lamkos and the Kalama survivors provided stability about midway between the mouth of the river and Fort Vancouver.

The tragic winter had aged Cassino markedly and part of his inner spirit seemed dead. Though he was unable to reconcile the loss of his family, friends and tribes, one happy miracle stood out and brought him joy: his son had been spared. Little Cassino was now the principal person in his life. Cassino doted on the boy, planned for his future, and took him along everywhere he went.

The first summer they had lived at the fort, Little Cassino had missed his Wakanasisi friends, but now most of his playmates were the sons of employees of the Company. He had become a child of the fort. He shared the sorrow and the fear and the emptiness felt by his parents when his sisters died, but he was spared the sight of his boyhood friends back in the village dying one by one.

Seeking to learn as much about the white ways as he could, Cassino continued to study the many new traders who came to the fort. One such visitor, who had arrived not long after the fort opened, was David Douglas, called the Great Grass Man by the Chinook. Cassino paid no particular attention to Douglas until he saw the deference shown him by

Pee-Kin. As Douglas roamed around the country, often alone, studying plant life and collecting specimens, his closeness to nature was something Cassino and every other native could understand. Cassino's growing admiration and fondness for Douglas resulted in a strong friendship. Cassino would occasionally accompany the naturalist and help him gain acceptance from the natives.

The term "gentleman," which he had often heard around the fort, had always puzzled Cassino. At first he thought it was a title based on the importance of the job a man performed, but slowly he began to realize another, more basic, distinction. Dr. McLoughlin explained the white man's ideas about "breeding" and "education," and gradually the concept became clear. Cassino realized that every white leader he had admired had been a man of learning, a gentleman.

As Cassino tried to foresee the future his son would face, he concluded there was only one solution: His son must be raised in the ways of the white man. After much soul searching, he knew there would be no seeking of a tamanowos vision for Little Cassino.

His mind made up, Cassino went to see Dr. McLoughlin. When he was seated in McLoughlin's office, he said, "My son is of good breeding. His father is chief of all the Chinook, and his grandfathers also. His mother is a Chinook princess. I want my son to become a gentleman. He must be brought up in the white ways."

McLoughlin was taken by surprise. "But, Cassino, that would mean he would have to be sent away to school. Are you sure that is what you want? I suppose we could send him to Canada, but it would take years—you realize that."

Cassino looked at the floor stubbornly. "My son must become a gentleman," he said with finality.

"Then I shall look for the best place for him," McLoughlin replied.

Near the end of October 1832, an overland American party reached Fort Vancouver. The leader was Nathaniel Wyeth and of the twenty-four men who had left Boston, only eleven remained. Among the survivors was a teacher named John Ball. The Americans were warmly received by Dr. McLoughlin and given food and shelter.

About two weeks after the arrival of the Wyeth party, McLoughlin called Cassino into his office. "I have good news for you, Cassino. We are going to open a school for children of the fort, and your son will be enrolled. My youngest son, David, will also be a student. Mr. John Ball, one of the Americans, will by employed by the Company as teacher. He is well qualified to do this work."

About two dozen students attended the new school. Little Cassino was the oldest, and a six-year-old boy was the youngest. The task of teaching the students how to speak, read, and write English was a formidable one. Not only were a French patois and several native languages represented— Chinook, Klickitat and Nez Perce—but several dialects of these as well. Mr. Ball was undaunted. He taught the lessons entirely in English, and when an older student lapsed into any other language, a medal was hung around his neck and he stayed after school for an additional lesson. Mr. Ball reported that the students were "docile and attentive" and "making good progress." After two-and-a-half months, Mr. Ball was succeeded by Solomon H. Smith, who also had come to Vancouver with the Wyeth party.

Little Cassino turned out to be one of the best students in the class. Compared to his customary freedom, the routine and discipline of going to school every day seemed irksome, but as he progressed, Little Cassino began to enjoy school and the success he was achieving. Even better, he knew his father was proud of him, and this pleased him even more.

By this time, Fort Vancouver had become the heart of all commercial enterprise in the northwestern part of North America, and the political and cultural center as well. Newcomers were astounded to find such a fine settlement in the middle of the wilderness, and were quick to appreciate the dramatic achievements of Dr. McLoughlin and the Hudson's Bay Company.

Under McLoughlin's direction, the Company continued to expand its operations throughout the region. A few of the remaining Wappato tribesmen still fished at Wallamt, but for the past two years they had shared the area around the falls with a camp and sawmill established by McLoughlin.

After staying several months at the fort, Wyeth returned to Boston. In September 1834, he arrived back at Fort Vancouver with a large party of more than fifty men. A ship from Boston, the *May Dacre*, had sailed around Cape Horn carrying trading goods and was waiting in the Columbia River when Wyeth arrived. He planned to establish an American trading post on Wappato.

The *May Dacre* sailed upriver into Multnomah Channel behind Wappato, and anchored not far from the remains of the Clackstar village. Wappato had been virtually deserted since the fever had wiped out the tribes and it pained Cassino to see white strangers take over his beloved island. Cassino knew that Pee-Kin liked Nathaniel Wyeth, but there was something he couldn't understand.

"I'm leaving it up to you, Cassino," Pee-Kin had said one day, "to see that no natives in the lower river help Wyeth in his new enterprise. See to it that no furs are traded to them and they are not helped with their fishing. This assignment is very important and you will need to attend to it at once."

The new settlement, called Fort William, was located on the west side of Wappato, on the broad southern part of the island, across from the deserted and decayed Multnomah village and not far down the channel from the Willamette River. By the end of the first week of October, several buildings had been completed to serve as storehouses, dwellings, a smithy and a cooper shop.

All winter, through the spring and into summer, Cassino carried out McLoughlin's orders. As the Americans continued to build, it became apparent that the Columbia River Fishing and Trading Company was intended to compete with the Hudson's Bay Company. Cassino now understood why Pee-Kin wanted to thwart Wyeth's endeavor. Success in fishing required the help of the natives, because Wyeth's men did not have the proper nets for use in the river, but Cassino made sure that such help was not available. He also arranged a trade embargo of sorts against the Americans, and by the end of the summer, only a half-cargo of salmon had been packed. After incurring seventeen deaths among his men—some succumbed to    illness, others were killed by natives—and having considerable property stolen by the natives, Wyeth concluded that his enterprise would not succeed. He was forced to sell his business to the Hudson's Bay Company.

As the days warmed into summer, Pee-Kin told Cassino that the abandoned villages on Wappato must be burned for health reasons. Cassino understood the necessity for this action and made no objection, but his heart was deeply saddened. Out in his canoe—alone on the river— he watched the pillars of smoke lifting the spirits from the villages straight up into the blue sky. He spent the entire day on the river, eating nothing, lost in his own thoughts. *Multnomah tamanowos*— it was the end. In the evening, rather than return to the fort, he paddled to shore on Tomahawk Island and lay on his back under the canopy of stars until he fell asleep in the warm, summer night. He thought and dreamed about life on Wappato: of his mother, Tenastsil; of Pilmowitsh and Lopahtah; of Monsoe and Tanohah and all the others now in Memaloose Illahee. He traced his rise to power, his ascension to chief in one tribe after another, and his final achievement as chief of the Multnomah. Now it was all gone, disappeared into nothingness.

He was proud of his Chinook heritage. He was proud to follow in the footsteps of his noble brothers, Monsoe and Tanohah. No matter what else he might endure before embarking on his own long journey, he was a Chinook and he would be with his family and friends again someday.

In the early morning light, he returned to Vancouver, ate, and told Sateena to pack a canoe for the two of them. Telling Ilchee and Little Cassino not to expect them back for several days, Cassino and his first wife paddled down the great, smooth river. The sun was warm and comforting, and Cassino said very little until the canoe neared Wappato.

"We will not go near the villages," he said. "They are still smoking. We will go to Pilmowitsh's place, then to the camp of the Niakowkow. We are returning home, even if only for a short time."

Sateena turned slightly to look back at him. "It will be as the first time I came to you, that night so long ago," she said.

"No," Cassino gently corrected her. "It will be as the first night I brought you back to the Niakowkow as my wife." He leaned forward to stroke her hair.

By his third year at school, Little Cassino could do simple reading and writing, and some arithmetic. Because his schooling was considered more important than assisting his father, he rarely accompanied Cassino on any of his trips. Now nearly sixteen, Little Cassino was beginning to have a life of his own. He spent much of his free time with his friends, and was mostly concerned with his own ideas and aspirations. Before long, a lovely young girl named Waskema caught his eye and held his attention. She lived a considerable distance above the fort, and Cassino became concerned about his son's inclination to slip away to visit her. Ilchee, who sensed that the girl was replacing her in her son's affections, agreed with

Cassino's decision to keep the boy close to the fort. The stage was set for a major confrontation between parents and child before Sateena, with her usual skill and sensitivity, negotiated an uneasy truce that settled things down for awhile.

As the newly appointed Chief of Indian Affairs for Pee-Kin, Cassino extended his influence far beyond the banks of the Columbia River. He helped to ease the way for white settlers who were moving into the fertile Willamette Valley and retiring employees from the Hudson's Bay Company who were establishing farms on the French Prairie. McLoughlin had built a landing and warehouse at Champoeg on the Willamette River, where farmers could exchange their grain for supplies. Some missionaries under Jason Lee, who had arrived with Wyeth on the *May Dacre*, had settled further south. The settlement around the sawmill at Wallamt grew rapidly as increasing numbers of white settlers moved in.

The influx of new settlers further displaced the natives who had survived the sickness. The roving bands became dangerous and unpredictable. McLoughlin relied increasingly on Cassino to mediate disputes and preserve the peace.

One day, messengers came from a Cathlamet tribe that had taken over part of the old Cowlitch territory downriver. The young men reported that the Hudson's Bay Company's fort at Nisqually on Puget Sound had been attacked and its inhabitants killed to the last man. McLoughlin summoned Cassino to listen to their story. When he had spoken to the messengers, Cassino said to McLoughlin, "Their story appears to be truthful, but you should be cautious, Pee-Kin. Because this fort is so far away, the story should be confirmed."

"I quite agree," replied McLoughlin. "I will have my second-in-command, James Douglas, visit the Cathlamets as my representative. I would like for you to accompany him, Cassino."

The meeting with the Cathlamets made Cassino uneasy. Though he couldn't say what it was, he felt in his heart that something was amiss in the tribe's story. Douglas agreed with Cassino's assessment and recommended to McLoughlin that a scouting party, rather than a full contingent, be sent north to investigate.

McLoughlin was perplexed. "I believe we must go ahead with sending a brigade to Nisqually," he said. "We cannot ignore our people when they need help." He ordered the men to continue to muster a force to depart the following day.

The next morning, just as the Company contingent was preparing to leave for the northern fort, two traders from Fort Nisqually showed up at the main gate. Dr. McLoughlin was quickly summoned to interview the men. They said that when they had left Nisqually, there had been no sign of trouble, and their journey to Fort Vancouver had been without incident. Under closer questioning by McLoughlin, the men confirmed that they had not yet left the fort at the time of the alleged attack.

When Cassino heard this new report, he quickly dispatched a trusted scout to visit the Cathlamet village and gather more information. When the scout returned a few days later, he reported that the story of the attack at Fort Nisqually had been a hoax designed to weaken the defense of Fort Vancouver. The Cathlamets had planned to attack the fort as soon as the brigade went north. McLoughlin commended Douglas and Cassino for their caution and sound advice regarding the Cathlamet story, and it wasn't long before James Douglas was made a chief trader for the company. Cassino suggested several plans for teaching the Cathlamets a lesson, but McLoughlin chose not to provoke another incident with the tribe.

All winter and into the spring of 1836, Little Cassino continued to slip away from the fort to be with Waskema. Her family always made him welcome. They knew that should Little Cassino take Waskema as his wife, fortune would smile on her family and the village.

At sixteen, Little Cassino felt invincible and paid little attention to the weather during his frequent visits to Waskema. Often he would return to Fort Vancouver soaked to the bone and thoroughly chilled by the wet winter conditions. One rainy March evening, he returned to the fort, waterlogged and coughing. That night, he had trouble breathing and his temperature soared.

He was confined to bed for the next few days, and his fever finally subsided, but the cough persisted. Princess Ilchee nursed him faithfully and requested medicine from the Company doctor. Despite the careful treatment, Little Cassino grew weaker and began to cough blood. Ilchee became frantic when she recognized the symptoms of what the white doctor called "consumption," a malady common to the natives and nearly always fatal. Little Cassino became delirious and spoke more and more about his trip to Wappato with his father. "I will never forget my

Multnomah home, Father," he whispered, "the place where I was born. I promise. I promise."

As he listened to his son's labored breathing, Cassino could see the Multnomah house and the rest of the village as it had gone up in smoke. He grieved for the old days and what had been lost. Then the rasping struggle ceased, and Cassino mourned the loss of his only son. Desolation and bitterness welled up in him, and he withdrew into himself to contemplate how to honor the memory of his son and ensure his safe passage to Memaloose Illahee.

*The long journey must be made successfully and in comfort*, he thought. Gathering the special clothing, weapons, and prized possessions was simple enough, but Cassino became obsessed with the idea that his son should not travel this journey alone. Remembering Lopahtah's decision to die with Pilmowitsh, Cassino desperately wanted to make his last great journey with his son. He was tired; what was left for him to do? He decided that his death would be the final great tribute to his son and his people. But then he remembered his tamanowos. He could not make the long journey with his son. He must stay and fulfill his destiny. Taking his own life would be cowardly—and act unworthy of the last great chief of the Chinook.

The thought that his son must not travel alone continued to plague him throughout the night. If Cassino himself could not go, then there was only one other suitable choice: Princess Ilchee, the boy's mother. The more Cassino thought about it, the more certain he became that this was the right course of action. Hadn't the princess nursed her son faithfully? Was she not the most prominent woman among her people? Not only would her death be a worthy tribute to her son, but it would also represent a great sacrifice for Cassino. He made up his mind—the princess must travel with their son.

Cassino asked Pee-Kin to have the burial in the fort cemetery—the only suitable place to bury a young gentleman. McLoughlin took care of the details, even requesting that the fort's carpenter make a coffin of great size, sufficient to include everything Cassino wished to place in it.

That evening, Cassino informed Princess Ilchee that she would have the honor of accompanying their son on his long journey. He was shocked when his wife screamed and ran out of the house. *How disgraceful*, Cassino thought. He was certain that she had loved their son as much as he had, and he was disgusted by her vain and selfish response. How could a noble Chinook mother value herself above her son—and the son of a great chief of her people? Overwhelmed by grief for his son and loathing for his wife, he called for several of his warriors and sent them in pursuit.

He knew he must find a solution that evening. Even in his mourning, he had to act. He sent for his Skookum, the greatly feared secret executioner and son of the Skookum who had taken care of the medicine man Leutcom and the renegade chief Shanum years before. Under Cassino's direct order, the executioner was sent to bring back Waskema. In death, Little Cassino's interest in the girl would be preserved, and she would be available to him at the end of the long journey.

Meanwhile, the terrified Princess Ilchee fled into the woods. She knew that Cassino would send men after her and she knew she would be killed. Under cover of the darkness, she slipped into the fort through the back gate and implored Pee-Kin to protect her. When he heard the circumstances, he quickly agreed to hide her until a suitable escape plan could be worked out. McLoughlin had great fondness and respect for Cassino, but he would not be a party to murder.

The next day at the burial, "good words" were spoken over the open grave by the Reverend Mr. Samuel Parker, who was visiting the fort. The grave was left open at Cassino's request so he could place additional articles in the coffin before covering it over. During the ceremony, there was great wailing by Sateena and the other Chinook women, but Cassino stood stoically, in true male Chinook fashion, while tears coursed silently down his cheeks.

As darkness fell over the fort, the Skookum returned with the body of Waskema and helped Cassino set her in the coffin with Little Cassino. His purpose fulfilled, Cassino solemnly shoveled dirt into the grave and buried the coffin.

The following week, when McLoughlin heard that Cassino's warriors had returned empty-handed, he made quiet arrangements to ferry Princess Ilchee down the river and return her to the protection of her people in the Chinook village.

# THE
# DECLINING
# YEARS

In the spring of 1836, after the death of Little Cassino, a small sailing ship, the *Beaver,* arrived at Fort Vancouver. Built in England the previous year, the *Beaver* carried a great new magic in her hold: a massive piece of intricate iron called a steam engine. Cassino was intrigued as he watched the engine being installed, because it was said that, with this engine, the Beaver could go through the water without wind and sails.

McLoughlin invited Cassino to join the excursion for the trial run of the first steamboat on the Columbia River and in the Northwest. Cassino dressed with great care that day, and when the time came, he proudly went aboard with the many officers of the Company and other special guests.

What a show the *Beaver* put on! First, a great puff of smoke belched out of the tall, single funnel. Then, a shrill whistle startled everyone on deck and on the dock. Gradually the little steamer pulled away from the dock. The apprehension on board eased as she smoothly gathered speed and ran down the river. The helmsman steered into the mouth of the Willamette, rounded the tip of Wappato and steamed down the channel behind the island. Their destination was Tom McKay's farm, located between the channel and the Scappoose Hills across from the lower part of Wappato.

After a stop at the farm, the *Beaver* proceeded downstream to the Columbia and turned back upriver toward the fort. Cassino was thrilled to be able to see all the way around his beloved island in an unbelievably short time. As he passed the old places—at once familiar yet so remote from his present experience—he thought of Pilmowitsh

189

and remembered the look on the canoe builder's face as he stood at the wheel of the great sailing ship so long ago. What would he have thought of this magic—the smoke, the churning paddles, the piercing whistle? Cassino was fascinated, but the ever-increasing power of the white man was also overwhelming.

Despite the occasional adventure and the momentary delight of a new experience, Cassino slipped deeper into melancholy after the death of his son. Sateena did everything she could to console and comfort him, but his listlessness and disinterest concerned her. She was beginning to feel her age and didn't know how long she would be there to care for her husband. *If only he could be given another son*, she thought. Thus began her search for another, younger, wife for Cassino.

One day, Sateena spied an especially attractive young woman at the fort with a party of Klickitats. Palletta, the daughter of a chief, was strikingly beautiful and one of the tallest girls Sateena had ever seen. Her black hair was drawn back from her face and plaited into two long braids that hung nearly to her waist. She drew admiring glances from men wherever she went, yet seemed to be unaware of the attention. Seeing the lovely round face and shy smile, Sateena decided immediately that this was the one. She contrived to have Cassino see the girl and casually suggested that he take her for his wife. It did not take long to convince him.

Palletta was humble in her role as wife of the greatest chief in the area, and she brought joy and the exuberance of youth to Cassino's household. It was precisely the tonic the old chief needed. Cassino had seen his fifty-eighth winter, and though he was old for a native, he was still strong and active. Before long, Palletta gave birth to a son, and with his hope restored, Cassino became his old self once again.

The proud, delighted father decided to name his son Tanohah. Of greater significance was the decision not to use the cradleboard to flatten the newborn's head. Cassino was firm in his resolve to look forward to the future instead of back at the old Chinook ways. "Tanohah must be prepared to live a life very different from the one his father has known," Cassino declared. "He must go to school and learn the white ways. Palletta, you and Sateena must promise to carry out these plans when my time comes to go on the long journey."

Although he was committed to raising his son in the ways of the white men, he also wanted Tanohah to understand and appreciate his Chinook heritage. Cassino spent many hours around the fire with Palletta and Sateena, telling the old stories and teaching them the Chinook ways so that they would be able to pass this wisdom along to Tanohah after Cassino was gone.

One evening, when Tanohah was still an infant, Cassino told his two wives the story of how he and his mother, Tenastsil, had come to Wappato. Sateena was astonished. She had never heard that Cassino's real father was the great chief of the Chinook. Palletta was proud of the fine heritage of her son, and she carefully committed the stories to memory.

On December 22, 1836, an American named Captain Slacum arrived as a passenger on the brig *Loriot*. McLoughlin received Slacum courteously, but Cassino sensed that Pee-Kin was wary of the newcomer. His perception was soon confirmed, when McLoughlin approached him with a new assignment. "I want you to observe this man Slacum, but do not interfere with him in any way. Report back to me where he goes and what he does."

Of greater concern to Cassino was the arrival of Ewing Young and his partner, who settled at Nathaniel Wyeth's old place on Wappato. Cassino heard that the two men intended to make firewater and trade it to the natives. Knowing the longstanding policy of the Hudson's Bay Company neither to sell nor trade liquor to the natives, Cassino reported the situation to McLoughlin immediately. "Pee-Kin," he said solemnly, "these men will cause trouble. If you wish, I will take care of the matter myself."

McLoughlin shook his head emphatically. "We both know that our policy must be enforced, but it would create more problems if these men were harmed. Your quick response is appreciated and I can assure you that Mr. Young will not be permitted to carry out his plan."

Shortly after the first of the year, McLoughlin placed a canoe and six men at Captain Slacum's disposal. At Pee-Kin's request, Cassino accompanied the captain to the French Prairie mission. As he followed Slacum around the Willamette Valley, Cassino began to understand why Pee-Kin was apprehensive about the man. The captain was outspoken in his criticism of the Hudson's Bay Company—but only in the presence of other Americans. When the party returned to Fort Vancouver later that month, Cassino reported to McLoughlin and learned that the captain was suspected of being an American agent.

Cassino shook his head. "Why not arrange an accident for the captain? I could take care of it easily."

"You know that is not our way, Cassino." McLoughlin reproved him. "Besides, such an 'accident,' as you call it, could start a war between Great Britain and the United States, and that is the last thing we want. This is a great land; it has a great future. We must develop it peacefully, all of us."

"So be it," Cassino sighed. "Your vision, your *tamanowos*, is strong and will prevail. I have known this from the beginning."

"Thank you, Cassino," McLoughlin replied gravely. "You have been an important part of it—from the beginning."

That evening, around the fire, Cassino told his wives about his conversation with Pee-Kin. As he spoke, the memories came flooding back. He closed his eyes and saw himself as a much younger man. "It was very near to this place where I first met Pee-Kin," he said. "We called it Skit-so-to-ho. I was wearing my red coat when we paddled up the river to meet the Great White-Headed Eagle. We exchanged presents, and I immediately saw his greatness. When I saw him next at Fort George, I knew that his *tamanowos* would prevail and that I must join with him in his vision. He is like no other white leader we have seen. He loves the country and the people. He has made much wealth for his company, but his love is for the country. He treats white man and native alike and he is a father to us all. No one knows more than I do how Pee-Kin has grieved for our people. He is the great chief, the greatest by far that I have known."

The three sat quietly around the fire for a long time, until the wise Sateena said gently, "My husband, I have seen another great chief. He is the most famous chief of the Multnomah and all other Wappato tribes—and now I know that he is a great chief of all the Chinook as well. He, too, has been a father to native and white man alike. He began as a boy in one of the smallest tribes, and through his unequaled leadership became chief of tribe after tribe until he was chief over all. He loved the people and the country more than anything else, and always used his wisdom and his wealth to help his people. Great chiefs see the greatness in others, and you are the only chief that Pee-Kin has trusted from the beginning."

The pace of life at Fort Vancouver ebbed and flowed with the ongoing arrivals and departures of a wide array of people. Early the following spring, the time came for Dr. McLoughlin to return to England. Cassino stood stoically at the water's edge as his good friend and mentor departed toward the east. They had said their farewells earlier, and now the great Pee-Kin was surrounded by the officers of the Company and the colorful voyageurs. Everyone at the fort had come to see the express off and the dockside was a merry hubbub of activity. To the piercing wail of the bagpipes, the departing chief factor of the Hudson's Bay Company stepped into the bateau. With a final flurry of shouts and farewells, the express was off. The voyageurs began their song as the line of boats began the arduous journey up the Columbia and across the continent. In McLoughlin's absence, James Douglas assumed control of the fort and he quickly and wisely enlisted Cassino's loyalty and help.

The second winter after Pee-Kin's departure, Sateena fell deathly ill. Weakened by fever and racked with chills, she spoke wearily to Cassino, who had come to her bedside to comfort her. "The time for the long journey is very near. Do not be sad, my husband, for I am leaving you with a young wife worthy of your greatness, and she has given you a son who is the joy of your life." She closed her eyes and sighed deeply. "It will be good to see my people again. Promise me that when the time comes you will take me to Wappato. It is from there that I wish to depart."

During the night, the last breath slipped from Sateena's lips, without pain and without a struggle. When he found her the next morning, Cassino gently wrapped her in her finest robes and summoned his tribesmen to help him take her to Wappato. The wind on the island was brisk and biting as Cassino tenderly transferred Sateena's body to a small canoe and hoisted it into a tree near the site of their old Multnomah house. He pointed the canoe toward the northwest, and within the glorious view they had once enjoyed from their doorway.

After an absence of nearly a year and a half, Pee-Kin returned to Fort Vancouver on October 19, 1839, his fifty-fifth birthday. Bountiful food and the good rum of the Hudson's Bay Company greeted the returning leader, and Cassino played a prominent role in the welcoming ceremony. Later, in the dining hall, Cassino sat at his chief's table and listened as Pee-Kin spoke about Canadian politics, the voyage to London, and the many facets of the Company's business—news meant for the ears of the highest officers. Cassino looked forward to when he would be able to speak with Pee-Kin alone and renew their longstanding friendship.

Chief Cassino was a familiar figure to all who visited Fort Vancouver. His quiet dignity and the favor shown him by Dr. McLoughlin marked him as a man of importance. He resented the references to "old Chief Cassino" made by newcomers or "greenhorns." The old-timers knew his history and the remarkable life he had led. His main responsibility now was to supervise the furnishing of fresh game and fish to the burgeoning fort population. As more white settlers came into the area, Cassino had to send his skillful band of hunters ever-increasing distances to keep the fort supplied.

Most of his native friends were gone. Sohowitsh still lived near the mouth of the river, but he was ailing. Laquano had died the second winter after leaving Wappato. Tenastsil and Olahno were long dead, but their two sons, Cassino's half-brothers, still lived with the Calapooya and had taken up farming in the Willamette Valley. Lamkos remained strong and held the Kalama tribe together. Princess Ilchee had fallen ill and died soon after her escape to the Chinook village, herself a victim of consumption. Cassino's heart was hardened toward her and he shed no tears when he heard of her death.

During the summer of 1840, Cassino and Palletta took the toddling Tanohah to visit Palletta's tribe. Instead of traveling up the river, they undertook an arduous journey by horseback, with a large party of Klickitat hunters, to the tribe's summer quarters high in the meadows on the south side of Klickitat—or Mt. Adams, as the white explorers had named it. When they arrived in the Klickitat camp, they were welcomed with great fanfare and accorded the honor of staying in a chief's lodge for the duration of their visit. Cassino had long been an honorary chief of the Klickitat, and Palletta was the daughter of one of the tribe's distinguished chiefs. Little Tanohah was greeted with great enthusiasm everywhere he turned.

Far from draining Cassino's energy as he had feared, the trip invigorated him and the return to the old pace of life was like a shot of youth serum to the old chief. He traded stories with the Klickitat chiefs and reminisced happily about the days on the river before the coming of the white men. Huckleberries grew in great profusion and Palletta joined the other women in harvesting the bounty. When the day became too hot, they could wade in the icy cold stream that flowed through the meadow near their camp. Every evening, the soaring crown of the great white mountain was bathed in the soft glow of the moon, and Cassino sat with Palletta under the brilliant shower of stars in the night sky. When the season ended, they said their farewells with great reluctance, but promised to return the next summer.

Back at the fort, the hustle and bustle of daily commerce was an unwelcome change, but they were glad to be home in time to prepare for the fall fishing. This year, Cassino planned to send a large party to the Cascades of the Columbia instead of Wallamt, because too many white settlers were living in the vicinity of the old fishing grounds.

In the days prior to his trip to Klickitat country, Cassino had not seen much of Dr. McLoughlin. Pee-Kin had been busy with the business of the fort. Jason Lee had returned at the end of May with another large group of Americans aboard the sailing ship *Lausanne*. McLoughlin welcomed them with his customary hospitality and put them up at the fort until they were ready to move on to various missions throughout the region. Cassino knew that Pee-Kin was apprehensive about the arrival of so many Americans, but it wasn't until he returned from his summer sojourn that he began to understand why.

One night, he tried to explain it to Palletta. "Pee-Kin is worried about the Americans—especially the missionaries. He thinks they are more interested in settling on the land than in caring for the spiritual needs of the people. He does not think this way about Father Blanchet and the blackrobes, only some of the Americans."

"It is hard to tell the bad white men from the good ones, because all of their ways are so different from ours," Palletta said.

"Yes, you are right," Cassino continued, "and now a new American named Waller has started a mission at Wallamt on land claimed by

Pee-Kin. Do you know what the Americans call this country? Oregon! I don't know where this word comes from, but they use it all the time. Pee-Kin thinks it comes from a French word that the voyageurs use to describe the stormy waters of the Great River. Yesterday, I heard about some white settlers on Swan Island, up the Willamette River. A man called Gale and several others were in the cottonwoods on the east shore and plan to build a sailing ship with tools from Lee's mission."

"Does Pee-Kin know about this?" asked Palletta.

"He had not heard this before I told him. He was greatly concerned, but he said we must not interfere. He said if these men wish to build a ship, it is their right. Sometimes I do not understand the ways of the white man."

Late that fall, a message arrived from downriver that Sohowitsh was gravely ill. Taking Palletta and Tanohah along, Cassino began the trip to the mouth of the river. He stopped at the Kalama village along the way to enlist some strong paddlers for the journey. When Lamkos heard the news about Sohowitsh, he decided to come along as well.

When Cassino arrived, Sohowitsh was lying on a mat near the fire, heavily bundled in fur robes. When he saw his brother, he raised his hand weakly. "Cassino, Lamkos, my brothers, it is good of you to come. The long journey awaits me and I am glad to go. It will be good to see my brother Tanohah and tell him about your son, who carries his name with honor. The wonderful days of Wappato, we will have them again in Memaloose Illahee. I should never have left my brother behind. I have always regretted my decision."

"You were needed here," Cassino said gently. "Tanohah followed his *tamanowos;* he did the right thing. You have held together what is left of our people here at the mouth of the Great River. Tanohah would be proud. We are all proud." Cassino quickly looked away into the fire as the emotion welled up in him.

During the night, Sohowitsh drew his last breath, and in the morning Cassino gave instructions for preparing the funeral. When the canoe with the chief's body had been safely lodged in a large tree overlooking the river, Cassino and his family headed upstream immediately to avoid an oncoming storm. At the Kalama village, he said good-bye to Lamkos and thanked him for his help.

"We are the last two, Cassino," the Kalama chief said quietly.

"Yes," replied Cassino. *And I am the only one left of all Wappato.*

In May 1841, Lieutenant Wilkes, an American naval officer, reached Fort Vancouver. Dr. McLoughlin spent a lot of time with the newcomer and traveled to Fort Nisqually in July to meet with him again. About the same time, Cassino, Palletta, and Tanohah left to join the summer camp of the Klickitats. This time they stayed until the days turned crisp and the nights were cold.

When they arrived back at the fort, McLoughlin had not yet returned. James Douglas was in charge and he was making preparations to receive Sir George Simpson, governor of the Hudson's Bay Company. Simpson arrived in grand style, with an impressive array of gentlemen in his retinue. The lively songs of the voyageurs echoed along the river as they made their colorful approach to the dock. At the landing, Simpson was greeted by Douglas and the other notables, including Cassino. Governor Simpson remembered the old chief and greeted him warmly.

Later, Cassino told Palletta all about the day's festivities, then added, "Something is not right. Pee-Kin's absence is a puzzle to me. It is not like him to miss the governor's arrival. Douglas says that Pee-Kin has much business at Nisqually and along the Cowlitz, but I find this story hard to believe. What business would be more important than the arrival of the governor? Pee-Kin has been away for longer than ever before. I don't like it."

When another week passed with no sign of McLoughlin, Cassino was certain that something was amiss. During the week, Lieutenant Wilkes had returned to Vancouver with three of his warships and had been received by Sir George. By the end of the week, Governor Simpson left for Fort Nisqually, accompanied by Douglas.

Dr. McLoughlin finally returned to Fort Vancouver, but he said nothing to Cassino about his absence. After a lengthy northern sojourn touring Company posts, Governor Simpson also returned to the fort. Things seemed to return to normal, but Cassino sensed that Pee-Kin was preoccupied most of the time. The chief factor and the governor were cordial with one another and seemed to get along despite occasional disagreements. Cassino sensed that their differences centered around the Americans, and he wasn't sure how he felt about them himself.

"Pee-Kin is changing," he said one day to Palletta. "He loves the country and he knows that the Americans wish to settle here and live. Pee-Kin understands this and supports the idea, but Sir George wants only to trade and make profits for the Company. He wants to keep things as before and does not want the Americans to settle here. But the Americans will continue to come, more and more, just as their great chiefs Lewis and Clark said many years ago. I know that Pee-Kin has made a difficult decision, but I do not know what it is. In due time, he will reveal his thoughts, and he will be right. It is his *tamanowos*."

In December, McLoughlin, Simpson and several other gentlemen from the Company sailed for California aboard a Hudson's Bay bark, the *Cowlitz*. When McLoughlin returned, it was without Simpson, and for a while life at the fort was much like old times. Then tragedy struck. Word was received that John McLoughlin, Pee-Kin's son, had been killed by his own men at a small Company trading post in the far north. The anguish that consumed McLoughlin was so great that Cassino feared for his old friend. As one of the few close associates to whom Dr. McLoughlin could turn, Cassino listened and understood as the Great White-Headed Eagle unburdened his grief.

The following summer, the ship built on Swan Island sailed down the Willamette, proudly flying the American Stars and Stripes, and anchored off Fort Vancouver. She was named the *Star of Oregon* and was what the Americans called "clinker-built on Baltimore clipper lines." The fifty-three-foot ship soon set sail down the Columbia, across the bar, and south to California. When Cassino heard later that she was traded for cattle in California and would not return to the Great River, he shook his head in disbelief. How could these Americans build such a lovely ship—their first in Oregon—and then sail her off and dispose of her? She belonged here, in Wappato country, where she was built. Forever after, Cassino would think of the *Star of Oregon* as the supreme Multnomah canoe. After all, hadn't she been created on the Multnomah? He knew Pilmowitsh would have been impressed.

Fall arrived and Dr. McLoughlin received word that Mr. Waller was again extending his operations onto the British claim at Wallamt. Angrily, he went to talk to Waller and Jason Lee, but the men were unable to reach an understanding.

Back at the fort, McLoughlin told Cassino, "They are not being honest with me, and I am afraid that Lee cannot or will not do anything to stop Waller. To end this controversy, I am going to have my claim surveyed into building lots and I will officially name the place Oregon City. A new sawmill will be built on the river bank and soon there will be a grist mill."

Cassino was pleased to see the old fire return to his friend's eyes. Founding the new settlement of Oregon City seemed to chase the last bit of despondency away from Pee-Kin—and it was just in time. In October of that year, 1842, the first group of American settlers in covered wagons arrived overland from the east—about 125 persons.

# 23 TAMANOWOS

"**I**n time the Americans will come. At first, they will come by ship, but later from the east over the land." These words, spoken by Lewis and Clark, were often repeated by Cassino over the years. Now, he was seeing the fulfillment of this prediction with his own eyes.

The first group to reach Oregon—with 125 settlers—was nothing. By the following year, 875 settlers arrived in November and December alone. And the year after that, 1844, more than fourteen hundred Americans came by covered wagon to make their homes in the Oregon country. Most settled in the Willamette Valley, across the Columbia and south of the fort. Oregon City soon rivaled Vancouver in importance, and ships were sailing up the Willamette as far as the falls. As early as 1840, Captain John Couch had sailed his brig *Maryland* to the falls, and he returned two years later with the *Chenamus* and reached the Clackamas River where it joins the Willamette just below Oregon City. The ship's cargo was transferred from there to the settlement by flatboat.

The time arrived for Tanohah to start school at the fort, and he moved easily into the new routine. While her son was at school, Palletta maintained the family's neat, comfortable cabin outside the fort, and Cassino moved about the stockade, quietly fulfilling his role as Indian advisor to Dr. McLoughlin.

Cassino had become an institution at Fort Vancouver and enjoyed telling stories of his past—his rare experiences as chief of the Wappato tribes—to anyone who wanted to hear, old-timer or greenhorn, native or white. He knew his services were no longer really needed, but he was quite aware that, in the eyes of many old-timers, his importance to the

Company was unquestioned. One day, Pee-Kin called him in for a conference. With the sudden influx of new settlers, Cassino's standing had suddenly changed, and his value to the fort was reinforced.

"Rumors are that the tribes around The Dalles are getting restless," McLoughlin said. "You must get word to them that no harm must be done to the 'Boston Men' and their families. I want the tribes to hear directly from you that I will deal quickly and harshly with any native who harms the white settlers. Tell them it makes no difference whether they are Americans or British."

"I will go and I will speak directly to the chiefs," Cassino said. "I will make it clear that it is their responsibility."

"They will listen to you, Cassino. Leave as soon as possible and take gifts if you think they are needed. We cannot afford to have any trouble."

Cassino traveled upriver with a group of Klickitat warriors in the late fall of 1843, just as members of the "great migration" began to push into the area. The Klickitat were a strong and well-respected tribe from east of the mountains. Cassino contacted all the major chiefs and made Pee-Kin's position clear. The great overland migration along the Oregon Trail in 1843 and 1844 proceeded without any serious trouble from the natives, a remarkable testimony to the influence of Pee-Kin and Cassino. Peace was maintained, even though the settlers flooded into and over the entire region.

When Cassino finally returned to Fort Vancouver, a new sadness settled on his shoulders like a dark cloak. One night by the fire, he spoke mournfully to Palletta about the old days. "Soon there will be nothing left to show that our people once lived here. Even our names for the places are gone. The Multnomah have lived on the island called Wappato for generations. But one day, in the early years of the fort, Pee-Kin sent a Frenchman named Jean Baptiste Sauvie over to Wappato to run a herd of dairy cows, and now the all the white men call it "Sauvie Island." Wallamt, where we gathered year after year for the fall run of salmon, is now called Oregon City. And they took our name for the falls, Wallamt, and changed the name of the Multnomah River to "Willamette." Skit-so-to-ho is now Vancouver; Wyeast is Mt. Hood; Klickitat is called Mt. Adams; and even the lovely Loowit they now call St. Helens. It is sad and it is not right. Our people were on the river long, long ago, and our names should remain."

"The new names are even hard to remember," said Palletta.

"The only one to keep our name was Tom McKay, and he is an old-timer. He named his farm down the channel 'Scappoose,' the Chinook name for the hills behind his land. McKay was fair; he came to ask me for the land and paid for it! The few Clackstar survivors in the village were happy to have McKay come. He took care of them. If only all the white men had been like Tom McKay."

During the winter of 1844 and the spring of 1845, Cassino often was dispatched to settle trouble with the tribes—or what was left of them—on both the Columbia and Willamette Rivers. With all the new settlers in the country, there was constant friction with the natives. Because Cassino's sympathies lay with the natives—though he represented the white traders at the fort—he was able to intercede for them and correct injustices. McLoughlin was still firm in his determination to deal fairly with everyone—native and white alike—but at times he hesitated or did nothing. To Cassino's surprise, Pee-Kin seemed reluctant to confront the Americans to the south. He was losing control in the Willamette Valley.

One breezy afternoon in late spring, McLoughlin confided to Cassino that he had made his decision: he was leaving the Hudson's Bay Company. "I will stay on here another year," he said, "but my heart is not in it. For some time now, Sir John and I have not seen eye to eye, and the Company has not been fair with me. Say nothing about this, but I have decided for Oregon. I have already begun plans for my permanent home in Oregon City. You will be able to stay with the Company as long as you live, Cassino. I will see to that. My hope is that James Douglas will be named successor. You two are old friends; there should not be any trouble for you. But remember, old friend, you can always come to me. Oregon is the land of the future!"

That night, as Cassino listened to Tanohah eagerly report on his lessons for the day, his mind drifted to Pee-Kin. Palletta saw that he was preoccupied and wisely said nothing. After Tanohah had been put to bed, Cassino said to his wife, "Tomorrow, when the boy has gone to school, we will go out on the river."

The small, light canoe knifed cleanly through the high water in the morning mist as Cassino and Palletta crossed to the south shore, close to the long island upriver from the fort. The current in midstream was strong, but it slackened close to the shore, and Cassino steered expertly to hold the canoe where the paddling was easiest.

"We will go up to Broughton's place," he announced, "and I will tell you the story of the boy who followed the white chief long ago."

Cassino leaned back in his seat and breathed deeply of the clean, fresh air. He thought once again about his younger days and the uncomplicated life of a Chinook boy along the Great River. The sun became warm as it rose above the narrow layer of clouds that sat on the peaks of the mountains, and the trees showed off their spring coats of green. A gentle breeze from the northwest brushed over their shoulders as they continued upstream.

Reluctantly, Palletta broke the silence. "Is there something you wish to tell me?"

At first, she thought Cassino must not have heard her, because he remained silent. Finally he said softly, "Pee-Kin is leaving the Company. He will move to Oregon City next year. It is a secret, so tell no one."

He paused as a sleek white gull took off from the water directly ahead of the canoe, voicing its annoyance as it flapped away. "It can never be the same without the Great White-Headed Eagle," Cassino continued. "Much can happen in a year, but Pee-Kin will not change his mind. It is his *tamanowos*. His heart and all his being is in the country and its people, not the business. It has always been so."

Cassino looked around at everything he loved: the shimmering water; the craggy, snow-covered peaks; the fresh green trees; the budding plants and flowers; and the beautiful woman in the front of the canoe. "I can no longer change," he said. "The white men want to take the country and change it to make it fit their ways. We have always accepted the country as it is and changed our ways to fit the country. Our people have died because of the changes brought by the white man—but the ways of our people are right. Some day, the white man will learn this lesson, but it will take a long, long time. They will not learn in our time, and they may not learn in Tanohah's time. They may not learn until they have spoiled the beauty of everything they touch, but someday they will learn. Of this, I am certain."

The little canoe passed the head of the long island and Cassino and Palletta were able to see another island on the north side of the river, where a great flock of white birds was rising noisily from the shore. Cassino steered past the Quicksand River where it emptied into the Great River, and a doe and two little fawns stood at the edge of the water on the mainland and paused to watch them pass. Across the river on the north shore, they could see the Company sawmill at Camas. Here the river made a great curve, and they stayed close to the south shore, passing one small island before beaching the canoe on a second small island.

After securing the canoe on the beach, they carried their basket of food up to a high grassy spot that afforded a breathtaking view up the mighty river. The Great River, the Columbia, had cut a deep, majestic gorge through the Cascade Mountains, creating a scene of unparalleled beauty. Ribbons of cascading waterfalls tumbled down the cliffs, and endless forests of deep green ran up the mountain slopes. Unusual lava rock monoliths stood guard along the shore. Upriver, well beyond Beacon Rock, the largest of the stone sentinels, lay the Bridge of the Gods and the thundering rapids of the Cascades. Overlooking the entire scene—one to the north, the other to the south—stood the towering rivals, Wyeast and Klickitat, looking longingly across the way to the beautiful, seductive Loowit.

Cassino and Palletta shared a leisurely meal, then napped in the warm midday sun. When they awoke, they sat in the shade of an alder tree and Cassino repeated the age-old story:

"Long ago, when I was a young stripling of a boy, my friends and I followed the first white man's boat ever to come up the river. This island was as far as they dared to come. We camped on that island across the river and watched them. The men came ashore and raised a flag and had some kind of ceremony that we could not understand. After I had been with other white men at the fort for a while I understood that the men that day were claiming this land for King George. But back then it was simply a strange ritual. After they left, we came over here, but we could find nothing to tell us what they had done. It did not bother us back then; we stayed up here for several days, hunting and fishing and having a good time. We didn't know that the white men would soon have a settlement up here and that most of our people would be dead."

Cassino relived those days in his mind for a few minutes before turning back toward Palletta with a serious expression on his face. "There is something else that I must say, and it bothers me to speak of it, but I must face the truth. I am getting old. The long journey must come to us all, and my journey is not far off."

Palletta stiffened as fear crept into her bones. She tried to place her long fingers over his lips to silence him, but Cassino brushed her hand away.

"Do not be afraid. We must speak of these things. You are young and so beautiful. We must decide what you will do—and Tanohah—when I leave you. I may have many more years—who can say?—but Pee-Kin's decision to leave the fort has caused me to think. Up until now, I have planned for you and the boy to remain at the fort, but now I am not sure. I wonder whether you should return to your people, the Klickitat, where Tanohah can learn the ways of our people. At first, I agreed with Pee-Kin that our young people must learn the white ways; but for Tanohah, that is not enough. You must do for him what my mother did for me. He is destined to be a great chief among his people. From this day forward, we must think of nothing else for him. He must learn the native ways as well as the ways of the white man. Your father will understand, Palletta, and he will help, but it is mostly up to you. Do you understand? Our people must have a strong young chief who can lead them when I am gone."

Palletta was stunned by the sudden rush of information and new ideas. All she could think of was the bright-eyed little boy who was just starting school. She stared up the river and pondered Cassino's words. When she had settled in her heart that his way was the right way for their son, she turned to him and said, "I understand what you are saying, but Tanohah is still such a small boy. It is hard to think of him as a chief."

Cassino saw the small tears that formed in the corners of Palletta's gentle eyes. He stood up and held out his hand to her. "Our son," he murmured, "this is his country. Some day, when he is a great chief, he will appreciate it as we do."

The return trip in the strong current passed too quickly, and soon they were back amidst the bustle of Fort Vancouver. Over the next several days, they formulated a plan for Tanohah's future. It was decided that as soon as school let out for the summer, the boy would go to live with the Klickitats, and would remain with them until after they returned to their winter grounds east of Klickitat. When the time came, it was hard for Cassino and Palletta to see him go, but as he rode out the front gate of the fort with a band of Klickitat hunters, his eyes were shining with anticipation of the adventure ahead.

During the summer, McLoughlin dispatched Cassino on one last peace-keeping mission to the Willamette Valley. When he returned, he and Palletta took a leisurely canoe trip down the river, past Wappato Island, to the mouth of the stream where the Kalama tribe had its village. After visiting with Lamkos for several days, they paddled back upriver to the fort and settled back into the daily routine.

When winter came, Tanohah returned to Fort Vancouver accompanied by several Klickitat traders. His parents were overjoyed to see him and they marveled at how much he had grown and matured during his months away.

Evenings around the fire, Cassino carefully taught his son the important history of the Chinook people. "Listen well, my son," he said every night, "for some day you will follow in the footsteps of your father and your grandfathers, and you too will be a great chief and serve our people. You must never forget your responsibility." Tanohah listened intently to his father's stories and tried to imagine life on the river before the coming of the white man. He went to bed each night with visions of adventure and promise filling his young mind.

The winter of 1845 was the last at Fort Vancouver for Dr. McLoughlin. Cassino shuddered to think how things would change when the Great White-Headed Eagle was no longer in command. His strong personality and reputation for fairness was respected by the natives and the white settlers, and many incidents had been avoided just by his presence. The settlers were setting up enterprises in countless new locations and it was difficult to monitor them all. The tribes east of the mountains were still warlike and could not be trusted to keep the peace with the sudden influx of new settlers. Cassino worried that the Klickitats would be caught in the middle between the fractious tribes to the east and the white settlements to the west.

As he discussed the situation east of the mountains with Cassino one day, Pee-Kin said wearily, "I tried my best to warn Dr. Whitman against locating over there, but he was absolutely determined. He has managed to get along so far, but his settlement is too far away for us to defend. They will be vulnerable if there is any trouble."

When the spring of 1846 arrived, Dr. McLoughlin left Fort Vancouver and turned over his great responsibilities to James Douglas. "Serve him well," he told Cassino, "as you have always served me. Come to see me

in Oregon City. The door of my home is always open to you. And if you
need anything, I owe you more than I can ever repay. Douglas has assured
me that your place with the Company is secure, but you can always join me.
We have accomplished much, my friend, and we must never say farewell."

At the closing ceremony for McLoughlin's command, Cassino stood
stoically beside a group of Company officers stationed behind Mr.
Douglas. Dr. McLoughlin lifted his cane in a salute of quiet dignity and
stepped aboard his boat. The bagpipes wailed a mournful farewell, the
cannon at the fort boomed, and the voyageurs at the oars began their
rowing song. All eyes followed the erect, proud figure of the Great
White-Headed Eagle as he rode downriver, his white hair blowing in the
breeze. No one moved on the landing until his boat was well downstream
and out of sight.

Later that spring, but before the other children were out of school,
Tanohah rode off with the Klickitat hunting party for his summer with the
tribe. He rode as if he had spent most of his life horseback, and his
parents marveled at their son's evident skill.

"He rides like a Klickitat," Palletta said proudly.

"He handles a horse as he handles a canoe," Cassino replied.

Cassino had no problem working with his old friend James Douglas,
but he missed Pee-Kin. On two different occasions that spring, Douglas
thoughtfully dispatched Cassino to Oregon City on matters of Company
business. Cassino took Palletta with him and they were received with
joy and kindness at the McLoughlin home. During their days together
in Vancouver, Palletta had befriended Margaret McLoughlin, Pee-Kin's
half-Indian wife, and the two women were delighted to renew their
acquaintance. Life at Oregon City was lonely for the quiet Margaret,
and it meant a lot to her to see old friends from the fort.

Cassino was not prepared for the size and tempo of Oregon City. It
was much larger than Fort Vancouver and Cassino sensed an air about
the place that was completely new and foreign. The American town
lacked the precise organization of a Hudson's Bay Company fort, and
the pace was bewildering—too much activity and too much hurry.
Nevertheless, it was fascinating to the old chief.

"You would like it here once you got used to it, Cassino," McLoughlin said. "This is a new country, a great country, just beginning. Everyone feels it and has much he wants to accomplish. Certainly there are those who seek only to plunder, to gain wealth without honest work, but the great majority are good, solid, hard-working people. In the long run, they are the ones who will succeed." Cassino had his doubts, but he kept his thoughts to himself.

The McLoughlins' big new house looked out on the Willamette River. It was all white, with two levels and a big porch in front of the massive front door. Cassino counted nine large glass windows in front, five upstairs and four down, and there were small windows all around the front door. The inside of the house was even more impressive, with beautiful furnishings filling the many rooms. The house was much finer than anything at the fort, and Cassino was happy that Pee-Kin and Margaret had such a nice place to live.

It was always good to return to the simple cabin at the fort and the pace to which he and Paletta were accustomed. Even better was to return to the pace of native life. Soon they were off to join Tanohah and the Klickitats in the mountain meadows where Cassino felt the peace and quiet in his bones and where the stars came down at night to touch him.

Tanohah had become one with the tribe, racing with skill and daring on horseback and more than holding his own with the older boys. His hunting prowess was highly regarded, yet he was not boastful. The two old chiefs who had taken him under their wing were proud. They knew he had the mark of leadership on him. He took to the role naturally, without pretense or pride, just as his father had done before him. Watching his son, Cassino began to feel his age.

James Douglas was grateful when Cassino returned to the fort. There were rumors of impending trouble with the tribes east of the mountains, but the winter passed much as usual. Nevertheless, when the summer of 1847 arrived, Douglas told Cassino that he needed his advice and services, and asked him to remain on the Columbia. Tanohah went alone to the summer encampment that year.

Summer and fall came and went without major incident, but early in December, Douglas received word from the east of a massacre by the

Cayuse at the Whitman mission. He immediately summoned Peter Skene Ogden and Cassino, and sent word on to Oregon City. Ogden was dispatched with an armed party to rescue any survivors and return them to Oregon City. Douglas asked Cassino to do whatever he could to keep the other natives calm and prevent more problems. When Ogden arrived east of the mountains, he found that Dr. and Mrs. Whitman and ten others from the mission had been brutally murdered.

Meanwhile, in Oregon City, plans for retaliation were underway. A party of settlers wanted to attack the Cayuse and other tribes involved and hang the guilty parties. Because the posse would have to travel through Klickitat tribal lands to reach the east, Cassino sent hunters to the Klickitats with instructions and warnings. Though they were caught in the middle between warring tribes to the east and avenging white settlers from the west, the Klickitats were prepared and were able to maintain peace in their own area. Thus Cassino reinforced the traditional friendship and loyalty between the Klickitats and the Hudson's Bay Company, and possibly averted a spreading of the hostilities.

The tension remained high at the fort throughout the winter and spring. Palletta saw the toll it was taking on Cassino, how his strength was taxed and he was growing weary, and she worried about him. When the summer of 1848 arrived, Cassino again stayed at Fort Vancouver when Tanohah left to join the Klickitats.

Cassino had become something of a legend, even far beyond the banks of his beloved river. His portrait was painted for posterity by two prominent artists, Paul Kane and John Mix Stanley. Kane, in particular, became absorbed in the study of Cassino's people, talking at length about the Chinook with their greatest chief, sketching pictures and taking copious notes. Cassino was pleased by the artist's genuine interest and the two became good friends.

As the summer once again faded into fall, Cassino sat for hours in the warm sun, remembering old friends, old places, and old exploits. He was amazed by the exact detail that flooded through his mind, as if he had done these things only yesterday. He began to long to return to his people, the Chinook, and he knew the time for his final journey was approaching. He began to speak about it to Palletta more often—preparing her for the inevitable, and preparing himself.

"A good chief belongs to his people," he said. "There will be no wailing at the longhouse when I depart. You must be proud and dignified, in the white man's way, and Tanohah also. You must be strong, so that our son will be strong too. Though I must fulfill my destiny and return to my people, you and Tanohah must remain and fulfill your destiny. Our people need you and they will need even more the great chief our son will become. You must see to it that he is prepared."

When Tanohah returned to resume his schooling, Cassino rejoiced to see how mature he had become. Tanohah understood that the time for his father to leave on his long journey was fast approaching. The late autumn rains settled over the area, and with it came a bracing wind down the gorge. Cassino gradually grew weaker and finally it became necessary for him to take to his bed. Everyone in Vancouver knew that the famous old chief was dying.

One day, Palletta came to him, troubled, and said, "Father Blanchet, the blackrobe, is here at the fort. Mr. Douglas wishes him to say good words over you."

Cassino smiled wanly. He knew they desired to bring him to the white man's God. "It will do no harm," he said. "It is good they wish to do it. Invite him to come."

So Cassino was baptized into the Church, but the priest had no idea that, throughout the ceremony, the convert's mind was contemplating the preparations for departure to Memaloose Illahee. Cassino was Chinook, and never had his *tamanowos* been stronger.

Winter set in. The great old chief grew weaker with the fading days, but he felt no pain. His last days were peaceful and contented. He was prepared for his long journey and he knew that Palletta and Tanohah understood that his time had come. There was joy in his heart, for at last he was returning to his people, the Multnomah. He died on December 10, 1848.

Chief Cassino was buried at Fort Vancouver, with many in attendance. Good words were said over the grave and there was no wailing at the longhouse as in former times. His wife and son stood quietly and proudly at the graveside, and there were no tears—just as he had desired. After the grave had been covered, a light snow fell, laying a pure white blanket over the remains of the Indian Father of Oregon. Later that night, the snow melted when a warm Chinook wind blew out of the northwest—

an omen to speed the great Chinook chief on his final voyage home.

The next morning, a large Klickitat hunting party left the gates of the fort, heading east. At the center of the group rode a proud and beautiful young woman and a graceful young man. They rode silently toward the rising sun and did not look back.

Dr. McLoughlin was in his office when Margaret entered the room and silently laid a note from Fort Vancouver on the desk. Pee-Kin stared at the envelope for a long time before he picked it up. A look of surprise, then pain, crossed his face as he read the brief message from James Douglas. He had known that Cassino was bedridden and in failing health, but he was not prepared for his old friend's passing.

The Great White-Headed Eagle sadly put the paper down and leaned back in his chair. In his mind's eye he saw the proud figure of a young native man in a red coat and lone eagle feather standing by a fire. Pee-Kin closed his eyes and a single word formed on his lips.

"*Tamanowos*," he whispered. He and his native brother had shared the same destiny.

# GLOSSARY
# OF CHINOOK
# NAMES

| | |
|---|---|
| **Asotan** | Shoto medicine man and friend of Cassino |
| **Cassino** | Eventual chief of all Chinook |
| **Celiast** | Daughter of a Clatsop chief |
| **Comcomly** | One-eyed chief of the Chinook |
| **Concomsin** | Quathlahpottle warrior and chief, and friend of Cassino |
| **Coalpo** | Chief of the Clatsop |
| **Ilchee** | Daughter of Comcomly, and wife of McDougal and Cassino |
| **Immahah** | Sub-chief of the Multnomah |
| **Kinsenitsh** | Chief of the Clackstar, father-in-law of Cassino |
| **Klickitat** | Mt. Adams—also the name of a tribe west of Mt. Adams |
| **Konapee** | Legendary Iron Maker |
| **Leutcom** | Clackstar medicine man |
| **Little Cassino** | First son of Cassino |
| **Lohtahsen** | Second sister of Cassino |
| **Loowit** | Mt. St. Helens |
| **Lopahtah** | Pilmowitsh's second wife and daughter of Chief Taneeho of the Multnomah |
| **Memaloose Illahee** | Chinook afterlife or heaven |
| **Monsoe** | First son of Pilmowitsh and Tsultsis, best friend of Cassino |

| | |
|---|---|
| **Nanalla** . . . . . . . . . . | Pilmowitsh's youngest wife |
| **Nobsoic** . . . . . . . . . . | Sub-chief of the Clackstar |
| **Olahno** . . . . . . . . . . | Chief of the Calapooya, husband of Tenastsil |
| **Palletta** . . . . . . . . . . | Daughter of a Klickitat chief, Cassino's youngest wife |
| **Pee-Kin** . . . . . . . . . . | Dr. John McLoughlin, head factor of the Hudson's Bay Company, Great White-Headed Eagle, friend of Cassino |
| **Pilmowitsh** . . . . . . . . | Wappato canoe builder, father of Monsoe, Tanohah, and Sohowitsh |
| **Poleetah** . . . . . . . . . . | Cassino's wife from the Multnomah |
| **Posen** . . . . . . . . . . . | Chief of the Multnomah |
| **Sahale** . . . . . . . . . . . | Great Spirit of the Chinook |
| **Sateena** . . . . . . . . . . | Cassino's wife from the Clackstar |
| **Shanum** . . . . . . . . . . | Cathlahminnamin warrior and chief, friend of Cassino |
| **Shannaway** . . . . . . . . | Chief of the Cowlitch |
| **Shenshina** . . . . . . . . . | Pilmowitsh's fourth wife and wife of Soleutu |
| **Skit-so-to-ho** . . . . . . . | Place of the Turtle, site of Fort Vancouver |
| **Sohowitsh** . . . . . . . . . | Third son of Pilmowitsh, second son of Lopahtah |
| **Soleutu** . . . . . . . . . . | Chief of the Cowlitch, second husband of Shenshina |
| **Taneeho** . . . . . . . . . . | Leading chief of the Multnomah, father of Lopahtah |
| **Tanohah** . . . . . . . . . . | Second son of Pilmowitsh and first son of Lopahtah Second son of Cassino |
| **Tenastsil** . . . . . . . . . . | Mother of Cassino, wife of Chief Olahno of the Calapooya |
| **Tsultsis** . . . . . . . . . . | First wife of Pilmowitsh, mother of Monsoe |
| **Waskema** . . . . . . . . . | Native girl, friend of Little Cassino |
| **Wy'east** . . . . . . . . . . | Mt. Hood |

 BIBLIOGRAPHY

Beckham, Steven Dow. *The Indians of Western Oregon: This Land Was Theirs.* Coos Bay, Ore.: Arago Books, 1977.

Cleaver, J.D. Island Origins. *Sauvie Island Heritage Series,* 1. Salem: Oregon Historical Society Press, 1986.

Corning, Howard McKinley. *Willamette Landings.* Salem: Oregon Historical Society, 1947.

Cox, Ross. *The Columbia River.* Edited by Edgar I. Stewart and Jane R. Stewart. Norman: University of Oklahoma Press, 1957.

Hayes, Edmund, ed. *Log of the Union: John Boit's Remarkable Voyage 1794-96.* Salem: Oregon Historical Society, 1981.

Irving, Washington. *Astoria.* Portland, Ore.: Binford and Mort, 1967.

Johnson, Robert C. *John McLoughlin: Father of Oregon.* Portland, Ore.: Metropolitan Press, 1935; reprinted, Portland, Ore.; Binford and Mort, 1958.

Jones, Robert F., ed. *Astorian Adventure: The Journal of Alfred Seton, 1811-1815.* New York: Fordham University Press, 1933.

Jones, Roy F. *Wappato Indians: Their History and Prehistory of the Lower Columbia River Valley.* Privately Printed, 1972.

Kane, Paul. *The Columbia Wanderer.* Salem: Oregon Historical Society, 1971.

Montgomery, Richard G. *The White Headed Eagle.* New York: Macmillan, 1934.

Morrison, Dorothy Nafus. *The Eagle and the Fort: The Story of John McLoughlin.* Salem: Western Imprints, Oregon Historical Society, 1964.

Ronda, James P. *Astoria and Empire.* Lincoln: University of Nebraska Press, 1990.

Ruby, Robert H., and John A. Brown. *A Guide to the Indian Tribes of the Pacific Northwest.* Norman: University of Oklahoma Press, 1986.

Sampson, William R., ed. *John McLoughlin's Business Correspondence 1847-48.* Seattle: University of Washington Press, 1973.

Shaw, George C. *The Chinook Jargon and How to Use It.* Seattle: Rainier Printing, 1909; reprinted, Seattle: Shorey Book Store, 1965.

Spencer, Omar C. "Chief Cassino." *Oregon Historical Quarterly* 34 (1933): 19-30.

Strong, Emory. *Stone Age on the Columbia River.* Portland, Ore.: Binford and Mort, 1959.

Thomas, Edward Harper. Chinook: *A History and Dictionary.* Portland, Ore.: Binford and Mort, 1935.

To order additional copies of

# THE LEGEND OF WAPPATO

## CHIEF CASSINO OF THE MULTNOMAH

$16.95 US / $24.95 Canada
$3.50 Shipping & Handling

Contact:

**BOOKPARTNERS**
INCORPORATED

P.O. Box 922
Wilsonville, OR 97070
Fax: 503-682-8684
Phone: 503-682-9821
E-mail: bpbooks@teleport.com